Total-E-Bound Publishing books by Jude Mason:

Ghost of a Chance
Night Games
Jacob's Pony
Knight or Daye
Stiff Trick
Forever Mine
Jett's Gift
Sam, the Man

I0679737

Anthologies
Naughty Nooners: Lunch is Served
Pleasure Bound: Selene's Awakening

With Jenna Byrnes

Untamed Hearts
Feral Heat
Bear Combustion
Wolfen Choice
Stallion's Pride

Kindred Spirits
Ethan's Choice
Hunter's Light
Alex's Appeal
Quinn's Blessing
Dylan's Dilemma

Anthologies
Friction: Maximum Exposure
Over the Moon: Trapped
Gaymes: Good Cop, Bad Cop

DAYBREAK 2525
Volume One

Doc

Jazz

JUDE MASON

Daybreak 2525 Volume One
ISBN # 978-0-85715-782-9
©Copyright Jude Mason 2012
Cover Art by April Martinez ©Copyright March 2012
Interior text design by Claire Siemaszkiewicz
Total-E-Bound Publishing

Published in 2012 by Total-E-Bound Publishing, Think Tank, Ruston Way, Lincoln, LN6 7FL, United Kingdom.

Total-E-Bound Publishing is an imprint of Total-E-Ntwined Limited.

DOC

Dedication

To the dreamers of this world, without whom
speculative fiction wouldn't stand a chance.

Chapter One

Terror stopped Doc and froze him in his tracks. The scene confronting him was one he'd seen before but never dreamed he'd see here. Not his home. Not his tribe.

It was daybreak, and the view of his village from the top of Elk Ridge had always made his heart beat a little faster. The prospect of being home, in his lover's arms, had made the joy of returning a special occasion. Now, all he saw were smouldering piles of wreckage and bodies sprawled where they had no right to be. Bodies that, for a moment, he feared looking at too closely.

While his mind raced, he peered at those closest to him and tried to identify them. Unfamiliar faces, clothing he'd never seen before... He sighed, greatly relieved he didn't recognise any of them. The few wooden buildings in the area leant precariously, one way or the other, and smoke rose in winding columns of dark grey from many of them. The breeze picked up, sending pale wood ash into the air, and a new flicker of fire flared up at the base of what had once been the trader's cabin. The smoke drifted away from him, and Doc knew that was why he hadn't heard or smelled anything on his way in. Rags and paper blew around the central meeting square, which was empty except for the fire pit and its pile of split wood still stacked neatly beside it.

He dropped the satchel filled with his doctoring tools and herbs to the grass and unslung his bow. It was a small affair, made of some mysterious alloy manufactured before the big war. He'd discovered it in what remained of the old city to the north and found it easier to aim than the long bows he'd been using. With a great deal of practice, the small weapon had proven extremely accurate, and he rarely travelled anywhere without it. An arrow in hand, he automatically notched it but didn't draw it back. When he leant down to pick up his satchel, he saw movement below and again froze.

Doc squinted, hoping to see Jazz crouched amid the piles of rubble. His mother and father would be there, and his sister Robin—unless they were dead. Just thinking about it made him cringe. The warriors, where were they?

He noticed several of the bodies ahead were very small. His stomach churned.

More movements below caught his attention. The familiar figure of a white-haired elder shambled out from under one of the heaps of debris. Each tribe in the region seemed to have at least one person who kept the histories of what had taken place over the last few centuries, passing on stories from one to the next. Seth was one of these 'Rememberers', keeping the records of their tribe. Being the oldest person, he'd lived through much of what needed recalling.

The wind turned, and Doc got his first whiff of the fire and of the burnt flesh. His belly rumbled. He swallowed bile and gagged.

Straightening up, he squared his shoulders and looked carefully around. The woods surrounding the village remained undamaged and quiet. There were a thousand places to hide. He watched for several heartbreaking moments, knowing he had to be sure those who'd attacked were gone before he ventured in.

When he was confident no one remained in hiding, he returned to the path leading down the hillside. His pace quickened until he was jogging. He scanned the brush on either side as he hurried on his way. Visions of the atrocities he'd seen, mingled with flashes of his family, and Jazz, his darling, sexy Jazz, leapt into his mind.

Jazz, the man he'd grown up with and had fallen head over heels in love with a handful of years ago, kept returning to his thoughts. If these were simply marauders, Jazz would have fought and probably died trying to protect the tribe. But if the attackers were after slaves or trade goods, the outcome might have been much different.

He thrust both of those thoughts aside. He couldn't bear to think of Jazz dead. Captive or slave might be worse in some ways. Doc's heart lurched. *At least you'd be alive, my love.*

"Just let it go," he muttered under his breath. "Wait until you know what's true."

He knew his own advice made sense. Hell, he'd preached it enough to others. Until now, he'd understood the message — but never so deeply or how important it was to follow.

Nearing the outer edge of the village, he noticed the well and gave a huge sigh of relief. Undamaged. They would at least have clean water. He'd need it if there were survivors to care for. He prayed there'd be an ample supply of those.

He slowed his pace, unwilling to rush into the horrors he knew awaited. The smell of blood filled his nostrils, and he wished he could wake up from the nightmare.

Damn the outlander family he'd been tending the last three days. *If only...* His thoughts wandered from the young father and the leg the man had broken when he fell from his horse. Doc had set the fracture and stayed to make sure no infection took hold.

If only I'd been here instead of miles away. If only his mother had accompanied him, as she sometimes did. If only Jazz had talked him out of going or urged him to go food fishing instead.

He went around a corner into what should have been the market street. As he'd seen from the ridge, the sellers' stalls and alcoves, or what remained of them, were in shambles. Food littered the ground and the stalls lay shattered on their sides, most of them burnt beyond repair.

It was the bodies that tore a sob from Doc. The stink of death wrapped around him like a cloak of sorrow, tight around his neck, his chest.

He saw the bodies of a young family first, lying sprawled in the remnants of the doorway to their home. Doc knew them well. He'd helped his mother with the child's birth three short years ago. She'd been preparing him, then, to take over when she died.

He turned away from that thought. *She can't be dead. I'm not ready for her to be dead.*

He refocussed his attention on the three villagers, rushing forwards to see if they were indeed gone. He dropped his satchel and touched his fingertips to each, to where they should have a pulse below their ears, quickly discerning the grisly answer. Doc closed the eyes of the dead and moved on.

It didn't take long for him to come across the next victims. The warriors of the tribe hadn't been idle. Doc had just made it to the corner of the next building when he saw half a dozen half-starved bodies strewn along the roadway. Unshaven, filthy, all of them seemed young, and that disturbed him. He checked to see if any were alive, but none was. A few paces on, he saw why. Trey, a middle-aged man who'd been a boon to the village and had a large family, lay dead from myriad wounds. A long slice from groin to sternum told the tale. Thankfully, Doc knew the death would have been fast, if painful.

"Goodbye, old friend," he whispered as he dropped to his knees beside the man. He reached out and closed Trey's eyes.

A noise from his left brought his bow arm up. Satchel thrust aside, he rose and turned all in one smooth motion.

"Son, it's only me," the ancient Rememberer said in his gruff, raspy voice. His long, white hair hung in tangled strands down his chest and back. His snow-white beard reached halfway to his waist. Doc always thought it made him look like a wizard from one of the ancient children's books his mother had rescued. A well-worn hat and long, flowing robes, so unlike Doc's own snug leather pants and rough wool jerkin, added to the whimsical effect.

"Seth!" Doc quickly lowered his bow and stepped forward. "I nearly shot you, you old fool." He drew the man into his arms, and a wave of relief filled him. Even though Seth barely reached Doc's chin, and his back was bent from age, the Rememberer held a special place in Doc's heart. Seth had been the one to teach him about the old towns and cities, about the grandeur as well as the catastrophic plagues that had nearly wiped humanity from the face of the Earth. For some, the lessons held little meaning, but for Doc, they tore at his soul. He wanted to see more of the people who'd survived the great devastation, while others seemed happy just to scratch a living from whatever they could.

"You'd never shoot me, unless you meant to." Seth hugged Doc with desperation, fingers like claws digging into the muscles in Doc's shoulders. "It's hellish bad, though. They came before dawn and…" He pushed Doc away and looked up into his eyes. "The children. They killed…" Tears streamed down the many crags in the old man's face.

Doc slid his bow up his arm, snuggling it tightly over his shoulder, and returned the arrow to its place in the sheath. He reached for his friend, gripped the man's arms and squeezed as if trying to force some of his own strength into the frail form. "I saw the tiny bodies from the ridge and knew it was going to be horrible. They didn't take us all, though, and that may be their undoing."

Seth closed his mouth and nodded. "You're right." He stepped back and straightened up as much as his body allowed. "I've managed to find a couple of people. We'll have to see how many were spared."

"Come on, then, we'll stick together." Doc handed his satchel to Seth. "We'll need this, I'm sure. If you carry it, I'll be able to protect us both a lot better."

Seth gripped the smooth, wooden handle and nodded. Heading back the way he'd come, he started off. "I've searched the outer area. There's no one alive there." He didn't turn, but Doc saw his shoulders shudder.

"My mother, father…my sister? Jazz, have you seen him?" Doc fought back the fear looming just below the surface. They couldn't be dead.

"I haven't found them." Seth looked over his shoulder and added, "Doesn't mean much. There are a lot of places to hide or escape to. And the bastards took many of us."

"Took?" Doc felt as if someone had kicked him in the belly. "Do you think they were slavers?"

"No, they didn't take just people. They took food and anything of value that wasn't too heavy." Seth resumed his walk towards the wreckage of the nearest building.

Doc followed, eyes constantly moving around the remains of the village and beyond. He couldn't take the chance of anyone returning to plunder the ruins. Pulling his bow off his shoulder, he slid an arrow free and held it in his other hand, prepared to load and fire at a second's notice.

Another body appeared, and Seth bent to check for life. He sagged and shook his head, closing the eyes of the dead man. He rose to his feet and hurried on.

"Slow up, old man. I can't watch you well enough if you go scampering away from me." Doc increased his pace but refused to let Seth's eagerness push him too much.

"There are injured." The Rememberer scowled, which was his own form of chastisement. "We really need to find them, and quickly."

"True, and I'll do all I can. You know that. But we do no one any good if we're hurt or attacked by returning marauders in our haste." Doc tried to be as kind as possible, knowing the man was suffering the loss as deeply as he was. "We'll find them."

Seth nodded but didn't say anything for a few moments. He ducked through the threshold leading into the next home only to let out a yell. "Doc, get in here."

Without thinking of the danger, Doc rushed under the half-fallen roof and knelt with Seth beside a middle-aged, dark-haired woman. She sat with her back against a wooden crate which had, no doubt, kept the roof from completely falling in. Her loose fitting pants were smeared with blood, mostly her own. Her shirt hung in rags, baring her breasts. He'd seen her many times before. Her name was Lily, and she'd been one of the women who made bread for the community. A task she wouldn't be doing again for some time, he thought when he saw her hands. They were burnt so badly the blistered skin had sloughed away, leaving great bloody, seeping holes.

"Clean cloths, Seth, we need to find more," he grumbled as he took the satchel from the man and opened it. He had some sterile cloth, but not enough to handle what he was sure he'd need.

Seth slipped away, saying, "I'll be back with bandages as soon as I can. Care for her."

Doc watched him go for a moment, hoping the old man knew where to look. A moan from Lily brought his attention back to her. He went about the task of smearing salve onto her hands then bandaging them carefully. "It's all right, Lily. You're safe, now. Old Seth and I will take care of you all. You'll see, it's all right."

He went on and on, talking nonsense yet knowing it would soothe her. He needed her calm. If she panicked and began screaming, and there were still marauders in the area, they'd be lost.

Lily seemed only half aware of what he was doing, and that probably helped her. She looked at him, then down at her hands, then back. Her eyes held that blank stare he'd seen only once before, when a babe had been stillborn. The mother had looked like Lily did now. He wondered if her mind would come back soon.

When Doc had tied the final knot and returned his meds to their place in his satchel, Seth reappeared, a cloth bag over his shoulder.

"Perfect timing." Doc got to his feet and approached the old man, holding out his arms. "Where did you find these?"

"The supply centre. It's not unharmed, but it's still standing," Seth replied evenly. "It's one of the few places they didn't destroy completely."

"Okay, did you see anyone on the way there or back?" Doc took the bag and set it on the ground between them. Inside, he saw dozens of rolled bandages wrapped in the usual tan coloured, tightly woven material.

"No, but I—"

Behind him, Lily moaned. Doc's attention shifted instantly to the injured woman. "We've got to get her to decent shelter. She's going to start making noise soon, and that'll endanger anyone around."

He stuffed the bandages into his satchel and handed it to Seth. "I'll carry her, if you can pack my bow and this thing." He nodded towards his bag. "We'll make the first place we find intact our headquarters."

"Course I can." Seth hefted the satchel and added, "There's a house not far that looks like it's still in good shape."

Doc bent to pick up the woman. Her breast slid over his arm, and he wondered where her man was, her children. "Lead the way."

Seth guided Doc to a house that turned out to be very close indeed. They skirted around one pile of rubble, and there it stood. Doc remembered it well. An elderly couple had lived in the one room building, both avid gardeners who'd loved nothing better than to get their hands dirty weeding the village's vast vegetable garden. There was no sign of them, and Doc refrained from asking.

Once Doc got Lily settled onto the large bed in the corner, he straightened up and surveyed the room. "You said you'd found a few others around. I need them here."

"If you'll stay with her, Doc, I'll go and get them. I only found two, both elderly but still feisty. Dent and his wife, Rose." The old man hurried out the door, his robes swaying around his lower legs. He stopped and peered back at Doc. "We're all right now, aren't we?"

Doc forced down his misgivings and tried to smile. "We'll make it. Just go find Dent and Rose."

Seth nodded and turned, scuttling off in the direction of the centre of town. Doc watched him skirt a burnt out house before vanishing around the corner.

"Doc." Lily's weak voice pulled him back inside.

He crossed the room and sat on the edge of the bed. The woman had managed to sit up but still had a blankness about her that worried him. Once he made sure the quilt covered her decently, he looked into her eyes. "I'm here. You're safe now, Lily."

Her brow furrowed. "Nils, is he here, too?" She looked around the room, her face going from hopeful to sorrowful resignation when she saw it was empty except for the two of them. "My little Danny, he's not here either, is he?"

"No, he's not. He might be somewhere in the village. I haven't had time to search, yet. But I will." He slipped his fingers under her chin and lifted her face. "You know I will."

Lily blinked then nodded. "Find my Danny, please."

He couldn't lie to her. Her child might very well be one of the dead he hadn't discovered yet. Releasing her chin, he simply whispered, "I'll do my best."

The woman closed her eyes and again nodded. As if the short conversation had stolen the last of her energy, she lay back. Her breathing deepened, and he wasn't surprised when he saw she'd fallen asleep. The events of the day and her burns had taken a huge toll on her. A body could only sustain so much before it shut down. His assurance must have been enough to allow her to let the stress go, at least for the time being.

Doc went to see what the cupboards and shelves held by way of supplies he'd need. Fresh water was a must. He'd have Seth and whomever he brought back get some when they returned. He set about cleaning the counters and table then found a dozen bowls he could use for mixing meds.

He'd just finished searching the cupboards when he heard Seth's voice at the door. "I found them. Dent's fine. Rose is limping, but it doesn't seem to be serious."

Doc hurried over to see if Rose's injury needed attention. Dent, a short, round man with almost no hair, had his arm around his wife and was taking most of her weight. Rose, who appeared a little younger and more slender than her man, grimaced when she put any amount of weight on her right foot.

When Doc reached for her, she pushed him away, saying, "It's nothing. I twisted it when I was running from those mongrel bastards ransacking our home." She slumped into a chair and gazed around the room, as if getting her bearings. She spotted Lily and looked up at Doc. "She hurt badly?"

From the look on her face, Doc knew she'd seen her share of death and injury that day. "Burnt her hands. She'll be okay, but she's worried about her man and little Danny."

"Her man's dead," Rose said in a dull, flat tone. She sat looking at the floor and for a few seconds was quiet. She finally added, "I don't know about Danny. Zoe, the young warrior woman, she herded a bunch of kiddies into the woods." Looking up, she found Doc's eyes and whispered hopefully, "He might have been one of them."

Doc squatted in front of her. "Did you see where she went?"

"Towards the cold storage cave we keep the produce in." A tear trickled down her cheek, which she either ignored or didn't feel.

"I know it well," he replied and patted the older woman's hands she'd clenched in her lap. "I remember you chasing me from it when I was a child. Apples always were my downfall, 'specially early in the fall."

"I remember." She smiled tentatively.

He got to his feet and looked at old Dent's face. "Will you be able to take care of things here so I can go in search of more survivors?" His thoughts went to Jazz, but he forced them down for the moment.

"Yes, of course I can," Dent's deep voice reassured him. He took Doc by the arm and led him away from his wife and Seth. He glanced back then put his head close to Doc's and whispered, "There aren't many of us left, Doc. Those they didn't shackle together, they killed, or tried to."

"That's what I figured." He glanced down at Dent's side, seeing a knife strapped to his belt, but nothing else. "Is the knife all you have?"

"Yes, but I know where there's a bow here." He strode over to a tall cupboard near the back door and flung it open.

Inside, Doc saw a well-used long bow as well as an old rifle that he'd seen a townsman show off. Ammunition was rare, so he'd never actually seen it fired.

Dent retrieved the bow and a half-full quiver of arrows from a hook on the inside of the door. "Seth and I'll be just fine here." He grabbed Doc's shoulder and whispered urgently, "I haven't seen Jazz."

Doc's heart slammed against his ribs. "Haven't seen his body either, right?"

"That's right," Dent nodded. "No body, nothing. He could have been taken with the others, cuffed."

"Thanks, Dent." Doc pulled free of the man's hand and headed for the doorway. He grabbed his bow, the quiver of short arrows and a small pouch filled with emergency meds for his belt. Once he'd tied that at his hip, he glanced over his shoulder at the small group and said, "Be careful and keep Lily quiet. I'll be back as soon as I can."

He hurried out and began his search. Methodically, going from the remains of one dwelling to the next, he found only bodies and became more and more discouraged.

He worked his way towards the cave where Rose thought Zoe had taken the children. He passed the body of a man he'd known, Gus, a warrior of great repute. The man was obviously dead, and Doc took a few seconds to mourn him.

The ruined homes, the mounds of broken brick and burnt timbers, made him want to weep. He, along with the others of the village, had worked hard to create a safe place to live — a place where families could grow and prosper. All that was gone, now.

Where's Mother, Father? What's happened to Robin?
And where's Jazz?

The thought brought him up short, and it took a few moments before he could force himself to go on. Jazz was alive, he had to be. Doc just had to find him.

When he came across a grisly pile of dead, he realised they weren't villagers and smiled. It seemed some of the tribes' warriors had been successful in defending their families, at least for a time.

A throaty male voice came from beyond the bodies. "Doc, help."

He rushed into a nearby hovel. The familiar face of a warrior looked up at him. The man's body lay across a mound of rubble, his right leg trapped beneath the collapsed roof.

"Fin, where are you hurt? Your leg. Is everything else all right?" He knelt beside the man and reached for a pulse point at his neck. The drumming of the man's heartbeat bumped steadily against his fingertips.

"Yeah, leg's maybe broke, but I'm okay," the man replied in a hoarse voice. "I need water. Got any?"

"No, but hang on and I'll get some." Doc checked him over, assuring himself the leg wasn't broken, just trapped beneath a large block of stone, possibly twisted from the big man's pulling and prying. After a quick exam of the rest of his body, Doc scrambled over to the water bucket he'd seen on his way in and dragged it to where Fin lay. Gratefully, Fin dunked his entire head in and, after a moment, came up sputtering, water streaming from his long, black hair. He drank then, until Doc pulled the pail from his mouth.

"Take it easy. You'll puke it up if you drink too much, and you know it."

Fin nodded and set the bucket aside then placed his gnarled hands on the block trapping him. "Any thoughts on how to get me out of here?"

"Yeah," Doc said and went for one of the least damaged wooden beams. He chose one that was a good deal longer than he was tall and pushed it under the corner of the block. He lifted it, and the stone moved. Fin grunted, but from his reaction, Doc figured he wasn't in any more pain than before.

Doc looked around and went to pick up a chunk of rock to use to pry the block higher. He placed it a couple of paces away from the tip of the beam and nodded his head at Fin. "When I lift it, you pull yourself out."

Fin's jaw tightened, and he nodded. "Go for it."

Doc heaved down on the beam. The rubble lifted off Fin's leg, and the man pulled himself out. It all went exactly how Doc hoped.

Once he was free, Fin scrambled away from where he'd been trapped and rubbed his leg. He looked up and asked, "Have you found others?"

"Yes, a few. I just got back from the outer farmstead." He bowed his head, biting back his anger at being away when he was most needed. "Did you see my family? What about Jazz?" He again bent to assess the man's injuries.

"I saw him, but not since it all went quiet. I don't know if he's alive or dead." He gazed into Doc's eyes and added, "I'm sorry."

Taking a deep breath, Doc patted Fin's leg. "Don't be. Shit happens. I'll find him." He pushed himself to his feet and extended a hand. "Let's see if you can get around."

Fin grabbed Doc's hand and pulled himself upright then tested his legs. "A bit sore, but it'll be as right as rain in no time." He made his way to the entrance and peered outside. "Which way are you going?"

"Left. The storage cave."

Fin headed that way, and Doc quickly followed. A few minutes later, they came to where the trail led towards the base of the small mountain against which their village backed. Several caves offered cold storage for fruit and vegetables, as well as protection for themselves from the winter snows and other dangers—if they could get to them. Obviously, there hadn't been time.

"Zoe's supposed to be in here with some of the children." Doc thought about Zoe and her affinity for knives. "We'd better be careful, too. She's all woman, but she's also a warrior to be reckoned with."

Fin nodded and slowed his pace, looking around as he went.

Brush surrounded them, the trail grown over in the last couple of months. When Doc spotted the cave's mouth, he laid a hand on Fin's shoulder to halt the man.

"Let me go in first. Zoe knows me and hopefully will realise who I am before she skewers me."

Fin stepped aside, allowing Doc to brush past him. The footing was uneven as Doc made his way closer to the cave. He stopped and turned towards Fin. "Wish me luck."

"You got it." Fin hunkered down, and Doc knew he'd be there until he came back—or was sure he wasn't coming back.

Taking a deep breath, Doc stepped out of the brush into the cleared area just in front of the wide, black opening. He slung his bow over his shoulder and cupped his hands, funnel-like, in front of his mouth. Before he could call out, a woman's voice came from his left.

"Just hold it, right there."

Doc froze and smiled. He'd known she'd be ready for him, or someone, so this wasn't a shock. He moved his hands away from his face, hoping the woman would recognise him. Something sharp pressed against the side of his neck.

"I said, hold it, asshole."

Doc did as he was told, trusting she'd check to see who he was before sticking him with whatever blade she held at his neck.

"Put your hands behind your head."

He quickly complied, pushing his bow out of the way. The muscles in his belly tightened. He knew Zoe would be on edge, her nerves strung taut.

"Lock your fingers."

Again, he followed her orders quickly. The hand on his elbow came as a surprise and, when she spun him around, he nearly fell over his own feet. She grabbed his arm and steadied him. When he straightened up, he faced her.

An abundantly curved and, if he ignored the hack job she'd done on her dark hair, quite beautiful Zoe stood before him. A tan vest and leggings along with the brown skirt and loose-fitting blouse camouflaged her well against the stone behind her.

Recognition brightened her exhausted face. "It's really you, Doc," she murmured, as if hardly daring to believe he'd come. Haunted eyes looked up into his.

He reached for her. "Yes, it's me. How many did you manage to get up here?"

Nestled in his arms, the knife laid against his back, she took a deep, shuddering breath before replying. "Seven. Not enough."

Doc stroked her hair. Her breathing slowly calmed, her body relaxed into his. He noticed his cock thickening but fought the urge to thrust against her.

Jazz, think of Jazz, he reminded himself.

"Seven more than if you hadn't been there," he said in a soft voice. "Seven the bastards didn't get hold of. You did well, Zoe."

"Not enough." She looked up into his eyes. "Too many died. So many more were dragged off by those..." Her face crumpled and tears streamed down her cheeks.

"Yes, too many," Doc said for her, and his own eyes misted over. He let her weep for a moment then remembered Fin still crouching in the brush. "Come on, sweet lady, let's see to those children. And, I'm not alone. I found Fin. He's hurt, but not badly."

Stepping away from Doc, Zoe wiped her eyes with the back of her hand. She slipped her knife into the sheath hanging from her belt and squared her shoulders. "Yes, seen him in the village many times. Don't know him well, though, other than to say hello." She locked eyes with him and added, "Never found much need of a warrior before." A small grin curled her lips.

Over his shoulder, Doc called, "Fin, come give a hand. I've found her."

Fin entered the clearing and nodded. "I'm very glad you're all right, Zoe. Equally as glad you didn't slit our Doc's throat."

"As is he, it would seem."

"Let's see to the young ones," Doc interjected and strode past Zoe into the cave.

Inside, around a small fire, sat the children. Doc recognised them all and frowned when he understood not all he'd secretly hoped were there had made it. With the help of Zoe and Fin, they gathered up all of them, plus a sack of dried fruit they found in the nearly emptied storage alcoves.

The trip back to their makeshift headquarters didn't take long. Even with their arms full of children and supplies, the going was easy. Children who were much too quiet. The loss they'd suffered would take time to heal, if it ever did.

When they approached the home Doc had designated as their headquarters, he was surprised to see more people there than when he'd left. At least two dozen came to meet them and help with the youngsters.

An older woman, Claire he thought her name was, came and took the two boys from Doc's arms. She cooed and cuddled them and, before they'd gone far from him, they were less sombre looking. Wide eyed and grubby, they'd all get baths soon and hopefully fed shortly after that. Getting back to something close to normal would go a long way to help their healing.

He turned away and focussed on those who were injured. He bumped into Dent, who took his arm and led him to the side of the crowded room.

"Where'd they all come from?"

Dent smiled and shrugged. "They wandered in, mostly one at a time. They just seemed to arrive and stay. None of them have homes, now."

"Well, it'll save me finding them, I guess."

"We'll need to find more undamaged houses." Dent scratched his head. "We can't all stay here for long."

"Yes, I know." Doc ran a hand over his brow. The responsibility of caring for the small group weighed heavily on his shoulders. "There are a couple in this part of the village. Not homes, but buildings that are still standing."

"Did you find any others out there?"

"Just these few." Again his thoughts went to his family and Jazz. He shook himself and added, "Tonight, I think we should stay close. The children will need people around them, and the elders will, too. Is Seth all right? What about Lily?"

"Seth is fine. He's been organising spaces for anyone who comes in. Lily...her hands are giving her hell, but she's a brave one. She'll be all right, I'm sure."

Doc nodded and ticked finding space for everyone off his list of chores he needed to do. Finding out about his family came high on it. Tomorrow, there would time for other things, or so he hoped.

He glanced through the open door and realised the light was fading. Settling everyone down wasn't going to be easy.

"I think we'd better get them sorted out for the night. It's going to be a rough one for most of them."

Fin looked around and nodded. "Dent and Rose are the only couple who made it, so far."

"Yeah, we might find more, but not tonight."

He strode past Fin, making for the centre of the room, where he'd spotted Seth.

"Hey, old man, how are you holding up?" He laid a hand on Seth's shoulder, gauging his strength.

"I'm all right. Better than many here." Seth's eyes shone, as if he were close to tears.

"Hang on. I need you to help me get them tucked in."

"Yes, it's growing dark. I wish we could start a fire in here, but smoke coming from a chimney looks different than if it comes from burning buildings. I don't think we should take any chances of drawing attention to ourselves until we're stronger."

Doc nodded his agreement. "At least the well is safe, so we've got water. Food next. In the morning, we'll sort out more." Over Seth's shoulder, he saw Rose handing out blankets that must have been recovered from a number of ruined houses. It seemed he wasn't alone in his thoughts.

In a surprisingly short time, they'd washed and fed the children what they could, and everyone found a place to lie down. It was crowded, but no one complained. Talking fell to a low hum for a while, but even that died when the light faded to the total darkness of night. Snores followed a few minutes later. A child's whimpering was quickly hushed by the soft cooing of a woman.

Doc, who'd been sitting next to the front door, rose and slunk out into the ruin of the village. He made his way down a relatively undamaged alleyway, heading for the small dwelling in which his family had lived. Rubble tripped him up repeatedly along the way. There were few bodies around, but he checked each one to which he came, just in case any were alive. None was. He stopped often to listen for the sounds of survivors but heard nothing but the hissing crackle of the few fires still burning. His heart grew heavy with dread.

It didn't take long for him to reach the familiar stretch of street. The devastation took his breath. Few structures remained intact. Even so, he knew exactly where he stood.

When he reached the doorway of his family home, he paused, hand on the doorframe, and peered into the rubbish strewn interior. The smattering of moonlight didn't help enough, and he eased inside. After only a few paces, he saw the shape of a man propped up against the far wall in the largest of the rooms.

His heart sank, but he hurried forward to see. He knew before he'd even reached the bulky form. The long, flowing, grey-streaked hair was the give-away. A large, black smear across the man's face and the wide-eyed vacant stare told the story.

Doc dropped to his knees beside his father's body and let go the full force of his grief. His head back, tears streamed down his cheeks as a howl of agony tore free. "Father!"

He'd known, deep inside, his father would be either dead or badly injured. The man had always been too much the warrior to let in the invaders without fighting and too old to be of value to them as a slave or to sell. But seeing him crumpled against the remains of the home they'd all shared was an agony for which he hadn't prepared. How could anyone prepare themselves for this?

Doc wept, stopping only because he knew he had to search even deeper into the house. His mother and sister were still missing. And Jazz. Where was the man?

With a surprisingly steady hand, Doc reached out and closed his father's eyes. "I swear, Father, I swear, I'll find the villagers and bring them home," he said to the man who'd raised him.

He struggled to his feet then searched the rest of the house. The pantry door was open, empty jars and broken pottery littering the floor and shelves. The three bedrooms all bore signs of struggle, but Doc found no one else in the place. His mother and sister were gone.

Doc raced out into the street and headed for Jazz's tiny hut on the outskirts of the village. It took him only a few minutes to find his way to where Jazz's home should be. In its place only burning timbers glowed.

Stomach in knots, Doc searched the area but came up with nothing. No body, no evidence of Jazz at all. Hope surged, but he forced himself to think clearly. Jazz could very well be dead somewhere else in the wreckage. Yet, he prayed his lover was safe, somewhere.

"I'll find you, my love," Doc murmured to the wind. *I have to find you.*

He turned his back on the fire and made his way to the relative safety of the group. Once there, he didn't go inside. Instead, he curled up on his side beside the door and hugged himself against the cool night air.

Sleep came eventually and took him into its embrace.

Chapter Two

Something warm and smooth slid across Doc's cheek, making him smile. He rolled onto his back and stretched out his legs, splaying them wide. Clenching his right hand around his crotch, he pushed his left under his head. He sighed with pleasure.

Lips pressed to his, a tongue flicked across them, wetting his mouth and giving him the taste of his lover. A hand strayed over his chest, found and pinched each nipple into excited hardness before Doc groaned. He thrust his chest out.

The hand moved on, parted his shirt front and slipped inside. The fingers were cool, the palm a little warmer moving over his skin.

Doc gave his cock a healthy squeeze and hoped the straying hand would wander downwards. It did, and he squirmed again, his excitement rising. His heartbeat drummed in his ears like a tune he'd dance to later, after the orgasm he approached had run its wicked good course.

"Get your hand outta the way," a man whispered with an urgency that surprised Doc.

"Yeah," he mumbled and pulled away from his cock. Thrusting his hips upwards flattened his shaft against the tight leather. He held that position for what seemed like hours, straining, arse clenching.

The tug of laces, dragged through the holes in the front of his pants, pulled at him. Another kind of tug, firmer, more insistent, shifted his hips, his arse. Cool air caressed his lower belly, his pubes and upper thighs. His balls pulled up.

"Oh yeah." The same male voice came from somewhere south.

Doc wanted to speak, to encourage a little oral action, but his body seemed frozen. No matter. A moment later, the smooth, wet softness of a tongue slithered along his cock shaft. His dick pulsed, thickening. It pulsed again, the head lifting into the air.

"Yess!"

The pleasure amazed him, darting like snakes' tongues towards his sac. Wet heat wrapped the head of his cock in softness. Suction pulled at his flesh, and soft, tantalising moistness slithered around the crown and down the shaft.

Doc thrust his hips upwards, striving to bury his cock deep between the soft, wet lips. It worked. The man above him, it had to be a man, allowed Doc's shaft to enter his mouth then swallowed when the head touched the back of his throat.

The automatic clenching of the man's gullet sent a lightning bolt of bliss straight to Doc's balls. He reached for them, but something, or someone, knocked his arm aside long before his hand got there.

"Jazz, don't fucking tease me."

A moment's silence followed while the man's mouth slid up and down Doc's shaft. The tongue flicked back and forth across the head before sweet heat swallowed him again. Taking it all in one slow, deliberate stroke, the man had Doc's toes curling in moments. Just when Doc was sure he couldn't hold back another second, the mouth slipped off his throbbing cock head.

"Fuck, Jazz." Doc's balls ached. His cock pulsed, its head tapping the chin of the man who'd been driving him insane with pleasure.

"Yeah, I like fucking, too." Jazz grinned up at him. His blue eyes seemed more brilliant than Doc remembered them. His unruly mop of dirty blond hair gave him the look of a wild animal.

"Suck it," Doc growled, his frustration beginning to get the better of him.

Jazz nodded, pursed his lips then leant forward. The crinkled mouth pressed against the head of Doc's cock then parted, taking him in, inch by shuddering inch, until Jazz's chin pressed against Doc's ball sac. The blond man waggled his head, sending Doc's cock into a wild dance inside his mouth.

"That's it, suck it. Lick it." Doc laid his head back and closed his eyes, letting his lover perform his oral magic.

Jazz sucked hard then relaxed his jaw muscles, withdrawing until just the tip of Doc's dick rested against his lips. Warm breath washed over the tip, and it throbbed in response, only to be taken in and swallowed again. In and out, slowly at first but quickening as did Doc's heartbeat. Soon Doc found himself thrusting in and pulling back, fucking his lover's mouth.

A warm hand slid along Doc's inner thigh, coming to rest just below his balls. He shivered and strained upwards. He was close, so very close he could taste the climax.

He thrust again and grunted. His body clenched. Every muscle grew taut as he spewed his load into Jazz's mouth. Just then, his lover pressed the knuckles of his fist into the underside of Doc's balls. A guttural groan escaped Doc as another stream of cum erupted into Jazz's throat. Stars flashed, and he lost his vision. He shuddered and trembled and could barely get a breath as his world flashed and whirled.

When everything calmed down, Doc opened his eyes and saw only the darkness of the village street. He sat up, his heart racing. The lane was quiet, the only movement was himself, the only sound, the mad beating of his heart.

"Jazz," he whispered, feeling the loss much greater now that he'd dreamt of the man he loved. There was no reply, and he sighed.

Struggling to his feet, he gazed around then down at the front of his pants. The fly lay open, his cock curled over the top. A dribble of cum oozed from the tip.

Doc strode over to one of the many bushes scattered around the village and pulled off a large leaf. Carefully, he wiped off the remains of his climax and checked the front of his leather pants. He couldn't see anything, but it was dark, so he'd have to remember to check again in the morning.

The fires had died down. The smell of them had faded to just a hint of smoke. He walked to the end of the street and peered along the next. Nothing stirred.

Rather than bunk out for the rest of the night with his memories and fears for his lover's safety, Doc entered the house shared by the survivors and found a corner just inside the door. Someone stirred to his left, but that was the only sound. He crossed his arms over his chest and was soon asleep.

* * * *

"Never mind, Doc. I'm well enough to help gather food." Lily scowled and shook her bandaged hands at him. "We all have to help, not just you men who think us women need to be protected. We fought the bastards who razed the village, too, you know!"

Doc ducked his head and finished off the meal of dry bread and the carrot someone had retrieved from the storage cave. Lily was right, but he hated to see the injured woman struggling with her heavily wrapped hands. He'd checked them twice a day for the past two and was sure healing was taking place. Stuffing the last of the carrot into his mouth, he frowned and looked up at her. "Yes, we all know you fought and fought well, Lily. All of you did."

"And we need to build up the stores for winter," chimed in Seth.

Doc turned and glared down the rough wooden table at the old man.

Seth didn't look away. "You know I'm right, and so's Lily."

It was Doc who looked away. "Yes, I know. It's just going to be so much harder with the few people we have."

"We all know that." Lily rose from her seat at the table and stood looking down at Doc. "We also know you'll find our families, those who are still alive."

"That's the plan. As soon as I'm sure you are all going to be okay." Doc pushed away from the table and paced across the room. The children sat along the wall diligently munching away at the sparse fare they'd been given. Bread and vegetables would keep them going for a time, but they'd need meat or fish soon.

Fin came to stand with him, and together they looked down at the small band of youngsters. "We'll be fine, Doc."

"Yeah, I think you're right." Doc faced Fin and laid a hand on the man's shoulder. "I'll have to take a few supplies. I can forage for food, but there's a few things that I just can't find...out there."

"No need to even ask. Take what you have to."

Lily joined them and gazed up at Doc. "Find my Danny. He's all I have in the world, now."

Her eyes shone with unshed tears, yet Doc knew they were close.

The small group at the table joined them. Rose put her arm around Lily and hushed the woman. "Doc'll do his best. You know that. We'll keep the wolf from the door and gather as much as we can for stores while he's gone."

Seth cleared his throat and, when everyone turned to see what he wanted, said, "We've got work to do. Let's all get busy." He looked up into Doc's eyes and winked.

"Thanks, Seth," he mouthed and, as quietly as possible, eased himself away from the gathering.

Decision made, Doc wanted to get on the road as quickly as possible. He retrieved his bow, quiver and med satchel from its corner before leaving the house. He made his way to his family's home and refilled his bag from his mother's stores, making sure he left plenty for the village.

Memories of her teachings thrust into his thoughts and, for a moment, he let his mind wander. She used to say he had a talent for healing. He didn't know what she meant, but he did know he loved that he could care for people in a way not many others could. His sister also had the gift, and it had been a tossup as to whether he or she went to the outlander family.

Guilt tore at him. If only she'd pressed a little harder, he was sure she could have persuaded him she deserved to go. Instead, he'd bullied her into letting him.

"Doc, I want to go with you."

Whirling around, Doc just about fell over his feet in his attempt to see who'd sneaked up on him so easily. The woman, Zoe, stood in the doorway, her arms crossed under her ample chest.

"You what?" Doc fumbled with the buckles of the satchel.

"Go with you, dumbass," repeated Zoe with a stubborn scowl on her face.

He knew that look. She'd made up her mind, and it would take some doing to talk her out of it. "There's too much to do here, Zoe. I need you to stay and protect these people. Help them get ready for winter." He finished securing his meds and hung the satchel from his belt, the weight a reassurance. "I'll be travelling fast. You'll never keep up."

"Listen, I'm as capable as any of the warriors. And of course I can keep up." She took a step closer and uncrossed her arms. Pointing a finger at him, she used it to punctuate her next words, stabbing him in the chest. "Fin and Dent are quite capable of taking care of these people. Rose isn't any slouch, either. Nor is Seth when it comes down to it."

Taking a step back, Doc rubbed his chest where she'd jabbed him with her finger. He knew what she said was the truth. He'd seen her best several of the village warriors and admired her skill. "Dent is old.

Fin can't do it alone. What if the marauders come back? What if some other band of cutthroats decides to take advantage and attacks? The survivors would be easy pickings."

Zoe apparently couldn't answer those last questions and stood with her arms at her sides, a dejected look on her face. She wiped a hand across her forehead. After a few more moments of silence, she looked up at him again. "And what if you can't do this alone? What if you need help?"

Doc knew she was right in so many ways. He just needed to know the villagers left behind were safe. She could protect them. "It's settled. You're staying."

She didn't argue or try to change his mind. She simply looked up at him and nodded then turned and walked out.

He watched her, taking note of the supple sway of her hips, observing how the material pulled tight across the flesh. He tore his gaze away and looked around the room. He spotted the earthenware jar in which his mother kept dried fruit. He reached out and flipped off the lid. Inside, he found a good-sized handful of dried apples. He deposited them into one of the pockets of his jerkin.

On his way out, he picked up one of the old style canteens from its hanger behind the door. Once he filled it from the well, he'd be on his way.

He passed the safe house, as they'd begun to call it, but didn't stop other than to wave towards Seth, who busily piled rubble into a wooden wheelbarrow. The old man returned his wave and bowed his head, as if offering some kind of blessing on Doc.

Next stop, the well. He lowered the pail over the side and listened for the splash. A second later, he heard it and peered down. The pail tipped.

Once he'd filled his canteen, he capped it and turned towards the road leading out of the village. He'd followed the marauders' trail for about half a mile the day after his return, so he knew where to begin. Tucking his bow a little higher over his shoulder, he started off.

It didn't take long for the noise from the villagers to fade into silence. Ferns and small berry bushes encroached onto the old roadway, grass and weeds pushed their way up through the broken tarmac. Maples and alders towered over him, long spindly trees that would one day take over. The evergreens had reclaimed their places farther along, and he hurried on.

Doc saw traces of the villagers' forced march. Discarded clothing, packs, blankets and all manner of things carried then later tossed aside when the going got rough.

The first body came as a surprise. He'd assumed once they were taken, the villagers would be babied until they got to their destination. Apparently not.

The woman's name had been Ruth. Her body lay like a rag doll at the edge of the pathway, the clothing torn and ragged. He didn't linger to see more. Wild animals would take care of her soon enough.

Two more corpses dotted the day's travel, but he didn't stop to bury them. Only to make sure they weren't his mother, sister or Jazz. Once satisfied, he hurried on, tracking the others easily.

When darkness fell, he ducked off the path and found a clearing large enough to make camp. A small stream meandered over the rocks not far away, so he knew he'd have water. He gathered dry grass and sticks then a few bigger pieces of wood.

He'd just settled down with his back against a large, fallen tree, the tiny, nearly smokeless flame directly in front of him, when a branch snapped nearby. Before he could notch an arrow, Zoe stepped out of the darkness into the circle of light on the other side of the fire.

Doc's jaw dropped open, and he let his hand fall to his side, bow untouched. When he could get his mouth working, he stammered, "Where in hell did you come from?"

Zoe smiled and took a few steps towards him and the meagre blaze. "The village. I followed you."

Doc blinked, his anger on the rise. "Well, no shit. I thought I'd made myself clear. You were going to stay in the village and help there."

"Yes, I remember. I just didn't agree with you." Zoe hunkered down on the other side of the fire and grabbed a branch poking from the flames. While thrusting the stick in and out of the blaze, she added, "I also knew it'd be useless to argue with you. You're a stubborn man used to getting your way."

Anger faded to annoyance. Doc settled back against the log and crossed his arms over his chest, glaring at the beauty across from him. "So you just decided to ignore my advice?"

"Yeah, pretty much. Fin, Seth and Dent are capable. The women left aren't likely to let anyone harm the children there, either." She tossed the stick into the fire and sat down, her legs crossed, Indian fashion. "Besides, I'm still sure I'll be more help to you when you find the villagers."

"And you know so much about rescuing people and the dangers of these bandits." Doc reached into the pocket of his jerkin and pulled out the slices of dried apple. Chewing on the first, he looked up and saw Zoe eying his meagre meal. "Did you bring any food with you?"

"No, I didn't want to deprive anyone back there." She looked into the fire. "The kids need it. I thought I'd snag a rabbit."

"With what?" Doc looked close and didn't see a bow or any other form of weapon.

Zoe reached behind her and pulled out a sling shot, a small but deadly device from what he recalled. "This. My bow was broken. This works."

"Yes, I've seen you use it." Doc held out his hand, offering her a share of his meal. "This isn't like a hunting trip. You could be killed. Or captured, which could very well be worse."

"I know, but I couldn't just sit and do nothing."

"So, you thought you'd tag along and get in my way."

Zoe's eyes darted to his. "No, you can't think that."

"I can." The woman thought much too highly of herself, in his opinion. Working together was one thing, running off to find adventure, at a time like this, was something entirely different.

Under her breath, Zoe said, "I can take care of myself. If you prefer, I'll travel alone. I'd hate to be a bother." She rose and made as if to leave his camp.

"Hold it." He stopped her before she'd taken a step. "You wandering off isn't going to make my life any easier. I'll simply worry about you getting eaten by some wild animal before the horde captures you."

Eyes flashing, she glared at him. "Well, it seems I've really made a mess of things for you."

"It would seem so." He slid another piece of apple into his mouth and chewed.

"What would you have me do?"

He could see how much those words cost her. Her shoulders sagged, and her face took on the look of someone whose hopes had been shattered.

"Sit, eat some dried apple," he said and held out his hand. He had no desire to hurt her, but he did want her to understand that her actions affected not only herself.

Zoe walked around the fire and squatted next to him. "I'm sorry." She chewed another piece of apple then sat down, her body touching his at hip and shoulder. "I honestly didn't mean to make your life more difficult." She turned and faced him. "I really can help."

Large brown eyes peered into his. Her hair curled over her forehead and framed her face, making her look too young to be here alone. Her cheeks, flushed from the day's travel, gave her a cherubic look he dared not think about too long. When she blinked, her long lashes swept down and kissed the upper part of her cheek, as he wished his lips could do.

Doc dragged his gaze away, pushing down the feeling of lust suddenly on the rise. Thrusting another slice of apple into his mouth, he pondered his feelings for the woman. He loved Jazz with all his heart, yet he found Zoe incredibly attractive. She was small, but he knew she was more than able to take care of herself. She'd proven that when she tucked those children away safely in the cave and been ready to lay down her life in order to protect them.

His anger at her rash behaviour vanished. She might very well be able to help him after all.

"If you want me to go back, I really would be all right."

"No, you'll stay with me." He glanced at her then back at the small, hot fire. "What's done is done."

Frowning, Zoe chewed. "Thanks, Doc."

"Best let the fire die down. Less chance of being found."

"Did you see the signs of the villagers along the way? The dead?" Zoe kept her eyes towards the flames.

"Yes, of course. They didn't travel fast, but for the wounded, it was too much."

"Jazz, there's been no sign of him."

Doc looked at her and tightened his jaw. "No. No sign, nothing. I'll find him."

They sat in silence until they'd finished their meal and the flames had died to embers. Zoe leant forward and, after picking up a stick, stirred the glowing coals then scooped them all into a pile. "That should take care of the fire. I'm bushed." With that, she scooted around to the other side of the fire pit and lay down, facing him. "Good night, Doc."

"Night, Zoe," he said, and almost added, 'I'm glad you followed me.' He rose from his place and did a quick scout of the area around their small camp before he, too, settled in for the night.

He tossed and turned for a while, worries about Jazz and the location of the remainder of his family plaguing him. Finally, sleep crept in, and he sank into restless slumber.

* * * *

"Wake up. Wake up before you hurt someone."

The urgency in Zoe's voice dragged Doc out of the dream, kicking and groaning. He sat up and peered into the darkness while trying to slow his heartbeat. Around them, the forest lay in its pre-dawn dimness. The sun had barely begun its morning journey into the sky, but there was light enough to see his campmate clearly. Her sleek, black hair clung to her head in tiny waves. Its shortness left her neck exposed, and the shirt she'd worn to bed had somehow come unfastened, revealing a beautiful valley of shadow between her pale tits. The mounds tempted him, but the last vestiges of the nightmare from which he'd woken shattered any thought of romance. Images of the dead villagers, Jazz among them, had made his heart race. He reassured himself it had indeed been just a dream.

He gazed around the clearing and was sure they were alone.

"Damn," Doc muttered and scrubbed his eyes with the heels of his hands. Behind the flashes of brilliance, his mind went into overdrive. Food came first. They needed to trap something or they'd be too weak to fight. Zoe's strength was a question he wasn't prepared to ask, but he'd seen her scrap and knew she'd be an asset if, or when, he needed her.

He lowered his hands and looked up at her. "Sorry. Nightmares." He shrugged and appreciated her quick nod. She appeared to understand.

"I've got a line in the creek just over there." She pointed to where the trickling stream meandered into the underbrush. "Water's deeper in there, and I spotted movement under the surface. Let's hope for fish."

"You must have been up early." He looked at where she'd lain down the previous evening, but the ground showed nothing, no mark or indent from where she'd rested. Looking up at her again, he asked, "What did you use for bait?"

"I carry a couple of hooks and a line in here." She thrust up a small, leather pouch from her waist to show him. "And there are all kinds of bugs and worms for the fish to eat, if there are any fish."

"Smart woman." He nodded, admiring her resourcefulness. "Let's go see if you caught anything." He pushed himself to his feet and held his hand out.

Zoe took hold of him and headed off towards the brush close by. Bending at the waist to get under the branches, Doc became very aware of the curve of her butt so close to his face. Just because it was rounder, more supplely muscled than what he was used to, didn't necessarily mean he couldn't appreciate the flexing. Branches scratched his cheek, and he ducked often to get free of them, each time bringing his nose closer to the firm swell of her arse.

A few dozen paces brought them into a clearing he hadn't noticed the night before. Serene came to mind. A soft breeze brought the scent of the water to him, as well as that of the mud and the ferns growing along its edge. The smell of wild mint perked him up, and he quickly found the plant. He plucked a leaf and sniffed it, sighing with pleasure. An herb for stomach pains, he thought and determined to return for more to dry for the winter.

"Here, come quick." Zoe darted away from his side and raced for the makeshift fishing pole. A short, flexible stick, strung with a bit of braided hair, bounced in the crook of the forked branch where she'd obviously left it.

Zoe grabbed for the rod just as it skittered towards the water's edge. Snatching it up, she gave a good tug. Her eyes widened. "It's a biggun," she called and slowly walked backwards, dragging the 'biggun' towards shore.

"Careful," Doc said, standing beside her, his fingers itching to wrap around the stick.

Once she'd backed up enough, the fish leapt into the air and flashed its silvery sides in the morning sunlight. Doc stepped forward and quickly grabbed it around the middle. It was so fat, his fingers couldn't go completely around it.

"Yes, breakfast," cheered Zoe from beside him. She dropped the makeshift rod and reached for the hook. A precious item, she apparently wanted her hands on it before his. Deftly, she flipped her wrist, freeing the silver metal from its mouth. After rinsing and drying both it and her line on her shirt, she stashed them in her pouch.

"Nicely done, Zoe. Breakfast it is. Let's get it cleaned and back to camp. You want to start a fire while I do the messy bits?"

"You bet. Small and hot." The woman was soon lost to his sight, and he set about cleaning the fish.

Not many minutes later, they sat enjoying a meal of flaky white flesh and licking their fingers.

"We should get moving," Doc said, guilt tearing at him for taking the few moments of peace and quiet when he should have been on the hunt. He tossed a few bones into the fire then shoved himself to his feet.

Zoe looked up at him and nodded, a serious expression on her face. She tossed the remains of the skeleton into the fire and pushed herself to her feet. "I'm going to wash the stink of fish off me." She strode towards the creek and squatted.

After pulling up a handful of mint, he joined her and handed her a few leaves. "Rub this on your hands and face. It'll take the fish smell away."

She complied, and it didn't take them long to be on their way again, the fire smothered by sand. Not even a wisp of smoke filtered through the trees.

They followed the sparse trail of the marauders, finding bits of cloth here and there. Once they thought they'd lost it, but the buzzing of flies alerted Doc to the grisly remains of another of the villagers half buried under a bush. He looked only long enough to see it wasn't Jazz or his mother or sister before grunting and moving on. He hated this trickle of death and hurried his pace.

It wasn't long before Zoe stumbled and went to her knees. "Hey, you trying to cripple me or what? Slow down a bit."

He looked back and watched her scramble to her feet and limp after him. "Sorry, it's just…I have to find them. Coming across a body every mile or so is killing me."

Zoe caught up and rubbed her knee. "Okay, I'm with you. But, if we go too fast, we're liable to miss a sign or get nailed when we make a noise or something at the worst time. We'll find them, and soon." She tried to smile, but it didn't come out well. Lowering her gaze, she said, "We're close, I just know it."

"I hope you're right." He brushed back a large branch and took off again, but more carefully. Zoe followed, her gait nearly as silent as his. They walked on, sometimes with her in the lead but more often him. By mid-afternoon, they were both nearing exhaustion but still moving ahead. He was just about to call a break when, in the distance, he heard someone cry out, followed by the sound of a whip striking flesh and another cry.

Dropping to his knees, Doc unslung his bow and notched an arrow before taking his next breath. He was sure it had been leather striking skin, and the yelp sounded tired, as if whoever cried out was near the end of his endurance.

Beside him, Zoe had a long, tapered blade in hand. "Ahead, through those trees," she whispered, confirming his determination. He nodded and pointed his chin ahead.

Zoe lowered herself and slowly crawled in the direction he'd indicated. Doc followed, inches from her hind end, but ignoring the tempting swell. Instead, he swivelled his head from side to side, trying to find any evidence of guards.

The wind had shifted, and the stench of unwashed bodies wafted their way. His partner squirmed beneath the branches, and he remained as close as he could without interfering with her progress. The only sound was that of the birds scattered in the underbrush and the sobbing of whoever had been struck.

Zoe halted, her body held rigid. Her hand rose, the knife held ready for throwing.

Doc paused, but only momentarily. With as much stealth as he could muster, he slithered forward until his shoulder came level with Zoe's. The brush thinned before them, and he saw what had made her stop.

Through a rift in the leaves, the movement of semi-naked people fixed his attention. Most of them sprawled, apparently exhausted or in pain from their injuries. The captives were bound hand or foot, some by the throat to others, and many had been beaten so badly they looked as if they'd never see the next day. Guards skulked among the prisoners, slashing down as they liked with their fists or makeshift clubs. Men, battered horribly, cowered beneath the onslaught of their captors. Women whimpered piteously as the guards mauled them at their leisure. Children ducked among the prisoners, scrawny and filthy, but still nimble enough to dart about, mostly escaping the marauders' fists.

"It's them," whispered Zoe, her mouth so close to Doc's ear her breath tickled his neck.

He looked at her and nodded. "Count the guards," Doc mouthed. "Look for weaknesses." He wanted to add, 'check for Jazz and my family', but refrained.

Across the clearing, against the forest backdrop, Doc counted a dozen carriages and wagons. Horses, oxen and the odd cow stood around each of the wheeled vehicles, tethered to them or to stakes in the ground, munching on the abundant grass. More men meandered around the camp, some dragging women, others molesting the weaker men. It was the picture of depravity.

Yet, he hadn't spotted anyone he knew. These prisoners appeared to be old timers, hauled around from one raid to the next for months, if not longer. They all needed to be rescued. If Jazz were there, he'd be ready to fight. All of them would—if they were able. *All they need is a chance.*

"Follow me," he whispered into Zoe's ear. He eased away from the grisly scene and made his way back to a small cluster of boulders they'd passed a short while ago.

Once they huddled against the rocks, Zoe let out a big breath and said, "I didn't see our villagers."

"Neither did I. But, we didn't see all of the camp, either. How many guards did you count?" Doc kept his voice down, sure the marauders would have patrols out.

"Sixteen. That's including the ones I glimpsed in the distance. They must have close to a hundred captives, if not more." Her voice quivered nervously.

It made Doc even more ill at ease. "I didn't see any women among the rabble. This looks like nothing more than a band of raiders. They attack whatever village they run into then take slaves and goods to sell to whomever will pay." Bile rose in Doc's throat. He hated the ruthless, blood-thirstiness of raiders. They didn't care about anyone or anything but themselves. That selfishness and lack of caring was also their weakness.

"What about the men in camp? They'll be occupied, for the most part. They'll consider raping our women just one of the perks of winning a battle, as well as training them for their futures as slaves."

"Let's rest until dark." Doc leant back against the boulder, and while he still held his bow, he'd unstrung it and let it lie against his thigh. "We'll reconnoitre again when we have a better chance of remaining unseen. I want to find our people. They'll fight for sure. These others I'm not sure of. It looks like some of them have been through a lot. They might not be in great shape, but they deserve the right to fight if they can."

Zoe sat next to him, her back to the rocks and her knife on the dirt beside her legs. "Not sure I'll rest much, but I agree. We need the cover of darkness."

The comfort of her arm against his made Doc think about how attractive he found her and how long it had been since he'd had a woman. Jazz was his love, and neither of them strayed far. At least they hadn't until now, he reflected as he admitted to himself how important Zoe was becoming. He prayed his man would soon be beside him again.

Chapter Three

"Keep down," Doc whispered urgently in Zoe's direction.

Ahead, small bonfires dotted the clearing where guards tromped between the prisoners. As each marauder reached a new captive, he'd bend down and roughly tie the person's hands behind their back. Done, he'd more often than not backhand the prisoner, sending them to the ground with another bruise to contemplate. Men, women and the children, caught now, all wound up restrained and shivering in their less than adequate clothing. Much of that had been ripped off and left along the trail.

"Looks like they don't get fed much. Just enough to keep them alive until they're sold off," Doc whispered harshly.

Zoe and Doc watched while the guards tossed the food among the captives, only to see it grabbed up by the few elders and handed out to the group. Zoe pointed at a young man who stuffed his meagre ration of a crust of bread into his mouth. Doc was proud of them. No one had much, but they shared what little they did have.

"Let's get moving." Doc pushed past the woman and made his way towards the end of the clearing. Keeping to the deep shadows, they'd managed to see a great deal of the camp without any of the ruffians spotting them.

Doc came to an abrupt halt, his eyes focussed on the back of a woman's head. He was sure he recognized the silken, white wave of hair. One naked shoulder poked out of what he knew was her smock. The very one she'd been wearing when he'd left for the outland farmstead. She had three of them, all identical but for the colour. This had to be her.

A woman beside her raised her head and peered over his mother's shoulder at the spot where he and Zoe lay hidden under the brush. Doc's heart stopped cold. The woman he knew well as his mother's best friend searched the undergrowth around him. A moment later, she lowered her head to the crook of her arm and remained there, either going to sleep or feigning it.

"Found them," Doc whispered and nudged Zoe.

"Yeah, got 'em," she replied, equally as urgent and as quiet.

The two of them settled in to watch and see how many of their fellow villagers they could pick out. Doc needed to know what kind of shape they were in. His mother seemed to be all right, but he hadn't seen her stand or move around much. Being as old as she was, perhaps the marauders had been easy on her. He hoped so.

Guards, at least a dozen of them, combed the area. The rest, most of them with captives bound to them in one way or another, lay sprawled near the fires still blazing in the semi-circle of wagons. Doc knew there would be more inside those carriages, but he had no way of determining how many — a dozen, perhaps more.

"Let's move along a bit, see if we can find my sister or Jazz." Doc scrambled to his feet but remained hunched over. Arrow notched but not drawn, he led the way. Not too far ahead, he saw two men he recognised from home. A little farther, a dozen more talked quietly while the guard slouched against a nearby tree. Women, children and a few of the elderly with special skills made up the bulk of the captives in this location. All of them wore bonds of some kind but looked in fairly decent shape.

Zoe tapped his hip, and he stopped, turning to look at her.

"Do you have some kind of plan?"

"Yeah, but I'd hoped to find Jazz, first." Worry ate at him. Had his lover been killed, and he'd just been unable to find the body? He imagined Jazz, his long, dirty blond hair stained with blood, eyes empty, wide and vacant, his face set in a grimace of a painful death.

Doc shuddered and forced the gruesome picture from his thoughts. Jazz had to be alive. The alternative was just too agonising to think about.

"I know, but there are so many captives. He could be anywhere. He might even be in one of the wagons." Zoe nodded towards the ramshackle group of dwellings on wheels.

"True, but I'd hoped. Let's get out of here before someone spots us. We've got some things to gather and a potion to make." He eased himself back, deeper into the undergrowth. Rocks bruised his shins and scraped his knees. Zoe must have been dealing with the same discomfort but neither slowed down nor complained.

Once they were far enough from the camp, Doc rose to his feet. Zoe joined him, and together they crept stealthily away. They didn't stop until they'd returned to the camp they'd shared earlier that evening.

"I'll need you to help me gather a few herbs," he said in a strained voice. His concern for Jazz, and for his female family members, wouldn't leave him.

Doc untied the pouch from his waist and squatted down. From the small, leather bag, he dug out a handful of white mushrooms and held them up so Zoe could see them. "I need more of these. You'll find them at the base of the biggest oaks."

Zoe held out her hand, taking three or four of the snow white fungi from him. She turned them about, eying them carefully. Mushrooms were nothing to play around with, especially the new breeds that had cropped up since the end of the old world. The wrong kind would kill. The right would do what he needed. "Got it. Anything else?" She handed them back and crouched down beside him.

"Yes, this," he said and handed her a sample of the herbs he'd use. Thickly leaved, the short branches held only enough of the drug to put four or five people to sleep. He'd require a good deal more of it and would have to get to the fire—without anyone seeing him—to deliver it effectively. "I'll need quite a lot of that—limbs from one of those miniature trees that have just begun growing around here. You know the ones—heavy stems, slow growing and tons of foliage up at the top of the plant. None at the bottom or up the stalk. Weird looking thing."

"Yeah, there's a small grove of them back the way we came, about half an hour's travel."

"That's right. There's got to be some here, too, or I'm baffled how just two of us can gain the upper hand with all those cutthroats. I'll need some of these, too." He showed her another type of leaf, one not so wide and much longer.

Zoe nodded. "I know that one. I think I saw it not far from here." She pushed to her feet and brushed off her knees. "Best get looking."

She went to one side of their camp, he to the other. Doc worked in a slowly expanding circle. It was a standard search pattern, so he knew Zoe would be doing the same. In the dark, it was slow going, and the chill soon made its way beneath his clothing.

He finally came to one of the trees he was looking for and said a silent thanks to whatever gods or goddesses might be listening. Reaching up, he pulled handfuls of leaves from the upper branches and stuffed them into the neck of his jerkin. They scratched his flesh, but he knew they'd do little damage, and he wanted to gather as many as possible. When his belly and chest bulged with the greenery, he nodded and headed back to where he'd parted ways with Zoe.

His thoughts went to her. She was an amazing woman, and he cared a great deal for her. More than he wanted to admit, even to himself. Several times, he'd fought the urge to lean down and kiss her, stopped only by the knowledge of how it might upset Jazz.

Yet, she piqued his interest, greatly. He'd watched her beat warriors of the tribe, not easily, but then many men worked as hard to get the same results. She'd taken no mate when other women her age rushed to do so. It seemed she wanted something else.

He wondered what.

His cock pulsed. He stopped dead in his tracks. "What the hell!" When his cock pulsed again, its head sliding farther along his thigh, he blinked. He rubbed the length of his shaft and shuddered at the intense pleasure. Visions of Zoe naked flashed in his thoughts. A fire by a lake at night, her dripping wet as she walked towards him, the flickering firelight dancing over her beautifully firm flesh. Her breasts swaying gently from side to side as she neared him. His cock throbbed to full erection in response. He wanted her more than he'd ever wanted a woman before.

Yes, he'd found her attractive for as long as he'd known her. But he'd never before actually let his thoughts linger on the lovely, sexy woman. Now wasn't the time or the place, he reminded himself, but his body refused to listen. He cupped his balls and gave them a careful squeeze, hoping to ease the tension building inside him.

Still in a state of lusty surprise when he heard a rustling in the brush not far from him, he simply looked up and stared. He pulled his fingers from his crotch.

Zoe emerged from the heavy foliage and raised a hand, saying, "It's me, don't shoot." She then walked towards him. The front of her simple cotton blouse bulged. Using the vest she'd had over it, she'd made a makeshift carryall and filled it with branches, too. "I came across a grove of this kind. Wasn't sure how much you'd want, so I brought as much as I could. I've got the other one stuffed down my back. It itches like…" It must have been about then she spotted the tent in the front of his leather pants because she suddenly stopped walking and talking.

Forcing his lustful thoughts aside, Doc strode forward and tried to ignore the hindering bulge.

"With what you—" He ceased speaking and cleared his throat. His voice had come out in a squeak. Trying again, he said, "With what you have and the bundle I found, we'll have more than enough."

Eyes apparently fixed on Doc's crotch, it took Zoe a few seconds to drag her attention away. She looked up into his eyes. Opening her mouth, she grunted. "Fuck!" she mumbled in a raspy voice.

"Now?" Doc teased. The instant she looked up at him, and he saw her lower lip quiver, he regretted saying it. "Let's get this concoction going." He shifted away from her, shielding his crotch, and looked around. The stone wall they'd spent part of the night against rose to their left a few dozen paces away. He headed that way, looking for a large rock to bruise the foliage. He dropped to his knees and continued his search.

"What now?" Zoe had followed him and quickly knelt beside him.

"I'll need a good-sized rock to pound these leaves along with the ones from my pouch." He scooped the foliage from inside his jerkin, depositing it onto a large, flat boulder.

"Here, found one." Zoe handed him a larger than fist-sized stone, and he immediately started pounding the pile of greenery. He didn't have to pulverise the leaves, he simply had to release their oils.

Zoe added her load to the pile, and in no time, he was done. He fumbled inside his pouch and pulled out a small flask of powder. After popping the top, he scattered the contents over the mound of crushed leaves. Done, he returned the flask.

"I need the other greenery, now." He reached to spin Zoe around. At the merest touch of her skin against his, it was as if a mini-bolt of lightning struck. The tingle raced up his arm, shot down his body and came to rest in his genitals. His cock, softened by the passage of time, throbbed back to full erection.

Stifling a groan, he bent forward. "These must have about driven you nuts." His voice didn't crack, but he detected a raspiness he hoped she missed.

"Yeah, but it needed doing. I'll survive." She apparently hadn't noticed or chose to ignore his discomfort.

The second batch of foliage cascaded onto the rock, burying the first in a slightly darker colour. He lifted his stone and pounded them all into a thick mulch that oozed green oil. When he was satisfied with the massive pile of emerald goo, he stopped and said, "We can wrap this stuff in some of the biggest leaves and tie them into bundles using that long grass." He nodded towards the heavy, dried weeds near the base of the trees nearby. "I'll grab some leaves, you get the grass. Make it as long as you can."

"You got it." A minute later, Zoe had an armload of straw nearly as tall as herself.

Doc searched for the largest leaves he could find and concentrated on losing the erection plaguing him. When he had as many as he thought he needed, he again knelt by the flat stone. Zoe positioned herself across from him.

"Watch," Doc said and showed her how to put a large handful of the green slop into the centre of a leaf then bind it up with a few long blades of grass. "Got it?"

"Yes, of course." She bent and retrieved a leaf, setting to work.

Silence stretched comfortably between them while the mound of round parcels of green got higher. Time seemed to remain still and gave Doc time to ponder his feelings. He adored Jazz and finding him remained at the top of his priority list. Yet, he knew Zoe meant something to him, too. He couldn't deny the physical attraction he felt for her. The past few hours told the tale.

"You're awful quiet, Doc," Zoe said in her deep, sultry voice. "Jazz will be all right, we'll find him."

He glanced at her face then down at the leaf he was tying. "I hope you're right. I'm not sure what I'd do without him."

"You'd go on. You're a survivor. But then, so is he." Zoe shifted from her knees to a cross-legged sitting position. "Hell, we all are, or we wouldn't be alive."

He worked for a while longer, watching the mound of green goo grow smaller. He looked up, meaning to say something nice, but didn't make it that far. The front of her shirt bowed open, offering him a nice view of her cleavage and the swell of her breasts. Once he spotted those treasures, he couldn't tear his gaze away.

"See something you like?"

Doc looked a little higher. His face grew warm, and he stammered, "Uh, sorry. Yes...err...No, I mean—" He closed his eyes and mumbled, "Fuck."

Zoe chuckled softly. "Never mind. I'm just glad I can distract you. You've shouldered a lot in the last few days. One man can't be expected to take care of an entire tribe."

Her words touched something within Doc. When he shifted his gaze and looked into her eyes, a sudden spark of emotion welled up inside him. His chest tightened, and his heart raced. "I haven't, not really. Seth and Dent and Fin. The women, you, everyone's helped. We're—"

"Yes, but it's been you who led us. Without you, I'd still be hiding in that cave with the children." She leant forward, her hands in the middle of what little remained of the green glop. When she was no more than a breath away from his face, she whispered, "Are we done here?"

"Yes," he said softly, pushing her hands away from the last handful of goo. "This is mine." He eased his fingers into the satchel at his waist, drawing out a small vial. With his teeth, he carefully pried open the top. The smell wasn't unpleasant, but he avoided inhaling the mixture and pulled his face away. He sprinkled the contents over the oozing mess of green then dropped the vial back into his pouch. Deftly, he bound the last leaf around the special mixture. That one, he pushed into a pocket of his vest. "Done. The rest waits until just before first light."

"Good, I'm going to wash up." She winked and smiled. "Care to join me?"

"You bet."

He followed her, knowing he'd enjoy the view. When she bent under a branch, he smiled appreciatively. The soft curve of her hips swayed beautifully as she walked.

When they reached the stream, she knelt and immersed her hands into the frigid water, scrubbing them with some of the sand from the bottom. He joined her, his thigh against hers.

"We'll get some rest until daybreak." He looked at her, just as she turned her face towards his. Eyes met and locked. His breath caught, and his heart slammed against his ribs.

"Yeah, rest, until morning," she murmured and leant closer.

The image of Jazz flashed into Doc's mind—a smiling face, bright with love. The man's eyes shone with passion. He nodded and winked then vanished just as Zoe's lips brushed Doc's.

Doc jerked back, but only for an instant. Jazz wouldn't mind. They'd both had lovers on the side and even shared them on occasion. They had the same taste in women, and Zoe was all woman. They'd just never cared for anyone else like they did for each other. That, hopefully, would change, with Zoe.

The kiss began slowly, the pressing of lips together tentative. Doc inhaled her breath. His cock thickened again, as if letting him know it liked the idea of her riding him. He did, too, and groaned as he darted his tongue across her lips then into her mouth. She suckled on it, drawing it deeper and stroking it with hers.

Breathless, he drew an arm's length away and whispered, "Finish washing. Let's go back to the rock wall."

Hands clean a few moments later, the two of them returned to the meagre camp they'd set up. The pile of packages lay waiting. The last of the smashed leaves lent a bitter smell that wasn't unpleasant. Doc took Zoe's hand and led her to where the rough stone rose from the ground. In the spot he chose, grass cushioned the soil and rocks.

He spun her around, stopping her with his palm on her shoulders. He slipped the fingers of one hand under her chin and tilted her face just a little, forcing her to look up at him. His eyes found hers and held them. "Are you all right with this? No man or woman going to begrudge you a little pleasure on the trail?" He traced his thumb over her lips, feeling their softness.

"No, no one to worry about me." She kissed his thumb then nipped at it with her sharp teeth. "I've wanted this for a very long time, Doc. Didn't want to come between you and Jazz, though. Still don't. Are you sure...?" She cocked her head, as if she were trying to see inside him.

"Yes, I'm sure. Very sure." He leant down and kissed her lightly on the tip of her nose. "When we find him, we'll ask him how he feels about it, together."

Zoe slid her hands around his neck and drew his face closer, bringing his mouth finally to hers again. The kiss grew hungry much quicker. Her mouth opened and his tongue darted inside.

Doc thrust his hips forward, his cock pressing hard against her lower belly. Sure she'd continue kissing him, he slipped his hands down her sides and reached around her. Cupping her arse, he had the perfect handholds to guide her against his crotch. Ecstasy, he thought, stabbing into her mouth with his tongue. *How perfect she is, how beautiful and brave.* And, in a sudden flash of insight, he marvelled at how much he wanted her and cared for her, this sexy, amazing woman. His cock pulsed, and he ached to free the underused tool.

He needn't have worried. In a matter of a few breathless seconds, her hands wandered downward, forced between their bodies. He eased away, just enough to allow them to unfasten the laces holding the front of his pants together. Loosened, the hide quickly splayed wide, allowing the tip of his erection to jut into the air. He shuddered, his hips jerking up, his dick reaching for more stimulation. Her fumbling with the laces soon opened the top of his leathers enough, and he wiggled his hips, causing the slick hide to slide lower.

Their kiss ended, broken by him and the frustrating slowness of his disrobing. He opened his mouth to curse his pants, their tightness, the way the leather stuck to flesh, but she smiled and pressed a finger to his lips. She apparently got the message and pushed them down. It took a little struggling, but soon enough, he stood naked from the waist down, his cock up-thrust and eager.

"I've waited for and wanted this for a while." She looked into his eyes then lowered herself to her knees, tits rubbing against him all the way down. They, and she, came to a stop when her knees touched the ground. She adjusted her pose, obviously getting comfortable, and kissed his lower belly. His shaft lurched and tapped her cheek.

"Sorry," Doc said and grabbed hold of his dick. "You seem to know exactly how to arouse the beast in me." She amazed him with her deep sexuality. He wanted her. No, it was more than that, he thought. She was becoming more important to him every second.

"Don't be sorry." She turned her head and, with obvious relish, sucked the tip of his erection into her mouth. The soft hum coming from her throat vibrated his cock head and sent another shiver through him.

He was desperate to get the rest into her mouth. A groan of frustration forced its way out of him, and the answering chuckle from her didn't make his predicament any easier. *The tease!* He pushed forward, carefully. Her tongue twirled around his glans, exciting him to a fevered pitch.

Inch by straining inch, his shaft disappeared into her mouth while he groaned and clenched his fists. Her tongue flicked across the underside, a torment that proved nearly more than he could take. His cock pulsed, the essence rising up the shaft. Sure his precum coated her mouth and trickled down her throat, he wondered how she managed to take his length.

Doc shifted his feet, spreading them as wide as his downed pants would allow. Then he placed one hand on each side of Zoe's face. Her cheeks were very warm against his cool flesh. His cock made her skin stretch taut, and her lips were nothing but a thin line of darker tissue surrounding the root.

"Oh, Zoe. You're driving me crazy. You're amazing!" He sighed when his balls touched her chin. The crown lay buried in her throat, and every time she swallowed, that glorious clench around his dick head made him shudder.

He took it for as long as he could before gently pulling her face off him. She dragged her teeth along the shaft, and he held his breath until they'd scraped ever so slightly over his glans before coming free of him.

Zoe looked up at him and grinned. "Want more?" She licked her lips and wiggled her tongue, which she'd stretched towards his throbbing dick.

"Damn, woman." He pushed her back a little more for fear she'd grab hold of him again and take him over the edge.

"I've wanted you for a long time. I plan to make it memorable for both of us."

"And me so blind, I couldn't see." He stroked his thumb across her skin, amazed at the smoothness. "That's changed, my sweet. Now and forever, I want you." Even as he spoke the words, his heart leapt, and he knew the truth of them.

With his hands still holding her face, she squirmed out of her clothing and tossed the pieces aside. The way her tits bounced made Doc's blood boil, which surprised him no end. He'd always loved the smooth hardness of a man's chest, always admired those who had rippling, muscular pecs he could sink his teeth into. But, at that moment, all he wanted were those lovely, soft, round, rose-tipped breasts. The crinkled nipples cried out for a good sucking or nibbling on. His mouth watered.

Looking up from his cock and away from those amazing nipples, he saw her face. Eyes half closed peered up at him, her nostrils flared, and her mouth seemed swollen, maybe bruised. Overwhelmed by his growing emotions, he sank down, kneeling, facing her, and kissed those bee-stung lips. His dick nestled between her thighs, the tip brushing against the soft down covering her womanly treasures.

Her lips tasted of him. Her breath gave a hint of manly musk, and he inhaled deeply as he sent his tongue exploring inside her mouth. The tanginess, the heady sweetness of her mixed with him, made his heart race even more. He clutched her arse cheeks tightly and ground himself against her.

Zoe let him go on for a time, but when she'd apparently neared her own peak, she pressed her hands against his chest and pushed. Breaking their kiss, she whispered, "Get out of your clothes. I need you naked. I need you inside me."

It took a second for Doc to realise what she meant. Naked from the waist down seemed fine to him. But, apparently, she wanted it all—or all of him. He scrambled to his feet and quickly stripped out of his clothing and boots, trying to ignore the painful erection slapping his belly and thighs as he did so.

He dropped to his knees in front of her and grinned. "Naked, ma'am. Now, can I have you spread out so I can get at that lovely, wet cunt I smell?"

Zoe blinked and looked shocked for a second, but then a smile brightened her face. "Yes, naked and very sexy. 'Fraid you're going to have to settle for rear entry, this time. Less chance of me lying on something that bites or is painful, and I really don't want to wait."

Doc chuckled and reached down to give his erection a couple of strokes. He watched her turn away, positioning herself close to the rock wall. She searched with her fingers for handholds, found them and wiggled her arse towards him. Over her shoulder, she said, "Come here. I'm going to scream if you don't do me right now."

"Better idea," Doc said and scrambled over to the log they'd leant against hours ago. He sat on it and spread his legs slightly. Holding out his hand, he crooked his finger, beckoning her. "Come straddle me. You'll save your knees, and it's how I daydreamed we'd do this." The log felt cool against his arse but not unpleasant. He hoped there weren't any splinters waiting to jab him but wasn't going to allow that thought to spoil the fun.

Zoe strode forward but stopped a pace or two away. "You want me this way?" She posed, facing him, her legs spread wide, her hands on her hips and a large, wicked smile on her face.

Doc smiled back at her and nodded but stopped when the sultry slut turned away and leant forward. Reaching behind herself, she ran her hands over the smooth, taut flesh of her buttocks. "Or, would you like me to back onto you, like this?" Zoe stepped to her rear, and with each shortened pace, she moved her legs a little wider. By the time her feet straddled his, she'd spread them more than shoulder's width apart.

"Oh fuck, yeah, like that," he managed to get out as he slid his hands up her outer thighs. The smooth, hairless flesh gave him a great deal of pleasure, the taut, muscular globes seemed to relish his touch when his hands finally got to them, and Zoe's sigh of approval made him feel amazing. *She* made him feel amazing.

His dick stood tall. The tip shone with a coating of clear pre-cum, and the shaft throbbed as if searching for a warm, snug place to enter. He thrust his hips upwards, grazing her inner thigh with his glans. At the touch, a shiver of excitement shook him, and he thrust his hips again, wanting more.

"Do it, fuck me!" Zoe growled and squatted, obviously trying to impale herself on him. She missed, and his dick head dragged along her flesh a little too roughly, a little painfully, yet he groaned his pleasure.

"Steady, girl," he murmured, taking hold of his shaft and her left hip. With her firmly in hand, he rubbed his cock head back and forth along her gash, wetting himself, then slowly guided her down on him. "Yess, fuck yes!" he hissed and closed his eyes. Multi-coloured lights flashed behind his lids, brilliant shards that made him gasp with each new burst.

Zoe gyrated her hips and clenched her inner muscles, gripping him like no man ever had or could. The soft, silken sheath holding him reminded him of a steel trap lined and coated with sleek wetness.

He fought down the urge to ram her hard and simply held still while she worked him. And work him she did. Expertly. Sinking down, clenching, she had him seeing stars in only a few thrusts. Withdrawing, holding just the tip of his cock inside her, soon had him clenching his jaw and growling his impending explosion.

"Yes, that's it. Fuck, just like that," Doc murmured in a non-stop litany of pleasure. "Such a snug little pussy, so sexy, fuck. More, swing your hips, more. Yes, like that." His grip tightened, his fingers no doubt would leave welts where his nails dug into the flesh, but he didn't care, nor did she seem to.

"Move your hips," Zoe said in harsh tone, demanding he pleasure her.

He thrust forward, the head of his dick brushing the curve of her cervix. Her body tensed, but an instant later, she strove for a repeat of the action. He slammed into her after that, swinging his hips and driving forward harder with each stroke. The slapping of his body against her arse made a sharp, staccato sound. Some tiny part of his mind hoped no one heard, but he wasn't sure he could have stopped even if someone approached.

His balls shifted and pulled up tight to his body. He thrust himself in deep, encouraged by the whispered sighs and moans drifting from Zoe's lips. She was so hot, so wonderful, yet so different from his Jazz.

The mere thought of his lover sent a cooling draft of dread through him. What if...and he shuddered. So many ifs, deadly things, might have happened. Yet, his body reacted to the sensation and shot a stream of cum into her depths.

"Yeah, oh fuck yeah." She slammed back against him. A steady bout of shivering gripped her, and even though he continued ramming his cock deep, she didn't seem able to control it.

Her pussy clenched, and he found it increasingly difficult to move in and out of her. Yet, the drag gave him an added note of pleasure. Enough to make him groan as his dick pulsed the last two or three times.

Letting out the breath he'd been unconsciously holding, Doc leant forward and wrapped his arms around his new lover. The soft flesh of her back pressed damp against his cheek, and he turned to kiss her shoulder blade before nuzzling her neck more insistently. "You're incredible, Zoe." He nipped her gently. "But we should get some rest. We'll need to be sharp later."

"Yeah, but I'm not lying naked on the ground." Zoe squirmed, easing out from under him.

His cock slid free and slapped wetly against his thigh. The sudden chill made him shiver, and he grabbed her tighter. With her held close, he straightened up and struggled to his feet, taking her with him. "Gotta agree with you. Too freakin' cold and too many prickly bits to stab tender skin." He lowered her to her feet and reached for some clothes.

It didn't take long for them to dress — even less time for him to settle down, his back to the cliff wall. Holding his arms out, he said, "Come here. I don't think I've had enough of you in my arms."

Zoe looked at him, sceptically. "What about Jazz?"

"What about him? He'll be as crazy about you as I am. You wait and see."

Zoe sank to her knees beside him and whispered, "I hope so. I've wanted..."

He pressed a finger against her lips, shushing her. "Time to rest, now. We'll talk later. I promise."

She turned and went into his arms as if she'd been doing it all her life. Perhaps, in her dreams, she had. Zoe rested her head on his shoulder. Neither said another word. He listened to her movements and sighs and wasn't unhappy when she snuggled deeper against him and her breathing deepened. He knew she'd fallen asleep. Doc liked the softness of her curves, but couldn't stop his longing for the man he loved.

They had to find Jazz. Simply had to.

Chapter Four

"He's exhausted." Zoe's voice sounded cheerful, yet strained, as if she were trying to keep from yelling. "He's been taking care of everyone — everything. You know what he's like."

"Yes, unfortunately, he's a control freak and thinks he can fix everyone's —"

Doc leapt to his feet and, before he'd even focussed on either Zoe or the newcomer in the near darkness, cried, "Jazz!"

The handsome young man with the mop of dirty blond hair shook his head and said, "Smart, too, as long as you don't ask too much of him."

Flabbergasted into silence, Doc stood gaping at the pair, afraid that if he moved, Jazz would vanish. His heart of hearts and the woman he was growing to care about tremendously. *He's alive. He's here. My love, my life is with me.* His mouth refused to work properly, still sagging open, and he tried to think of something at least less than stupid to say, but nothing came to mind. He finally managed to close his mouth and took a deep breath, annoyance tugging at him before love gained the upper hand again.

"You make me crazy." He glared at Jazz then turned his attention towards Zoe. "Both of you." There was no way he could hold back a smile of relief or stop from striding forward and into Jazz's arms. "My god, I thought you were..." He couldn't finish. The fears he'd pushed down for the last few days were too much. Tears threatened, but he refused to let them form.

"Yeah, I know," Jazz whispered before kissing the side of Doc's neck, just below the ear. "I'm all right." He pressed his lips more firmly to Doc's neck, kissing him again. A little louder, he said, "That's part of my charm."

"Part of why I keep you around, I suppose," Doc countered, although at that moment, his relief far outweighed any other emotion, except perhaps love.

"Doc," Jazz said in a completely different tone. "They killed so many. I've been trailing them, trying to find a way to—"

Still with an arm around his lover's waist, Doc interjected, "You did all you could." He turned and reached towards Zoe, taking her into their embrace. "Both of you did the best you could, and that's all anyone can do."

"But, I didn't stop them. I let them kill or herd the people—" Jazz's voice cracked, and he couldn't go on.

Before Doc could utter a word, Zoe said, "You fought. I saw you as did many others. You fought and killed dozens of the marauders. But before they had the chance to kill or enslave you, you escaped. You live. That's what will defeat these bastards."

Doc added, "You can't fight them if you're dead. Zoe's right. One man, under those circumstances, had no chance. Hell, even the might of all our warriors didn't stop them." He leant forward and kissed Jazz on the lips then pulled Zoe around until he could easily get to hers, as well, planting another on her mouth. "You both fought. You both lived and helped as many as you could. Our people have a chance."

Jazz took a deep breath and nodded. "Yes, they do." He gave Doc a quick peck on the cheek and, leaning down, planted a kiss on Zoe's lips. Looking back up at Doc, he added, "That is if you can keep your pecker in your pants."

Doc blinked then stammered, "You...you saw? But, we, I..." He lowered his head, shook it and shrugged his shoulders. "Well, fuck!"

"That's what I'd hoped you'd say," Jazz whispered. "If we have time."

Zoe squirmed in Doc's arms, pulling away from him just a little. "Doc, I could go down to the stream if you want some privacy."

Doc, who still struggled with the sudden appearance of Jazz, couldn't bear to have Zoe back away from him like that. He drew her close and let go of Jazz, but winked at the man over the woman's head. "Are you determined to make me crazy too, woman?" Her arms going around him again were a comfort—to them both, he hoped.

"No, of course not. I just don't want to get in the way."

"Bloody hell!" Doc stroked her back and cupped the smooth curves of her bottom. "You're not in anyone's way. I care for you, my sweet, sexy woman. Jazz will, too. Remember what I said?"

"Yes, but that was...well, before he appeared."

"Why don't we let Jazz decide who and what he likes?" Doc's heart suddenly raced. He looked at his lover, the man who'd stolen his heart, and turned Zoe towards him so she, too, would see his response as well as hear it.

"Our families, our villagers come before any of this." Jazz shifted his feet and looked uncomfortable.

"Yes, I agree," Zoe said, along with Doc.

"But, Doc's right. Love is love, the sex of a partner, someone you care about, doesn't matter. At least it doesn't to me, or him."

Zoe looked from Doc to the younger man, then slid into Jazz's arms and said, barely loud enough for Doc to hear, "Nor to me."

Doc gazed around and up at the sky, searching for the moon. From where the crescent shaped orb perched in the sky, he knew little time had passed since Zoe and he had fallen asleep. "We've got a long while, still. I've got our attack planned for pre-dawn."

"Good," Jazz replied and pulled Zoe more firmly into his arms. Holding her tight against his chest, he whispered, "Doc thinks I'll grow to care for you as much as he does. Might surprise him to know I've had my eye on you for some time."

Zoe slid her arms around Jazz's neck and dragged his face closer. Doc leant in, not wanting to miss a thing she said. He smiled at her next words.

"Never mind him being surprised. You're shocking the bejezus out of me. In a good way."

Doc moved closer behind her and bent forward enough to kiss her neck as he slipped his hands around her, between her skin and that of his man's. He cupped her tits and gently pinched each nipple between finger and thumb. The woman's gasp came to an abrupt end when Jazz pressed his lips to hers.

"Yeah, surprised, but not a lot, you horny dog," Doc murmured affectionately. He stroked Zoe's breasts for a few moments longer, drawing her nipples taut and pinching them hard enough to make her grunt — at least he thought it was his treatment causing the reaction. Jazz's eyes opened, and Doc saw the smouldering lust burning in them.

He released his grip on Zoe's breasts and moved around behind Jazz, making him the man in the middle. "I've been afraid I'd never have this again," Doc whispered into the man's ear as he ran a finger along the seam of Jazz's leather pants.

"And catching glimpses of you two made me as hard as a rock." Jazz turned his head and grinned at him.

Doc blinked then laughed. "Well, fuck me."

"Later." Jazz lifted Zoe and drew her against himself even tighter. "I want this tease, first."

Doc leant in, grinding his cock against Jazz's hide-encased arse. "Perfect. I'm sure she'll love every second of your attention."

Zoe finally piped in, saying, "A dream come true. Both of you. I never thought it would happen."

Jazz released her but only long enough to unfasten his pants and wiggle his arse towards Doc while pushing them down. Once he'd kicked them aside, he seemed ready and, from the size and sway of his erection, more than eager to get down to business.

Zoe reached for him, and Jazz quickly pulled her into his arms again. He bent forward, and for a moment Doc wondered what he could be doing. The answer came when Zoe's pants flew across the small clearing, coming to a landing next to the log she'd shared with Doc, not so long ago.

Without any foreplay or warming up, Jazz lifted Zoe. Her legs automatically wrapped around the man's slender hips, her heels brushing Doc's leather clad thighs. Her arms circled Jazz's neck, her lips found his, and Doc merely stood there, dumbstruck for the moment as the two made out.

While they kissed, Doc took the opportunity to explore and tease both of them. He knelt and reached between Jazz's legs to his dangling balls, cradling them for a much desired caress. The firm orbs shifted against his palm, as if trying to help in their pleasure-giving. Once he'd had enough of those, Doc moved on to the underside of Jazz's dick, lightly stroking as much of its length as he could reach. The tip lay buried between Jazz's body and Zoe's. The gentle pulsing of the shaft had his own cock thickening, eager to join the party.

The smell of Zoe was driving him crazy. Mixed with the more subtle, manly scent of Jazz, it had Doc's head whirling. He quickly struggled out of his own suddenly too tight clothing. Tossing it aside, he too was more than ready to have some fun. His erection throbbed, and he gave it a few quick tugs before refocusing his attention on his lovers. Doc slid his hand between Jazz's thighs then slipped his fingers into the wetness of Zoe's succulent pussy. He used that moisture to anoint Jazz's thick shaft but didn't stop there.

"Oh yeah," moaned Jazz when Doc's fingers probed his tightly clenched arsehole. Zoe's juices flowed freely, supplying Doc with an ample supply of lubricant for the task. He didn't rush his lover, there wasn't any need. Jazz adored being fucked, and the novelty of being between Doc and Zoe seemed enough to encourage his excitement. Within minutes, his nether hole opened, hungrily sucking Doc's fingers past the outer ring and farther in. Slick muscles clenched and relaxed, allowing Doc passage, until the flat of his hand lay against Jazz's bottom.

Doc remained still for a moment or two, allowing his lover time to grow accustomed to the intrusion. While he paused, Jazz squirmed and apparently shifted himself enough to position his dick head at Zoe's sopping pussy.

"Yes, push in. Fuck me."

Her guttural demand made Doc smile. She knew what she wanted and wasn't afraid to ask for it. He loved that.

And, apparently, so did Jazz. A soft moan of lust accompanied a hard forward thrust.

Doc was in the perfect place to know when the man's cock slipped easily into Zoe. Her grunt would have been a dead giveaway, if he'd needed it, but this was much better. With a little repositioning, he could actually see the action. Smell their heat. The sound their bodies made as one pushed into the other drew his face closer. He stopped only when his forehead brushed Jazz's flesh.

Fingers still buried in his lover's arse, he was ready for the next step in pleasure. Doc eased his digits out, nearly freeing them from Jazz's body, before thrusting the three of them back in. He twisted his wrist slowly, drawing his fingers out, then shoved ahead. He fucked his lover until he was sure he'd stretched Jazz's hole enough to accommodate the girth and length of his own erection.

Doc rose to his feet and shuffled closer to Jazz, pressing himself to the man's back. His cock pulsed as it nestled between Jazz's arse cheeks, as if seeking entrance to the well-remembered pathway to bliss. Doc thrust his hips, dry humping his lover, and enjoying every second of it. Zoe's feet moved, dropping to dangle along Jazz's thighs.

Doc leant forward and whispered in Jazz's ear, "Ready, stud?"

"Yeah, fuck yeah." Jazz shifted his feet, spreading them, thus opening himself to Doc's lustful advances.

Sensing Jazz's readiness, Doc pulled back just enough to reposition the head of his dick at Jazz's anus. The softness made him shudder. The gentle fluttering of the outer ring of muscle nearly drove him over the edge. Taking a deep breath, he readied himself then pushed forward.

"Yess," Doc hissed as the crown popped into the tight heat of his lover's rectum. He stopped, the head barely inside, but afraid to go deeper for fear of exploding too soon. The image of Zoe with her legs wrapped around Jazz's hips, her feet tapping at his thighs, was burnt into his brain.

He'd had her. The luscious smoothness of her. The slick wetness of her cunt and the smooth expanse of skin. Her gentle, caring nature had been what had attracted him in the beginning, but when they'd fucked, he'd wanted more of her. She'd cast her spell over him, and it seemed she'd done the same to Jazz.

Carefully, Doc began the timeless motion of fucking. In and out, twisting his hips to add more sensation to the already pleasurable dance they shared. Each time Jazz pushed into Zoe, he withdrew from Doc's cock. When he pulled free of her, he impaled himself on Doc.

"Oh my God," breathed Jazz as he filled Zoe with his shaft, his anus clenching down, apparently trying to hang onto Doc's erection. "Doc, don't just stand there. I'm dying."

Doc took firm hold of Jazz's hips and buried himself. The smooth clenching made him grit his teeth, it felt so damn good. He waited until his heart rate slowed a little then pulled back leisurely. With great care, he swung his hips while trying to match the movements Jazz made to fuck Zoe. For a little while, all went well. The pace increased, each of them groaning soft words of lust while the excitement soared. But, as it always did, Doc's thrusting became erratic, as did Jazz's. Zoe's sobbing turned into a soft keening that rose and fell.

"Yes, yes, now, more," Doc babbled and heard his words echoed by both Jazz and Zoe. His wild seesaw action did the trick, and in less time than he'd wished, that special feeling of fullness, desperation and need took hold. He grunted and held his breath, hoping to stall his release. Seconds later, Jazz growled, and his arse clenched tight around Doc's erection. The man sagged but managed to keep on his feet and swing into Zoe a few more times as she, too, sobbed her orgasm.

Doc followed a few seconds later. A gush of fire erupted from his dick, filling his lover's body. Doc shivered and thrust again and again, each time spewing more of his precious juices. His knees sagged, and he gripped Jazz's hips tighter while his orgasm came to a satisfying, shuddering finish.

When he could think clearly again, Zoe was on her feet and Jazz stood unsteadily before him. Doc kissed Jazz on the shoulder and whispered, "I love you." Before Jazz could respond, Doc eased out of him and stepped back.

Jazz turned and faced him, saying, "I love you, too." He held his hand out towards Zoe and pulled her close to his side. "And you, my pretty wench, are amazing."

Doc grinned and added, "She is indeed." He needed to wash himself but didn't want to leave either Zoe or Jazz just yet. "I knew you'd care for her, too."

"Let's go clean up." Jazz started towards the little-used trail. "There's a stream just through—"

Doc hurried ahead and said over his shoulder, "Yes, we found it already."

Washing up didn't take them long, and they were all exhausted from the days of terror. Reunited with Doc, Jazz seemed to relax and fell into a deep sleep nearly as soon as the three of them curled up together.

Not knowing if Jazz were alive or dead had taken its toll on Doc. Exhaustion plagued him, yet he felt the need to talk with Zoe before he slept.

"No matter what happens with our people, I just want to make sure you know that I do have feelings for you. Deep feelings." He leant across Jazz and kissed her tenderly on the lips.

"Yes, I know, but Jazz is your love." She took a deep breath, as if steadying herself for an enormous letdown.

"No, that's not what I mean at all," he reassured her. "I mean I care for you, and I want to spend more time with you and Jazz. There's nothing to say three people can't form a family."

Zoe's face lit up, and she smiled. "Let's just free our people. Then we can talk."

"But you like the idea. I see that." Doc readjusted his position, slinging an arm across Jazz, his hand coming to rest on her waist.

"Yes, I like the idea—very much."

Doc closed his eyes, a smile firmly planted on his face.

* * * *

Doc and his small team approached the camp. He led, Zoe followed and Jazz brought up the rear. They each carried a sack of the crushed leaves. He looked over his shoulder at the treetops and saw the first hint of dawn—that streaking of light then darkness that always preceded the full breaking of day.

Leaves brushed his sides, the noise sounding louder than normal to his oversensitive senses. He stopped and listened but heard nothing. Zoe touched his back and he turned, nodding at her questioning look.

He bent to her ear and whispered, "Time to spread out."

She nodded, and when Doc pointed to the left, she eased herself through the underbrush heading that way. He captured Jazz's eye and motioned to the right, knowing the man would be as silent as a breeze going through the brush.

Doc readjusted his makeshift sack and started forward again. He'd be the first to see anyone moving, if indeed anyone was up and about. He spotted people curled up together in small mounds. Children slept with whoever looked capable of protecting them among those of the village. Sadly, many he'd hoped to see didn't seem to be there.

Every forty or fifty paces, a small fire smouldered and spat, and that was what Doc had counted on. To his left, he saw Zoe crawling towards one. A man, who looked to be one of the ruffians and supposedly on guard duty, sprawled against the base of a tree, sleeping, a few paces from her. She stopped behind the fellow and looked towards Doc, her bright eyes and flashing, white teeth making it easy to spot her exact location.

"Good girl," Doc mouthed and nodded, unsure if she saw him or not. He crouched and worked his way ahead, only to freeze when he heard someone cough nearby. A splattering sound of water, or something else, striking leaves came next. Doc remained still. He smelled the man and heard him grunt when he had finished pissing. Doc didn't move. He waited for the fellow to return to his bed and gave him a few more minutes, hoping he'd settle down, before Doc moved on.

To his right, he spotted Jazz nearly hidden beneath the overhanging branches of a tree, smiling his way.

"Bastard," he muttered under his breath but smiled back good-naturedly.

Jazz moved from his hiding hole closer to one of the fires. He'd placed himself at the outer boundary of where they'd seen their villagers and the furthest fire.

Doc lowered his sack to the ground and crept forwards, determined to release as many of the prisoners as he could before they sent the drugged leaves into the flames. The group huddled together nearest him were familiar—how could they not be? He'd seen these people all his life. First he hushed them, knowing they'd assume he was one of the marauders come to do them some harm. When he was sure they understood, and realised who he was, he quickly unfastened the makeshift ropes holding a man's limbs then moved to the next person and the next.

Leaning forward, he whispered, "Jazz and Zoe are in the trees. Crawl out there. You must be silent."

Four men and two women nodded. The children simply sat wide-eyed and stared. The eldest man, Axel, stretched his arms out and almost herded the others into the bush. They went easily enough, but their will seemed to be gone.

Doc turned and went to the next gathering. The people there were awake already. Children whimpered, and Doc quickly shushed them, looking around to see if any guards lurked nearby. This time there were a dozen adults, and they melted into the undergrowth much more quickly than the first bunch had.

Twice more, Doc scurried ahead and unfastened ropes or rags from around people's necks and limbs, freeing them to join the others now hiding in the woods. He'd just reached for his mother's arms when a ruckus broke out from the direction Jazz had taken. Doc didn't look up. He quickly tore at the rough bindings holding his mother and pushed her towards the forest, whispering harshly, "Go, find the others." He tugged at more bonds, liberating another man, pulled at yet one more but failed to free the next.

Screams came from Jazz's direction—a woman, he was sure of it. He rose, ready to rush that way, but stopped when he saw a knot of men, mostly marauders, fighting. There didn't appear to be any weapons, thank whatever gods there were, but Doc's belly tightened in fear.

"Jazz, where the fuck are you?" he murmured and searched the area for his lover.

More people struggled out of their bonds, or Jazz had set them free before the fight had begun, and they, too, joined the ruckus. Children scuttled into the brush and women followed, fleeing into the early morning light.

"Prisoner escape!"

The cry came from the centre of the camp, and Doc knew their luck had run out. He saw Zoe dart into the woods and corral several refugees on her way. More saw her and made haste in her direction, while others seemed torn between joining the melee and gaining their freedom.

Marauders, dozens of them, came at a run, clubs and whips at the ready. They went straight for the disturbance, and that was when Dock saw Jazz. In the middle of the fray, his lover fought valiantly to free an old man, another of the elders, from the clutches of a guard.

The old man went stumbling into a clear spot and found his balance more quickly than Doc would have imagined possible. He shambled for the brush. Doc saw his determined look and applauded the man's tenacity.

Jazz went down under a barrage of fists and feet while all Doc could do was bite his lip and curse. To leap in and try to save his lover would mean only that both of them would be captured, or worse. They'd both known it was likely to happen, but he'd pushed the thought aside, hoping they were wrong.

"Jazz," he whispered, but only loud enough for himself to hear. He clenched his fists for a moment then bent to the next captive. The rope around her neck had burnt the flesh with its rubbing, but the woman leapt to her feet as soon as she was free. She didn't run but went to the next villager and worked on the ropes holding him.

More and more men, women and children worked to liberate their kin and friends, while the marauders bludgeoned Jazz. It seemed they were blind to anything but their task at hand, until a hoarse yell came from the other side of the camp.

"Bastards! Fucking morons, the slaves are getting loose!"

Doc crouched low and looked back to see how many newcomers were racing towards them. The sun chose that moment to rise over the treetops and gave him an even better view than he wanted — right down to the half-naked man bearing down on him with an upraised club. The marauder's semi-erect cock flailed against his thighs. He'd obviously been on the verge of sexual gratification. Doc hoped whoever had been the man's target of the morning had escaped any build-up to the man's attention.

With a grunt of anger, Doc straightened and faced the man. The club came down prematurely, but the blow didn't completely miss, sliding down Doc's arm with numbing force. A blood-curdling scream followed, and the man was upon Doc, kicking and punching as if he'd gone mad.

A fist connected with Doc's chin and sent him stumbling backwards over the prisoners still bound around him. He shook it off and crouched in a fighter's stance, approaching carefully while hoping to give others time to get free. The maniac hurled himself at Doc, arms pin wheeling and rage like a mask on his face.

Doc sent a punch into the man's cheekbone and heard a satisfying grunt of pain. Spittle flew as the man sidestepped, and his legs wobbled.

"Fuckin' bastard," the man slurred, approaching again. He shook his head, as if to clear it.

Doc realised his punch had done some good. A quick look around halted any thought of continuing the attack, though. More guards approached by the second, and they weren't too gentle with the captives in their haste to get into the fight. Women cried out when they were stepped on, and children screamed in panic. Men fought back, as best they could, but were hampered by the makeshift bindings.

Jazz yelled a vile curse, and Doc looked that way just in time to see several of the larger guards overpower his lover, beating him down with their feet and whatever weapons they held. Doc's heart stopped for a second longer than normal then beat wildly as he watched, mesmerised by the spectacle. He knew he couldn't *do* anything, but it tore at his gut, anyway.

The man approaching him leapt, and Doc barely managed to drag his attention back to his own battle, sidestepping the full weight of the guard with barely a hair's breadth to spare. The brute hit the ground hard. Doc attacked quickly, driving a knee into the scoundrel's back and bashing him on the head before he could even attempt to break free.

A wave of bellowing marauders lunged and lurched towards where Jazz fought. When they apparently saw the downed guard at Doc's feet, several turned his way, their anger revitalised. New weapons emerged, axes, long knives and well-formed clubs, all wielded with an accuracy that startled Doc. The guards cleared the way by simply swinging those weapons, killing or maiming anyone unlucky enough to be underfoot or even nearby.

A small child scrambled into the bush and was quickly snatched up by one of the escaped prisoners. Doc took a chance and glanced around, glad to see many of his villagers gone.

A few men, those who'd been captive, raced from the safety of the woods and grabbed still-bound women and a few of the children who were apparently too frightened to flee.

The guards were upon them then, using their clubs and feet. Doc forced his way forward, knocking aside the man who'd been after him and bashing down another guard's hands. His club dropped, and Doc reached for it. Another marauder took the fallen guard's place and swung at Doc, beating him back before he could retrieve the weapon.

Jazz was down. Others, too. But most of his villagers were loose. He had to free his lover. That was why he'd come all this way.

Doc started towards Jazz but stopped before he'd taken five steps. A dozen guards brandishing weapons patrolled through the remaining prisoners in the area, between himself and his lover. He'd never make it, and he knew he had to remain on the loose. That was Jazz's only hope.

He saw Zoe, a child in her arms, racing into the woods. People limped after her, and a guard followed.

Heart breaking, Doc headed after her. He vowed to return and free Jazz. He looked back and saw more villagers scrambling after him, blood and filth clinging to their limbs. Some were barely able to walk, but others leant over to help them.

"I'll come for you," he mouthed, then raced for the cover of the forest. He knew there were some who'd never see freedom again, but he vowed to help as many as he could. The cries and moans of those left behind tore at his soul. But he had no choice.

He took a last look back and spotted a large, fur clad ruffian standing over the pile of men where he'd last seen Jazz. Dark eyes and a ruthless snarl aimed his way made Doc cringe.

That must be the leader. The brute held up an antique rifle that showed more rust than metal and yelled, "Bastard. You'll pay."

Doc bent forward and slipped his arm under one of the elder's, helping the old man to the safety of the woods. From under the branches of an enormous tree, he glanced back and scowled.

"It'll be you who pays," he whispered. "And for every mark you leave on Jazz, I'll give you ten."

Around him, the newly freed people scurried into the woods. The guards ventured after them, but not far. It seemed their bravery came from their large numbers, not the individual.

Ahead of him, Zoe supported an old woman, and for an instant, his heart leapt. His mother, it was...No, it wasn't. But it was a woman of the tribe, and he consoled himself with that.

When they finally stopped, the injured and weak collapsed.

Chapter Five

"Fucking bastard!" Doc strode towards the fallen tree, kicking its rotten base, then he turned and stomped back towards Zoe, who leant against the trunk of an enormous oak. His rage, like a wild thing, threatened to scorch anyone or anything that came too close. He clenched and unclenched his fists, trying to calm his growing rage but having little success.

The only bright spot he could be happy about was those they'd freed were on their way back to the village. Three of the warriors they'd rescued had volunteered to escort the survivors. Even wounded as they were, the men would see the others safely home, of that Doc was sure. His mother was not among them. Nor was his sister.

His anger flared.

Jazz had been taken.

The worst of the worst possibilities had happened, and it tore at him. His lover, the man who meant more to him than any other, and his mother, the one who'd given him life, were both in the hands of those bastards. And his sister... *Where is Robin?*

"Doc, they're alive. We'll get them out." Zoe approached him with her arms outstretched.

He knew she meant well. She might even believe they'd have no trouble getting Jazz and the others free, now. He knew better. He glanced at the few men who'd remained with them. The strongest and most capable of the tribe's warriors huddled together, whispering, planning. Doc trusted them implicitly.

From the direction of the marauders' camp, a loud, rough voice bellowed, "Ya better show yourselves or I'll be orderin' a few executions."

"Damn his misbegotten birth and any offspring he might have," one of the men growled. His cursing continued but at a much quieter level.

Doc looked towards where the camp lay through the trees. They'd retreated only far enough to give the previous captives a feeling of relative safety from any marauders following them. It had surprised him when they'd had to run such a short distance before the guards returned to camp, telling each other the prisoners had vanished too quickly, there were too many rescuers, words that could only mean they were cowards when they didn't have the numbers advantage.

"Come on," Doc said to the dozen who accompanied him. "We'll get closer and see what the bastard has in mind." Without waiting for anyone's response, he headed for the camp. From the whispering sound of branches sliding across clothing, he knew they were following.

A few minutes later, they all sank down and crawled the last few dozen paces. The noise coming from the camp sent a chill through Doc's body. Men and women yelled curses and pleas for mercy, and children screamed and cried.

He looked to his left and saw Zoe. Directly in front of her lay one of the makeshift bags of crushed leaves. His initial plan could still work, sort of. He thought about the one packet he'd made differently.

Crawling to where Zoe lay, he whispered, "The leaves, I want all of them pushed as close to the camp as we possibly can. All of them. Make sure they're upwind."

Zoe turned, and a smile slowly spread across her face. "But how —"

Doc patted the pocket where he'd tucked the specially mixed pouch. "Don't worry about that. I'll make sure it gets where I want it." Doc saw the tribe's warriors slithering closer and moved towards them. "I'm going in. You lot, talk to Zoe. We had a plan, and it can still work. A slight variation of it. Do exactly what she says. Don't come in too soon. Wait until the guards are distracted"

"Doc, what are you going to do?" It was Max, the strongest of the survivors and the most level-headed of the bunch.

"I need to get next to the central fire." He nodded towards the camp and shuddered. If all went well, the last of the prisoners would be free soon. If not, he'd at least be with Jazz. "It's part of the revised plan."

"Shit, Doc," Max growled. "You can't go in there alone. They'll kill you, for sure."

Behind him, Alex nodded vigorously. "The Duke, that's what the arsehole who leads this bunch likes to be called, is insane. He'll kill whoever gets in his way or threatens his power. Hell, even the pack of murdering arseholes he has are terrified of him."

"Yeah, that's usually how it goes." Doc turned his face towards the camp, hoping to come up with another plan. He really didn't want to dive into this hornets' nest. Nothing came to him, and time was passing.

As if to punctuate that thought, another blaring yell came from the camp. "I know you're out there. Unless you want these people dead, you'll come forward."

Doc looked at Zoe and winked. "Get the leaves in the fire then get back here to safety. You'll know when to sneak in again. But for fuck's sake, don't come in until the smoke clears." He crawled forward towards the camp and the 'Duke'.

When he deemed himself close enough, Doc peered around the side of a boulder and froze. His heart slammed in his chest. His vision blurred for a second. Doc closed his eyes and fought to keep from groaning when he exhaled.

Jazz and five other young men knelt side by side in front of a mountain of a man dressed in a mixture of ragged denim and half rotten leather. The giant's scruffy, black beard reached halfway to his belt but couldn't camouflage a large belly. Behind each of the ones kneeling stood a guard, a hand gripping his charge's hair, a knife held across the exposed throat.

Doc's anger returned, but he controlled it. This wasn't the time to lose control. He had to find his mother and sister and somehow get both them and Jazz out of there.

He recognized others of his tribe, dozens of them. Most looked like they were in decent shape, but the hardships of the last few days had to have taken an enormous toll.

An old woman limped forward, grabbed one of the guards in her clawed hands and wailed, "Please, not our young. Take me, I'm old and used up."

Doc was close enough to see the guard glare down at the woman and hiss a curse that no man should ever utter to an elder. With his hands busy, the guard simply kicked her aside and returned his attention to his leader.

Doc chose that moment of inattention to slip closer to one of the bags of crushed leaves. Hoping the old woman had distracted the marauders for a short time, he eased the awkward bag ahead, moving it towards the large fire nearby. Once satisfied, he took a deep breath and got to his feet. Keeping low, he used his feet to kick the bag forward until it rolled into the blaze.

Nothing happened, but he'd known it wouldn't. The leaves were still damp, and sitting all night had compacted them even more, making them even harder to light. Yet, it was all he could do.

He turned and straightened up, facing Jazz and the others. The Duke's back was to him, but the guards holding the villagers saw Doc and, after the initial double take, yelled. The first few words came out as incoherent gibberish. The distraction, hopefully, would give Zoe and the others time to finish their tasks then escape before being discovered.

Out of the corner of one eye, Doc saw Axel lumber forward and thrust a mound into the nearest fire. The others, he could only hope, followed suit.

The man mountain, the Duke, turned and stumbled, barely managing to keep to his feet. "Grab the bastard!" he roared, a vicious sneer showing anything but humour. The guards close by lunged for Doc, snatching at his arms and shoulders, nearly knocking him to the ground in their haste to obey their leader.

Doc fought only enough to occupy them for as long as possible. That and to keep from being brutalised. He covered his head with his arms and bent forward. When a fist connected with his belly, Doc went down like a sack of fresh milled flour. The blow hadn't been all that hard, but he hoped they'd stop beating him when he was on the ground. He should have known better. As soon as he hit the dirt, the stinking lot of them began kicking and didn't stop until their lord and master commanded it.

"Get him up," the brute demanded in his gruff voice. "Got some questions for pretty boy."

Doc's head throbbed horrendously when the guards holding his arms dragged him to his feet. Blood trickled into one eye from a gash on his forehead, and his left ear rang. Agony on his left side indicated badly bruised ribs, or worse. Something to deal with later, if there was a later.

On his feet, he wobbled more than necessary, hoping they'd think he was hurt worse than he was. He didn't have to exaggerate much. He eased his hand into the inside pocket of his jerkin and palmed the packet he had hidden there.

With a guard on each side holding him, Doc was hauled towards the rotund leader. He let himself fall forward, his toes dragging along the dirt. The heat of the nearest fire warmed him, and he exploded upwards. At the same time, he tossed his small bundle of drugs into the flames.

Again the guards pounced on him, but he'd completed his task, making the new beating worthwhile in some weird way. Or so he thought until his vision blurred from another blow to his head. Instinctively, he curled into a ball and gritted his teeth.

"I said bring the bastard here, now!" snarled the Duke, who obviously didn't appreciate the delay.

The hitting and kicking ended, finally. He forced his body to relax enough so he could take a cautious, shallow breath. The pain wasn't as bad as he'd feared it was going to be, so he downgraded the damaged ribs to bruising. His thighs and back ached from the number of kicks they'd received, but his biggest concern was how woozy he felt.

Dragged the rest of the way, Doc didn't have to pretend semi-consciousness. He really was having a hard time staying alert. Forcibly knelt at the feet of marauder's leader, he allowed himself to weave from side to side. It wasn't a stretch.

The rotund giant wound his fingers into Doc's hair and thrust his head up, forcing Doc to look him in the eye. Duke bent down, and the man's putrid breath engulfed Doc when he spoke. "How many are out there?"

Flecks of spittle struck Doc's face, and his stomach heaved, threatening to empty itself right there on the spot. A fitting answer, he thought, but nevertheless he fought down the wave of nausea and glared into the man's face.

"I asked you a question, pretty boy. How may are out there and what are your plans?" He pulled Doc's head to the side by the hair, nearly tearing the long, shaggy locks from Doc's scalp.

Doc yelped and struggled against the hands holding him down. "Fucking bastard!" He got one arm free and swung with all his might at the filthy guard on the opposite side, aiming for his ugly smirk. His fist connected, and he had the momentary satisfaction of feeling teeth snap under his knuckles before the toe of a boot sank into his unprotected belly.

His pleasure turned to agony in a second, and he couldn't stop the grunt of pain nor the taste of bile rising into his mouth. He swallowed quickly and collapsed to the side, feigning unconsciousness.

"Arsehole, piece of shit townie doesn't know when to fuckin' quit."

A set of feet appeared in front of Doc, and a moment later, his hair again took on the role of handle as his head was pulled back. He worked at remaining still, giving the Duke no reason to strike him again.

"Shit, he's dead to the world." The Duke twisted and turned Doc's head, as if he could get information from him that way. "Slick," he bellowed, tossing Doc to the side. "Digger, tie this one up. I don't want to chance him escaping. He's a sly one, for sure."

The prisoners close by cursed their disapproval, and Doc heard the rattling of a few chains as well as flesh striking flesh. Moaning women and a few hissing oaths from men were enough to reassure Doc he needed to continue the charade. *The bastard!*

Doc slumped to the ground when the remaining guard let him go, but the respite was short-lived. Almost immediately, more hands grabbed him, wrestling his limbs behind him. His legs were crossed and tied tightly, then his wrists were secured to his ankles. Bound like a hog readied for the market, Doc found himself uncomfortably helpless.

He opened one eye just a slit. Around him, captives cringed away from the Duke and his men. They apparently knew how dangerous it was to be noticed, and Doc had to agree.

"Toss 'em over there, with the women I used last night." Duke turned away and went back to where the line-up of bound prisoners awaited their fate. "String these ones up, nice and high, so anyone coming to their rescue will get a perfect view of them dying, first."

Jazz and each of the others got a good back-handed blow from their guards along with the command to get up. Doc watched each of the six men struggle to stand. They'd obviously been on their knees for some time, and their muscles seemed to fight their every move. The continued punches and kicks from their handlers encouraged them to hurry, and in record time all six of them were on their feet.

Doc saw Jazz's face, and knew his lover had been watching him. He also knew Jazz would want to know what the hell Doc had gone and got himself captured for. Doc took a chance that his own guards would be paying more attention to their fat leader than an unconscious prisoner and nodded towards Jazz, then pointed his nose towards the nearby fire — the one into which he'd tossed the drugged packet.

Jazz looked quizzical but remained quiet, turning his attention to the Duke, who had climbed onto the back of an empty wagon, the better to be seen.

"Ain't no one got any hope in Hell of defeating us, boys. We're too strong and too organised. You know it, and I know it. We trashed villages all over this part of the continent and never had one bit of trouble. And we ain't likely to. With my brains and you following my orders, we'll sell enough of these fuckin' townies so we'll all be rich. We'll rule this entire country!"

A wild cheer went up from the guards and those who'd lost the ability to think of escaping the mad man's rule. Conquest and bloodshed, that was all they knew, and that seemed to be all the Duke wanted. That, and power.

Doc shook himself free of the guards' grasp, as if he'd just regained his senses. Nothing happened. The two men ignored him, too wrapped up in the speech their crazy-arse leader was making.

"Anyone who joins me will get their reward. You'll have women at your feet, or men if that's what turns your crank. You'll have land and slaves. Money. And power.

"Nothing will be denied you. I'll see that you have the pick of the best loot taken." He leant forwards and grinned conspiratorially. "After me, that is."

Men laughed and clapped. This seemed to be the speech they wanted to hear. The reassurance they craved. Doc lowered his head and shrugged. There was no loot. Not any more. Not since the wars. Not since the collapse of civilisation. They all knew it, but hope refused to die.

An enormous 'boom' sounded from the nearby fire pit, followed by a cloud of noxious gas. Doc got comfortable and listened to the coughs and screams of those around him. Most of the guards panicked, trying to get away from the horrible smelling fumes. Doc watched them run a dozen paces, maybe a little more, then a few dropped like stones.

The Duke stumbled down from the wagon but recovered all too quickly when a gust of wind cleared a swath of smoke around him. He screamed curses and ran from one guard to another, all the while ranting about how he'd kill anyone who tried to do him wrong. "I'll slit you from your gullet to your pecker," he wailed to no one in particular and drew a long blade from somewhere in his ragged clothing. The big man turned and peered around, as if seeking a target for his anger. His eyes came to rest on Doc but lingered there only a moment or two before moving on. He turned again, and Doc noticed a glimmer of a smile crease the behemoth's lips.

Doc looked in the direction the Duke faced, and his blood ran cold. A woman cowered in the midst of many others, young, beautiful with the same wavy hair Doc wound into a ponytail most of the time. Her large, dark eyes stared unblinking at the Duke, and Doc strained to break free of his bonds.

"Robin!" Doc yelled, but knew his voice would be lost among all the others in the confusion.

A slight breeze wafted among the trees and dispersed the gas almost as quickly as it spread through the area. More guards fell, but Doc saw others stumble among the prisoners while a few seemed unaffected.

More and more prisoners had somehow managed to get free of their makeshift bonds and either tried to free their companions or made for the relative safety of the forest. The guards slashed and pushed them down, but the haphazard effects from the gas hampered any real organisation. Fighting broke out in small groups.

The wind shifted again, pushing the gas back over the camp. Men choked. Guards cursed and swung whatever weapons they had at the prisoners still standing.

"Robin, get down," Doc bellowed and hoped she heard. His little sister, he'd found her, finally. *But, am I too late?*

"The whore!" the Duke growled and took a stumbling step forward. Spittle flew from his mouth as he staggered towards Robin.

Doc cringed and fought the twine holding him.

"The fucking whore," the Duke growled as he peered first at Robin, then back at Doc. "She your bitch?" A leering grin crept over the man's face. He blinked and shook his head, as if to clear it.

The ropes burnt Doc's wrists but didn't stop him from fighting to get free. He had to stop the lunatic approaching Robin.

"Bitch," the Duke muttered then waved his free hand in the air, nearly toppling himself in the process. "You lazy, good for nothin' bunch of freeloaders. Gather the fuckin' slaves, get 'em out of here. Get up and do as you're bid," he snarled as he kicked a downed guard at his feet. The dull thud seemed very loud against the insanity around them. "They won't do me any good if they're fuckin' dead, you dumbass son-of-a-bitches," the Duke snarled.

The smoke sank to ground level, and Doc knew he'd be unconscious very soon. At first, it clung to his lungs, sending him into a coughing fit that took his breath. *What the hell was the Duke rambling about?* The guard on Doc's right stumbled and fell, landing across Doc's back. The man's head hit the ground with a thud, and Doc looked down at him. He was out like the proverbial light.

Another guard coughed then crumpled to the ground a few paces away. Doc looked around and saw men and women falling haphazardly everywhere the smoke seemed the thickest. Many of the prisoners who were trying to get to freedom fell.

"Damn!" Doc would have said more, but after another coughing fit, his vision blurred.

Zoe's face appeared. "Doc, I'm here. Just give me a second."

Her hands worked the ropes holding him. His mind numbed. The drug dragged at him, but he refused to go under.

Something struck the side of his head, and the world went dark.

Chapter Six

"Get up!"

The words sounded like they came from the end of a tunnel, echoing inside Doc's head. The ringing in his ears drowned out the rest of whatever the woman said. He had to get his thoughts together.

Zoe!

Robin!

Mother!

Jazz!

Doc forced his eyes to open and then to focus. His heart raced, and around him the yells and grunts of battle continued. Zoe leant over him, a concerned look marring her beautiful face and creasing her brow. He pushed himself upwards, trying to sit. Hands gripped his forearms, helping him, steadying him.

"Where's Jazz, Mother, Robin?" He peered around, seeing dozens of bodies scattered in the surrounding area, hopefully slumbering and no more. None looked familiar. He couldn't see the Duke among those still fighting. He looked back at Zoe and opened his mouth to ask about the bastard.

"Jazz is nearby. He was right behind me. Your mother, I've seen her. I sent her into the woods along with a dozen or more others. They're both fine." She looked away and didn't add any more.

Doc waited for her to continue. Over her shoulder, he spotted Jazz, free and coming towards them. His face showed the signs of the beating he'd received, blood covering one side of his forehead and temple, one eye puffy and reddened, promising a nasty bruise later, and a long scrape down the other cheek. He hobbled as he ran, no doubt battered from stem to stern. But, he seemed whole, and that was all that mattered to Doc.

From out of nowhere, a beefy marauder appeared between where Doc sat with Zoe and where Jazz shambled towards them. The man held a large, well-worn club and wielded it with abandon at anyone who seemed to get in his way. He apparently thought Jazz was in the way. The club came down, connecting with a resounding smack against the side of Jazz's head, and sent Doc's lover flying through the air. When Jazz landed a few paces away, he didn't get up.

Doc saw red and pushed himself to his feet, thrusting Zoe to the side. The anger he'd felt upon the discovery of Jazz's capture was nothing compared to the fury raging within him at that moment. Oblivious to Doc's rage, the marauder who'd struck down Jazz continued advancing. Doc charged, his thoughts on nothing more than the death of that one single man and the emptiness filling his heart.

The distance between the two vanished in a heartbeat, and Doc was ready. One foot slightly in front of the other, legs spaced, he leant forward and braced himself for the impact. When the big guard hit, for a moment Doc thought he'd taken on more than he could handle. Then the man groaned and sagged.

"Fuckin' townie," the marauder mumbled, taking a stumbling step back to get his feet under himself. "Pretty boy goin' down." The man puffed out his chest and retreated a couple of steps before charging forward again.

His head lowered, the savage reminded Doc of a work horse or battering ram more than a man. Instead of standing and taking the blow, Doc waited until the marauder was a mere pace or two away then side-stepped and let him rush by. At the last possible moment, Doc stuck out his leg.

"Shi...!" The yell ended abruptly when the big man hit the ground with a thunderous thud. It didn't stop him, though, and after only a brief moment, he struggled to his feet and gave himself a good shake. Peering around, he spotted Doc and growled low and deep in his throat. "Fuckin' bastard, piece of shit," he snarled, lowering his head again. But this time, he didn't charge immediately. Instead, he glanced up as if gauging what Doc would do.

"Come on, my pretty. Come for that fuck I know you've been after," urged Doc in a light, sing-song voice. He winked and blew the man a kiss, adding more fuel to the fire.

It proved to be enough. The fellow bellowed like a wounded bull and charged. Hands like claws reached for Doc, but in his rage, the brute had lowered his eyes again and raced forward blind.

Again, Doc waited for the right time. He didn't trip the fellow. This time he brought his joined fists down hard right at the base of the fool's skull. Unconscious before he hit the ground, the big man skidded a few paces on his chin before coming to an abrupt stop.

Doc looked around and advanced on the closest guard, who'd crouched and held a long blade at the ready. Deftly, Doc feinted to the right and reached for the man's wrist. With a swift crack of Doc's knuckles on bone, the guard dropped his knife. Doc scooped the blade up and thrust it forwards, burying it between the man's ribs. The next man fell nearly as easily, as did the following. Blood spattered Doc's chest and arm as he made slow progress to where he had seen Jazz fall.

The wind shifted again. Smoke, thicker now and with a much harsher, acrid taste, wafted around him. Doc tried not to inhale much of the drugged air, but the exertion of battle proved his undoing.

He glanced around then took a hesitant step towards a large man lying on the ground. The Duke lay on his side, the body of a young boy clutched to him. Doc recognised two previous captives as they jumped in and grabbed the Duke's arms. The enormous man squealed as if he'd been struck in the groin, but otherwise remained still.

As Doc's vision blurred, he saw the child pulled out of the monster's clutches and ropes wrapped around the man's wrists, none too gently.

The world faded to black again. Doc dropped to his knees painfully on the rough ground. The side of his face stung like he'd been slapped.

* * * *

Doc groaned and tried to shift onto his side. A stab of pain brought him up short, and he opened his eyes. Blue sky and his mother's smile welcomed him.

He blinked. Her face came into focus a little more, and her expression shifted to concern. Her usually tidy grey hair poked out all over, and she had a large bruise on one side of her jaw. The dress she had on was torn and filthy.

Doc tried to sit up, but she'd read his thoughts. She put a firm hand on his chest, holding him down. "Stay put. You've got a hell of a bump on your face, and you inhaled a lot of that drugged smoke." She smiled again, her face awash with relief. "What on Earth gave you such an idea?"

"Jazz. Where..." Doc's voice sounded worse than he'd thought it could, rough, dry, strained. Yet, he was all right, he knew it. "Are you okay?"

"Yes, I'm fine. I've got a bruise or two, might have a sprained ankle, but I'll be right as rain in no time." She stroked his face, her fingers lingering above the sore spot on his cheek. "And, Jazz is fine. Bruised and battered—a few bumps on his head that I've bandaged. He's going to be all right. Like us, he'll mend."

"The others. I saw so many from the village. More from other places." The numbers both outraged and bewildered Doc. How could such a rag-tag group of marauders vanquish so many?

"There are dozens, maybe even hundreds, who are now free. They've been prisoners, more like slaves, for a long time. Most of them will heal. Some won't make it." Her face took on a haunted look.

Doc knew she'd seen things no one ever should. He also knew how strong she was. It was then he remembered the face of his father in death, and sadness, deeper than he could ever remember, came over him. *Did she know?*

"All of the marauders have either surrendered or fled," she said matter-of-factly. "The strongest will have to go after them, at least to make sure they don't double back on us later."

"There are warriors for that, mother," Doc reminded her and frowned. He had no idea really how many survivors there were.

"Yes, I know." She ran her fingers through his hair.

He winced. "Sorry. It feels like that dumbass pulled half my hair out."

"He better not have. That's my job." The soft voice of the man Doc loved came from somewhere behind his mother. Dirty blond hair appeared first, then the grinning face peeked around. A large bandage circled his head, and a small blotch of red marked the white cloth at the temple on one side. "Not that I'm after you being bald. I just like something to hang onto." Jazz winked and stepped out from his spot behind her. "Pearl, mother of the man I love, you need to rest. Let me take care of him for a little while."

She sighed and arched her back, a hand going to the base of her spine where Doc knew she suffered pain from time to time. "Yes, now that I'm sure he's going to be all right, you can take him. Just don't let him go traipsing around too much, yet. He's got some pretty ugly scrapes and bangs. He might need to have his ribs wrapped." She pushed herself to her feet and stood gazing down at Doc with an expression of the sort of love only mothers seemed capable of having. "Before I go, son, do you know about your father?"

"Yes, I found his body. He died well. He was an amazing man. I loved him very much." That was all he got out before a tear trickled down his cheek, and he stopped. He didn't want to set her off, and they'd talk later about the man who'd raised him.

"I did, too. Very much." She bent down and pressed a soft kiss on his forehead before she turned, ready to leave his side.

He stopped her with a touch of his finger to her hand. "Zoe, is she nearby?"

"She's tending some of the injured." His mother smiled and added, "She's been so helpful. It's almost as if she has the healer's touch."

Doc nodded and wrapped his fingers around his mother's wrist, gently drawing her closer. Tenderly, he kissed her palm.

She gazed down at him for a moment before freeing her hand and hobbling away.

Doc saw a large fire blazing in the pit close by, and several elders sat beside it. His mother joined them. Watching her, he realised how close the group of elders had become and knew she'd get comfort simply from being with them. It made him feel better.

He peered around as much as he could, trying to spot Zoe. He finally saw her bent over one of the women who'd been rescued. Blisters from a recent burn marred the side of the middle-aged woman's face. Zoe had some kind of salve and was spreading it on the sores.

Doc nodded and winked up at Jazz, a little weakly, but it was the best he could do. "So, you like to pull my hair." The man blushed, and that made Doc smile even more.

"Well, you know how it is. Had to say something, and it's been a tad hectic these last few days," Jazz said lamely. He sat next to Doc, facing him, then he leant down and pressed a kiss to Doc's lips.

The warm breath across his face had Doc wanting more.

Too soon, Jazz sat back and added, "I like kissing you, too, but didn't think you'd want me to do that while Pearl was here."

"She'd have moved aside. You know she loves you like another son." Doc slipped his arms around Jazz's neck, slowly but surely pulling him back down for another kiss.

"Yes, I know she does. She's been the mother I wish I'd had for...how long have I known you?" Their mouths touched, the words ended.

Doc slid his tongue along Jazz's lips, seeking entrance. An instant later, his tongue found itself inside, tasting and exploring the familiar teeth. Smooth wetness sent a shiver up his spine when Doc's tongue slid up and down Jazz's. He loved the pseudo fucking and licking, the sweet taste and smell of his lover.

Jazz pulled away, breathing hard, his face flushed. "I hate to stop, but we should wait until later for this."

"I know, but I needed that kiss." Doc trailed his fingers across his lover's jaw line, being extra careful where he saw bruising, and over the puffy wetness of his mouth. "Give me a hand up, would you? My ribs are really sore."

"Okay, but if you think I should get something to bind them, don't fuck around. Just tell me. Your mother will kill me if you're hurt unnecessarily." Jazz grunted as he got to his feet, his own body in less than perfect condition.

"We're in fine shape, for the shape we're in, aren't we?" Doc remarked, taking Jazz's outstretched hand and pulling himself upwards. A stab of pain forced a groan from deep inside, but Jazz reached down and wrapped his free arm around Doc, gently helping him to rise. Once he got his feet under him, things went easier. Not good, but better.

Jazz released him and stepped back. "You sure you're okay?" He eyed Doc from head to toe, as if waiting for him to fall on his face.

"Yeah, I'm good."

"I know you're good. I just don't want you to collapse in front of Pearl." Jazz turned and looked at where the elders had formed their own tiny bit of normal at the fireside. "A fine pair, indeed!"

"Sure are," Doc replied and grinned at his lover then over at Zoe. *More than a pair, perhaps.* "Let's see if we can get some kind of travel organised." He eyed the surrounding woods. "I'd like to get our people home. The others, I'm not sure what they'll want to do, but we've got to get them to shelter.

"The guards, those we've captured, they can carry the injured back. The children—give them switches. I'm sure they'll be more than happy to keep the marauders moving."

Jazz chuckled. "I'm pretty sure their mothers wouldn't mind, either. Not sure it's a good idea, though. Feels a bit like training young sadists to me."

Doc peered around at the dozens of people standing or sitting quietly, waiting for someone to tell them what to do. It was as if the short stretch of slavery had torn their sense of pride from them. He needed to help them get it back.

"Where are the guards, now?" he asked, unable to see any sign of the marauders.

"There's a cage affair over that way, between all the wagons. The Duke used to keep his prize catches in it." Jazz grabbed Doc's arm and lead him to where several ramshackle wagons sat in a circle around a central fire pit. The cage was approximately ten paces square and crowded with semi-uniformed men, who either sat or slouched against the rusted metal bars. Blood oozed from fresh gashes on many of those imprisoned. Some looked as if they could barely stand but were refusing to give in and sit down. Others snarled curses at their former charges, while rank fear shone in their eyes.

Doc walked around the cage, admiring the wounds and smiling as the marauders cowered away from him. The Duke wasn't among them, though, and he looked at Jazz. "Where's the Duke?"

His lover smiled. "A special place for a very special man. Come, and I'll show you." He walked around the biggest of the wagons, which Doc took to have belonged to the Duke.

On the far side, dangling from the branches of a very large oak, hung a cigar- shaped cage. Doc stopped and gaped. The Duke, stripped naked and bound to the many bars of the cage, was displayed at eye level.

Mostly women were present, but there were a few of the younger men, as well. Long slender sticks, whips and clubs taken from their former guards, anything they could use to swing at the Duke's flesh, seemed at hand.

"These are the ones the Duke took special interest in. It looks as if they didn't like his attention. Not one of them has offered to help set him free. All of them have been here since the men strung him up." Jazz crossed his arms over his chest and stood stony-faced, watching a woman wield a short-handled whip clumsily, striking the naked man haphazardly. His well-striped body swayed to and fro, and each stroke of the whip brought a new cry of agony from the former despot.

Doc felt no pity for him and doubted anyone else in the camp did, either. Even the Duke's own men showed little respect or loyalty, having been there only for the money or goods they could earn, beg or steal.

"The wagons, if they were emptied, could carry many of our tribe and the other captives home. We don't need luxury, just a way of transporting them all." Doc slowly spun around, surveying the number of people there might be in the camp, how many were injured or too weak to make the trek without help. A lot, he decided—children half starved, men and women beaten then forcibly marched for hours beyond reason. It'd be a slow trip.

Jazz nodded and slid his arm around Doc. "I think we should give them a night to rest up before we start back. Many of them haven't slept properly in weeks."

"I bet they haven't eaten properly in as long or longer. We'll break open the Duke's stores and see what we can find for everyone. I'm sure we can bag a deer or two. Perhaps there are warriors who have strength enough to join us." Doc faced Jazz and smiled. "We'll slip away. I've been so worried about you, my love."

"I thought you'd never find us." Arching his back, Jazz pressed his crotch against Doc's and moved his hips from side to side.

Doc's smile widened as Jazz's cock grew hard and slid against his. "Had to do what I could at the village. There were survivors, injuries, many dead. My father..." The vision of the man flashed into his thoughts and dampened the sensual heat growing inside him.

Jazz must have sensed it. He leant close and kissed Doc's neck, nipping at the skin below his ear. "He'd have been incredibly proud of you. You took on a great deal, caring for everyone, coming out here to the rescue. You really are crazy."

"Yes, and you love me for it," Doc said, adoring Jazz more than he could say.

"Yes, of course I do." Jazz nibbled on Doc's ear.

It sent a shiver along Doc's spine. "Before I drag you off into the bush, I think we should get these people fed and sheltered for the night. I want to make sure Zoe is all right, too." He eased out of Jazz's arms and headed back to where his mother and the group of elders sat around the fire. His erection was gone by the time he got there. He looked around, searching for Zoe, but didn't see her. She could have been anywhere in the makeshift camp, though, so he wasn't worried.

Crouching in front of his mother, he said, "I need to get as many warriors together as I can. I want you and the rest of the elders with me when I speak to the survivors here."

"Yes, of course, we're all ready to help." She held out her hand, and he pulled her to her feet. She turned and motioned the rest to join them.

Doc went to the back of the empty wagon from which the Duke had spoken, climbed onto it and yelled, "Everyone, I need your attention, now!"

His mother joined him, followed by a dozen elders from their tribe and others. None moved easily, but they all made it onto the wagon before the crowd had gathered. Jazz hopped up with a long, low bench and placed it behind Doc. The elders nodded their thanks and promptly sat down on it.

The gathering was large, much larger than Doc had anticipated. He'd thought possibly two hundred, but by the look of the crowd, there were double that, at least. He quickly re-evaluated what they'd need for the night, food being the number one concern.

Taking a deep breath, he raised his hands and yelled, "People, listen up, please!"

A soft rustling of speech carried on for a few moments but quickly faded. The sea of faces looked his way, expectantly, hope in each and every one of them. A child whimpered close by, and he turned towards the sound. A young girl — quickly picked up and hugged into a middle-aged woman's arms.

"The Duke has been captured and caged. His men will no longer harm you. Any of you." Doc gazed around the crowd, looking for trouble spots, people who might want to get their hands on the Duke or his men, anything that might disrupt a peaceful night for the majority. Small groups of people murmured softly, but he sensed nothing harmful or dangerous and went on. "Are there any hunters or warriors here?"

It took a few moments before anyone reacted. Finally, a dozen or so hands rose, and men stepped forward. Not all of them looked capable of a prolonged hunt, but they might be able to help.

"Good. We'll need meat for all of us." He looked at the small group of men who'd volunteered and pointed to two who appeared more 'damaged' than the rest. "Would you two find where the Duke kept his stores and bring them out? I'm sure he had food stashes that'll help." He checked the elders and smiled when he realised all of them were nodding.

He faced the survivors and marvelled at them. They'd taken so much punishment, lost everything and, in some cases, everyone they knew. Yet, they'd come through it all and would carry on. From the youngest to the oldest of them.

At the front of the crowd, he spotted Zoe and smiled down at her. Holding out his hand, he pulled her into the wagon. "Sit with the elders and my mother," he whispered to her.

"But—"

He pressed a finger to her lips and said more urgently, "I want to know where you are. Please, just humour me."

Zoe nodded and went to sit beside Doc's mother, who scooted over to give her a space.

Doc faced the gathering again and took a deep breath. *So many, how can I help them all?* He focussed his thoughts and said, "The children should be cared for first. The injured need attention, and you all need rest."

The sea of faces nodded their agreement. A hand shot up, and Doc gave it a moment before he indicated with a finger for the woman to ask her question.

"What's to become of us?" From her filthy appearance and the slenderness almost hidden by her torn clothing, he judged she'd been a captive for some time. She might have nowhere to go. There were probably many like her.

"No one will be turned away. Our village was razed. Many of our families were slaughtered, our homes burnt, but we still have the land and hope. You'll be made welcome there, unless you break our laws or wish to go on to your own places."

A smile turned the woman's face into a beautiful thing. He looked around and saw others reacting to his words in the same way.

"All righty, let's get the injured taken care of. Anyone here with medical training?" He looked around but saw no one for the longest time. Then, a small, elderly man raised his hand.

"Me , but it's been some time since I had anything to use to care for the sick or injured," he said in a surprisingly firm, masculine voice.

"We'll find meds, bandages, whatever we need." Doc turned towards his mother and said, "Will you assist him?"

"Yes, of course I will." Pearl got to her feet and shuffled to the back of the wagon where she waited for Jazz to help her down.

Doc bent to Zoe and kissed her. "Will you join the warriors? We need food, meat."

"You don't even need to ask. Of course I will." She leant up and pressed her lips to his again, running her tongue across his mouth then nipping at the wetted flesh.

He reached for her, but she darted away. "Later," she murmured over her shoulder as she stepped down onto the dirt. "We need to talk." She shifted her gaze towards Jazz and added, "The three of us need to get a few things straight."

Doc knew she was right and nodded, hoping to convey his deep caring for her. "Yes, soon, very soon. Thank you, Zoe."

She waved and headed towards where the warriors formed a circle.

The day fled by. The hunters and warriors brought in four or five large bucks, which were quickly butchered and spitted over the main fire pit. The Duke's stores provided a good variety of greens and savoury items, even a few sweets for the children to gobble up. Zoe appeared and disappeared with the hunters, busy at the task he'd set her.

When Doc was sure the survivors were being well taken care of, he grabbed Jazz by the arm and dragged him towards the bush. "Come with me, I've got this errand for you."

Jazz's face lit up. He smiled and called over his shoulder at the group he'd been helping carve the haunch of a deer, "I'll get back if I can, but don't count on me. Make sure the injured get their share."

"Now then, where are we off to?" Jazz slipped his arm around Doc's waist and pulled him close.

The easy comfort of his lover's body pressing so tightly against his was enough to bring Doc's stress level down. He sighed and whispered, "The stream, remember it?"

"Oh yeah, and I seem to remember a nice, big rock to bend over."

"You and I think so much alike, it's scary sometimes." Doc slid his hand down and grabbed a handful of Jazz's bottom. *Firm, taut and all mine*, he thought as they hiked along the pathway the Duke's horde had taken.

In no time, they found the stream and the boulder they both remembered so well. Doc spun Jazz around and touched the man's head. "Are you sure you're up for this?"

"It'd be a worse idea if you turned me down. I'm as horny as…well, just trust me, I'm turned on and need you." As if to punctuate the sentence, he skinned out of his shirt. Bruises marred the smooth expanse of flesh, but he seemed oblivious to any pain. His rough hide pants followed a moment later, and he chuckled. "You going to stand there watching, or you want a piece of me?"

Doc gave himself a shake and reached for the hem of his jerkin, quickly skinning it off. He'd left the pouch of meds behind in his mother's care, so he simply let his leather pants slide down his legs, and he, too, was naked. "Watching is fun, but I'm here for a piece of this." He grabbed hold of Jazz's cock and gave it a firm squeeze. It jumped in his hand, throbbing to its full size.

"Oh yeah, I thought we'd never get time alone." Jazz worked his hips, effectively masturbating himself with Doc's hand.

It was a game Jazz loved to play, and one with which Doc enjoyed teasing him. He tightened his grip for a few thrusts but loosened it when his lover's movements became frantic with need. Pre-cum oozed over his fingers, and he leant forward, licking it off.

"Tastes good, stud. I want more," Doc murmured between languid laps of his tongue.

Jazz trembled and shook, his hands going to the sides of Doc's head to keep him in place. "You're going to make me shoot if you keep that up."

"You're the one that's up," Doc mumbled around a mouth full of cock head. He sucked and licked, sliding a hand up Jazz's inner thigh until it bumped against the man's lightly furred balls. Once there, he rubbed them carefully.

Jazz grabbed Doc's ears and pulled, forcing him off the engorged cock. He kept pulling until Doc got to his feet. "You're driving me crazy." He dropped to his knees in front of Doc and sucked in the length of his erection. Nothing subtle or slow, he simply deep throated Doc's shaft, swallowing when it touched the back of his mouth.

"Fuck yeah," Doc growled, his blood pounding in his ears.

Doc knew Jazz loved making him happy, and the man seemed determined to send him into orbit. Yet, before Doc's spunk shot, his lover withdrew and smiled up at him. Bruised lips and dreamy eyes tormented him. "Spin around, lover."

Doc obediently turned his back on Jazz and bent forward. With his legs spread slightly, his butt cheeks parted.

"Hold still. Don't you dare move."

"Wouldn't dream of it," Doc replied in a raspy whisper. An instant later, a wet tongue slithered across his anus and sent a shudder of pleasure straight to his core. He gasped and reached for the boulder.

Jazz didn't spend long on his knees, but by the time he rose to his feet, Doc was delirious with pleasure. His cock pulsed wildly, its head slapping his belly with each beat of his heart. Warm wetness covered his balls, gently sucking at them and pulling them down. He wanted to scream his love and his need but refrained somehow.

Sensation and tension mounted, and he curled his toes. His sight faded. Sweat trickled down the sides of his face, his ribs. Fuck. His ribs ached, but he thrust that aside in need of the promised bliss.

"Fuck me. Jazz, please! Fuck!" His head spun, and he clenched his fists. He arched his back and spread his legs wider, inviting his lover to take him. Begging him with his body.

"Yeah, that's it. Spread for me," Jazz whispered.

With one hand gripping Doc's arse cheek, he positioned his cock at the wetted anus. A gentle nudging at the hole sent a shudder down Doc's spine. A little pressure and the head popped inside.

Doc saw stars and growled his joy. "Yes, oh my fucking lord, yes, fuck!" Nonsense dripped like honey from his lips as he worked himself backwards onto his lover's cock. Slowly Doc drew Jazz in. When Doc felt the man's balls touch his own, he came close to losing it. He held perfectly still while the feeling passed. Sure he'd last, at least for a few minutes, he worked his hips back and forth, fucking himself on Jazz's cock.

Jazz gripped Doc's hips and controlled the speed and depth, frustrating Doc tremendously. Shallow, hard fucks alternated with deep, slow thrusts until Doc couldn't hold back the scream of bliss he'd been fighting. His balls churned and blasted their cargo, sending a long ribbon of spunk onto the boulder. Another spasm followed, along with the second rope of juices. Jazz's cock pulsed, sending a stream of cum deep into Doc's hole. Another joined the first on the next thrust then one more.

"Yes, oh yeah, do it," Doc growled and pushed his arse back against Jazz's belly. He came until nothing was left, and still the pleasure gripped him. Blind and deaf, he wallowed in it for as long as he could until he finally collapsed on the boulder.

Jazz lay spent across his back, panting into his ear. They remained there for several minutes, basking in the afterglow. Jazz stroked Doc's sides and kissed his neck.

"I think you broke something," Doc said in a low voice, his body aching.

"Of mine or yours?" came the immediate response.

"Mine, I think." Doc shifted his weight and groaned. His ribs felt like someone had stuck a knife in his side. "I hate to ask, but could you move, please?"

"Sure." Jazz eased off him and moaned. "Might need to get Zoe to stand in for a few days. I'll watch, though, if that's okay?"

Doc chuckled then bit his lip. "You're going to kill me yet. But, I'm sure she'd be happy to oblige."

"You might want to ask me before you go assuming things." The female voice came from across the stream and was definitely Zoe. She stepped out from behind a large berry bush and stood with her hands on her hips.

Doc leapt to his feet and dropped his hands to his crotch in an idiotic attempt to hide what she'd no doubt already seen.

Jazz nudged Doc. "I think she's been watching, so what the heck are you hiding?"

Doc growled at the man but smiled when he noticed Jazz's hands were also covering his own crotch. "Same thing you are, dumbass." He chuckled and returned his attention to Zoe, waiting for her to speak.

"Mind if I join you?" The fully clothed woman didn't wait for an answer. Instead, she waded across the swiftly moving flow. The water reached almost to her knees.

Doc reached for his leather pants and pulled them on, motioning for Jazz to dress himself, as well.

"I gather you saw it all?" he asked when Zoe stepped onto the bank and held her hand towards him. He grabbed it and helped her up the slope.

"Yes," she replied in an unsteady voice. "I came close to joining you but thought you two needed some time alone together."

"Nice of you." Jazz reached for his multi-coloured shirt and slipped it on. "Next time?"

Doc looked at his lover and smiled. Jazz was serious. He looked back at Zoe.

"Yes, and soon, I hope."

Time seemed to stand still for Doc then. He wanted them both. He adored Jazz and would never give him up. He couldn't. Their bond was forever. He was sure Jazz felt the same. He knew Jazz thought highly of Zoe, their recent play had told him that. But, did he want her to join them more permanently? *Does my lover want to share? Forever?*

Jazz eyed him then turned his gaze on Zoe. All Doc could do was wait and hold his breath. And pray.

"Yes, next time you join us," Jazz said softly. "And the time after that. And the time after...well, you get the picture. Can't make you any promises, yet, but if desire and admiration mean anything..."

Zoe exhaled. That was when Doc realised how tense she'd been and how much she wanted them both to say yes.

"Of course, yes," he said and pulled her into his arms. Gazing into her eyes, he whispered, "The next time and the next. A lot of times. Lots of exploring. The three of us, together." He leant down and kissed her.

When he came up for air, he saw Jazz had moved closer. The man's hand slid around Zoe's back then halfway around Doc's. "This is going to be fun."

Doc chuckled and said, "Yes, it is, but we've got things to do first. Besides, I need a little time to recuperate."

"Poor men," Zoe lamented playfully. "Now women, we can go for hours and wear out several of you guys."

"Cheeky, just plain cheeky," Jazz remarked and smiled.

"Come on, you two," Zoe said. "Let's get back. We've wasted enough time."

"Never wasted time when I'm with you." Jazz winked at Doc.

Hand in hand in hand, they walked back to the camp, each deep in their own thoughts.

Zoe pressed her cheek into Doc's arm when they arrived, as if the feel of him solidified what they'd each said. She repeated the act on Jazz then, in a rush, said, "I wanted to tell you the hunting went well. That's why I was looking for you. I don't spy on people." She blushed.

"I didn't think you were spying, not really," Doc said. "But, I'm glad you did."

"Me, too," Jazz chimed in and gave Zoe a quick peck on the nose.

"We're pretty well organised now," Zoe went on. "Those with the worst injuries have been cared for. The rest can wait until we get back home, unless you want to see anyone."

Doc looked around and, in a more serious tone, asked, "Everyone get something to eat?" He focussed on the groups of people.

"Not quite, but there's more food coming," she answered.

"Where's my mother?"

"She's with the elders." Zoe pointed to the fire pit where his mother had taken her place a while ago. "Over there."

"Thanks, Zoe. I want to talk to her." Doc released both her hand and Jazz's and headed over to where his mother sat among the dozen other elders.

He waited respectfully for them to notice him. When she finally nodded, he sat beside her and said, "We'll leave in the morning. We should be able to get most of the way there tomorrow." He hesitated. "I haven't seen Robin since sometime in the middle of the fight."

Pearl sat quietly for a long moment then said, "She was taken to be given to someone. A traveller."

Doc leapt to his feet and cried, "What? When?"

Moisture brimmed in his mother's eyes. "When the fighting got really bad, the Duke sent her and several other young girls off to some traveller who'd asked about buying slaves."

"But, I was here. I didn't see—"

"I know. But she's gone." Tears streamed down the old woman's face. "When you were unconscious, I saw... I'm so sorry, Doc. She was dragged away by several of the Duke's men."

Doc had no choice but to go to his knees and comfort her.

I could have saved Robin. I was here!

"Do you know which way they were going? Anything?"

Sniffling, she swiped at her eyes with the back of her hand. "He said something about the city. But that made no sense. The cities are all dead. Aren't they?"

Doc's blood ran cold. The city. Dead, almost. There was still life in some of them.

"I'll find her. Mother, somehow, I'll find her and bring her home."

"What's wrong, Doc?" Jazz's voice came from behind him.

Doc turned and looked up into the eyes of his lover and his lady. Jazz and Zoe, his mates—would they understand?

"It's Robin. She's been taken to one of the old cities. As soon as I make sure these people are safe, I'm going after her."

Jazz's eyes grew wide, and he gasped. "Fuck. But, I saw—"

At the same time, Zoe said, "She was here. I talked—"

Doc interrupted them both in a voice as dark and loud as thunder, his hands raised. "I saw her, too. She was here." He wanted to scream to the heavens how unfair this was. His family had suffered enough. He had suffered enough.

"We're going to get these people back to the village. That's our first order of business."

Jazz nodded and said, "We'll leave at first light. They need a night of rest. They'll never make it without it."

"I know. Damn, I know." Doc slammed a fist into the palm of his other hand. "The city. Mother, do you know which one? Where it is?"

"I think so. The man, this traveller or trader, whatever he was, mentioned Victory when he was here yesterday. I think that's where he came from." The old woman gulped back a sob then buried her face in her hands.

"Mother, we'll find her. We'll bring her home."

Zoe dropped to her knees before Doc's mother and slid her arms around the woman's waist. "We've been through hell, but we survived. Robin is strong. She'll be waiting for us."

Doc went behind his mother and bent forward, his arms circling her upper body. Jazz joined him, and the three of them comforted the woman as best they could.

The sun slowly sank behind the hills, and the people settled in for the night. Those men who could set up guard posts. Most found comfort in the arms of the fellow captives with whom they'd shared space. Even his mother had taken comfort from the elders surrounding her and had finally succumbed to the rest she so desperately needed.

Only Doc and his lovers sat up and talked far into the night. The trip home should take a couple of days, at most, but they wanted to be ready for any eventuality that might hold them back. They spent several hours tearing the cupboards and shelving from the Duke's wagon and those he'd used to carry the plunder of the many villages he'd raided. Doc hoped they'd be able to send the wagons back later to collect all that might be of use to his tribe. At the moment, though, getting the people home safely had to be the priority. The animals the Duke had used to pull the wagons had been nearly as maltreated as the people, but Doc didn't object to using the guards, or the Duke himself, as slave labour. A fitting end to the man's reign, he thought, and justice for the guards who'd cared so little for their charges.

Morning came, and after a sparse meal of leftovers, the former captives mounted into the wagons if they needed to or took up places beside them if they were able.

Doc and Jazz walked up and down the line, helping the injured onto makeshift beds, while Zoe and several other women made sure the children weren't left behind. When the sun was high overhead, Doc strode to the head of the line and called, "It's time. Let's go home."

The cheering that followed shocked him but made him smile. The village would be full upon their return. Rebuilding would take time, but they'd have the people to do it.

Two wagons pulled by former guards led the way. Freed captives raised the whips they'd so recently felt themselves and brought them down on the backs of their abusers.

Doc stepped aside and pulled Jazz next to him. "I need you to lead the way. I want to make sure no one is forgotten."

"You got it, lover. I'll set the pace as fast as I dare."

"You're a mind reader. Thanks, sweetie." Doc hurried away, moving between the wagons. People walked along beside them or trailed behind. It didn't take him long to see they were all moving.

The day passed slowly, as he knew it would. They stopped several times for short breaks but found the people were eager to move on. Darkness crept up on them, and they stopped only when Doc was afraid someone would fall or injure themselves.

* * * *

The next day went much like the first, with miles of slow travelling. Children, the elderly and those injured but still on their feet were helped by those more able. They found water, and that seemed to provide the energy everyone needed to carry on.

That evening, Doc sat beside Zoe, and Jazz faced them across the small fire they'd lit. "We'll reach home in the morning," Doc said.

"Yes. I'd hoped we'd make it tonight," Jazz said evenly. "The small meal we managed to put together for them seems to have worked wonders, though."

Doc knew the man must be exhausted. Jazz's head still bore the white bandage, although it was now grimy with dirt from their arduous journey.

"I didn't dare push them any more," Jazz went on. "Food's pretty much gone, and with this many mouths, there's no way we can trap enough to feed everyone. So it'll be one hell of an incentive to get them all moving in the morning."

"All but the guards and the Duke. He looked good pulling a wagon with his guards behind him, urging him on." Doc would have laughed at the memories of seeing the defeated guards prodding the Duke with whatever they'd been able to reach.

"I'm sure the villagers will find tasks for them all once we get home. Grunt labour under guard for the time being. It's probably something the Duke and his cohorts understand only too well, but not from the position they'll be taking," Zoe said with venom.

"Time to call it a night, you two." Doc made sure the fire was well back from anything flammable before he slid down and pulled Zoe with him. Jazz quickly joined them, and they curled into a ball of warm limbs. It didn't take them long to fall into a deep sleep.

* * * *

Mid-morning, they saw their village from the top of Elk Ridge. Doc remembered less than two weeks ago when he'd returned from his trip to the farm to a razed home. Seth had been the first person he'd seen then.

Looking down from the Ridge, he noticed smoke rising from several chimneys and wondered how many homes were habitable. "We'll soon find out, and we'll make more," he whispered to himself.

On one side of him stood Jazz, his lover, his life, the man he'd spend the rest of his days with. A smile on the man's face made Doc wonder what he could be thinking. On his other side, Zoe leant against him. A new lover, one he'd wanted secretly for much too long.

He turned just in time to see his mother slip down from her place on one of the wagons. She scrambled over to where he and his lovers stood. "We made it. All of us."

"Yes, we made it. Almost all of us," Doc replied, his thoughts going back to his sister, Robin.

Jazz reached around him, and Zoe slipped her hand over Doc's chest. "We're home. We'll rest up and get these folks settled."

Doc watched hundreds of former captives walk past, some confidently, others hesitantly. They'd stay or go, but they were all free. He felt good about that.

He faced his mother. "I'll find her. I swear it."

Jazz said, "Yes, we'll find her and bring her home."

"We?" Doc looked at him.

Zoe blinked up at Doc and said, "All three of us are going. There's no more just you, mister. We're together now."

Doc's heart came close to bursting

JAZZ

Dedication

This one is for Janice, my former editor — a special
woman who encourages me with kindness and
patience — and for Jamie, who pushes, but never too
much, and understands, all the time. Thank you both.

Chapter One

"But, I want to go with you two," Zoe whispered into Jazz's ear.

Jazz rolled over, taking the sexy, dark-haired woman into his arms. Doc's warm butt pressed against his and he shuddered. Having two lovers, one male and the other a lovely femme, was about all the excitement one man could ask for — or take. He ran his nose along the soft curve of Zoe's neck and whispered, "I know you want to come with us. But we all know the people in the village still need guidance. Doc trusts you to be able to handle them all. And he—"

"Yes, yes, I know. He needs you because you've been to the city before. You lived there. You know where to go, who to ask and all the rest of it." A breath of frustration followed her small rant.

"You got it." Jazz ran his hand down her back and kissed her upper chest. He continued to slip lower, taking a nipple between his lips and flicking his tongue across the puckered nubbin. Covering his teeth with his lips, he tugged at the turgid bit of flesh until she shuddered. He cupped her arse cheeks and pulled her closer, the slick wetness of her pussy anointing his newly roused erection with her juices as it slid between her thighs.

"It's not fair," she murmured, then kissed the top of his head.

He nodded but didn't speak, too busy kissing his way across her chest to the other nipple. He tugged at it, knowing from their times together how much she loved nipple play. Only too willing to give her that pleasure, he'd added it to his repertoire and began many of their sessions toying with those taut morsels.

"I could help." Her hips jerked against him, as if a shock had gone through her.

Behind Jazz, Doc shifted. A moment later, a warm gust of air wafted across Jazz's arse. Hands—his lover's—pried Jazz's cheeks apart. A warm wet tongue slithered down the crack of his buttocks, zeroing in on his hole in record time. The soft tip flicked across the crinkled opening, quickly easing its way inside.

While his lover's tongue drove him crazy with desire, Jazz increased his onslaught of nibbling and tugging on Zoe's nipples. His cock pulsed and he pushed a little harder, seeking a refuge deeper between her thighs.

Lifting his lips from her breast, Jazz said, "You could help by taking my cock and moving it so I can enter you." He gently thrust his hips back and forth. His thoughts reeled. Doc's tongue slithered in and out of his arse, nearly driving him crazy with lust. When it pulled out and Doc moved away, Jazz could have snarled his frustration.

"Not yet, Zoe," Doc said when he popped his head over Jazz's shoulder.

"What the...?" Zoe's voice came out harsh, but not with anger.

"Just a second," Dock repeated and rolled onto his back.

Jazz sat up and looked down at his male lover — his other half, as he liked to think of him. He adored the man and, of course, Doc knew it. He'd told him often enough.

"Better make this good, babe. I'm ready to burst." Jazz took hold of his erection and stroked it a few times; hard jabs that made him grit his teeth.

"Zoe, I want you to climb on top," Doc instructed, holding his arms wide. "I want at those luscious tits."

"You've got such a way with words, Doc." Zoe clambered onto Doc's body. She swung her leg over his hips but didn't mount him immediately. Instead, she straightened up and said, "Show me how much you want me."

"You're crazy, sweetness," Doc said, a mischievous smile on his face. He wrapped his fingers around his cock shaft and stroked himself. He wasn't just teasing her — his torturously slow masturbation had them all eager in no time. Jazz loved seeing his man preparing himself for a good fucking. Zoe liked to tease them both, too, and had a way of getting them involved that amazed him.

Doc's mouth sagged open and his hips thrust upwards, a sure sign he was more than ready. Jazz found his hand matched the pace of his lover's and his hips mirrored Doc's.

"Better get on soon, sweet cheeks, or I'm going to dive in and take him myself," Jazz said in a husky whisper.

Zoe chuckled, a deep, lusty sound, but quickly straddled Doc's hips. While Doc held his cock upright, she eased herself down onto him.

Jazz knelt behind her and, reaching around, cupped her breasts, pinching the large, crinkled nipple topping each. Her soft intake of breath was like music to his ears, but his pulsing, eager cock felt abandoned. Ignoring his erection for the moment, he continued toying with Zoe's nipples, while she churned her hips and muttered incomprehensibly.

Doc reached up and pushed Jazz's hands aside. "Your turn, babe," he said to Jazz. "Fill the other hole, carefully." He eased her forward, and she followed his lead.

Jazz backed away just enough to allow himself more room to work. Zoe's buttocks lay spread, her taut little hole winking at him. He slid a finger along her crease, stopping at the pucker. She was tight—he knew that from other times they'd been together. He circled her crinkled opening and pressed in, ever so lightly, wanting to prepare her for the fucking she so richly deserved.

"There's cream," Doc said, as if reading Jazz's thoughts. "On the floor beside the bed."

"Where the...?" Leaving the question unfinished, Jazz scurried to the side of the bed and looked down. There sat the expected small tub. Taking it, he unscrewed the cap and scooped a dollop on to his fingers. Not wasting a second, he repositioned himself behind her and slid his fingers along her crack. Her anus opened beneath his probing touch, eagerly accepting the creamy lube. He thrust into her, one finger soon joined by a second. He spread his fingers, easing them in and out until the third slipped in effortlessly.

"Please, now. I need your cock in me," Zoe whimpered and raised herself, nearly losing Doc's cock in the process. She groaned and reached between her thighs, grabbing hold of Doc's shaft. Keeping it in place, she swayed her bottom, fairly imploring Jazz to hurry.

Jazz got to his knees between Doc's wide-spread legs and scooted forward. With the fingers of one hand still spreading her arse, he gripped his cock with the other and took careful aim. The tip of his erection brushed her anus and pulsed. He pressed the super-sensitive crown against her pucker and, while pulling his fingers out, he pushed the tip in.

"Yes. Fuck. Yes." Zoe froze, her body held between Jazz and Doc as if in some otherworldly stasis.

Jazz eased forward, her hips in his hands. Doc's hands joined his, guiding their woman down onto his cock while Jazz filled her from the rear.

"Oh, my God," Doc whispered, a deep, guttural sound of wonder. "Your cock is right there. Pushing against mine. Fuck, oh fuck."

"Slow, babe, let me do the work," Jazz said, and prayed he could control his lust long enough to bring them both off. His testicles shifted, rising closer to his body in the first steps towards taking him over the edge. He fought the surge of bliss enveloping him and slowly sank balls deep into Zoe's arse. His sac pressed against Doc's and it nearly took him too far.

The slow rhythm he chose soon had all three of them gasping for breath and begging to come, yet he controlled it and prolonged it. Sweat poured off him. He shuddered and groaned every few minutes, but still managed to hold the threatening bliss at bay.

When it finally overcame him, he gave a mighty shove and exploded deep inside Zoe. Her body answered with its own shuddering thrust, a cry of completion sending Doc into a quivering lunge of his own. Jazz's cock pulsed against Doc's and the answering throb was a signal for all three of them to cry out with pleasure. The rolling waves of bliss held them for aeons, each clenching and thrusting adding to the soaring, mindless wonder of it all.

Jazz's world imploded. His vision went from blinding flashes of brilliant colours to simply black. His body was cold, hot and covered in sweat. He gasped, couldn't get a breath, then inhaled as every muscle went weak from the exertion of the last few minutes, or hours, he wasn't sure how long.

Breathlessly, he collapsed across Zoe's back, even though he tried to keep from squashing her. She sighed and sank on to Doc, who gasped at their combined weight.

"I think I broke something," Zoe said, her voice barely loud enough for him to hear.

Jazz lifted himself off her, hoping he hadn't actually injured her. "What? Did I hurt you?"

She reached back, grasping his hip with a hand, and drew him against her. "No, not you. This was amazing. I just feel incredibly used up."

"Ah, I think we both agree with you," Doc said, and reached around both her and Jazz, holding them tight. "I love you." He gazed at Jazz over Zoe's shoulder and sent a silent kiss his way. "Love you, Zoe," he added, and pressed his lips to hers.

Feeling a little stronger, Jazz very carefully pulled himself free of Zoe's bottom. He crawled off the bed and cleaned up in the makeshift kitchen. With no running water yet, the large basin filled for washing up proved the perfect fix. He took a damp cloth back to the bedroom and used it to clean both Zoe and Doc.

Once he'd finished, he tossed the cloth into the corner and joined his lovers on the bed.

Doc lay in the middle, Zoe on one side and Jazz took up the other.

"Zoe, sweetness, I know you want to help us find, Robin. I know you'd be a help. Hell, you were amazing when the villagers needed you." Doc slipped his arm around her and pulled her close.

Jazz pulled the covers over them all and laid his head on Doc's shoulder. He gazed into Zoe's eyes across his lover's chest.

"It's my sister, sweetness. I can't stick around here any longer and get the village moving again. I have to go, and I need Jazz to help me in the city. Victory is a jungle, but not the kind I'm good at navigating. He's lived there. I need him with me." He leant down and kissed Zoe's head. "And I need you to take care of what needs to be done here. I trust you to do that for everyone."

Zoe looked up and, for an instant, Jazz thought she was going to argue more. She reached up and cupped Doc's cheek. "How can I refuse? Knowing you trust me means a lot. I'll do my best, but you have to promise me you'll be careful." She turned and gazed at Jazz, adding, "That means you, too."

"Course we'll be careful. Aren't we always?" Jazz smiled, although he gathered from her teary-eyed look that it wasn't as reassuring as he'd hoped.

"I guess that's why you have the bandage on your forehead, right?"

"Oh, that." Jazz touched the fresh bandage on his head and tried again, "Bumped my head is all. Almost time to take this stupid thing off."

"Jazz, you're a lousy liar. Besides, I know what happened. You two…"

Doc rolled Zoe over and rose above her. "Yes, we two. We'll be back as soon as we find Robin. I have to go. I—"

"Shh! I understand, love. I really do. I'll stay behind and see that all goes well here. You just find Robin and bring her home. Maybe find us a new playmate while you're there. "

Jazz chuckled and said, "Might just do that. Someone who doesn't get broken so easy."

Zoe's soft laugh was her only reply.

Jazz sighed contentedly and turned on his side, pressing himself against Doc's back. Peering at Zoe over Doc's shoulder, he whispered, "We'd better get some rest now, or we won't get much of a start in the morning."

Zoe flashed him a look that said it all. She hated that they were going without her. She'd follow Doc's wishes, but she wasn't thrilled. She'd be waiting for them to return—both of them.

They shifted around, Doc still centred between them, and finally slept.

The next morning came much too soon. They left before the village was awake, saying goodbye to Zoe and to Doc's mother, Pearl.

On the way out, Jazz saw Seth, the Remember, standing quietly beside the village's most important asset, its well. Memories of finding the old man, alone and grief-stricken after the raiders had struck, raced through his mind. The following rescue had been touch and go but, with Doc and Zoe's help, a success. Seth would remember all that had happened and pass it along to the generation to come. Zoe would be in those tales. He raised a hand in farewell and smiled when Seth waved back.

* * * *

"It's been years since I was here," Jazz said in a quiet tone. He hunkered down and reached forward, parting the mass of undergrowth. The wilderness had taken over much of the city since the collapse of the old civilisation, the rambling streets and alleyways barred by trees that could have been used to erect the largest of houses. Vines and runners adorned what remained of buildings long ago fallen, shattered by time and the elements, somehow softening the harsh appearance of decay. Windows, empty of glass, peered down at them or glared from their drunken lean as Doc and he crept forward, trying to remain hidden by the underbrush. The sun touched the horizon and, judging by its position and the reach of its golden rays, would be down soon.

Beside him, Doc nodded and slunk behind an uprooted stump, its root ball looking more like a work of art than anything else. "Yeah, it's been one hell of a long time since either of us was here. You were bor — "

A noise behind them stopped Doc's speech cold and had them scrambling for cover under some nearby ferns. Jazz bit back a yelp of pain when his knee landed on one of the many pieces of broken brick littering the area. He gritted his teeth and listened for a repeat of the noise that had sent them to cover. Nothing stirred.

Doc faced him and gave the tiniest of shrugs. Jazz nodded but didn't rise. Neither did Doc. They'd both been around long enough to understand stealth and patience.

Jazz shifted his weight, easing his knee off the sharp point of the brick. He carefully manoeuvred himself towards Doc. Once his leg touched the bigger man's,

Jazz whispered, "You ever think you'd come back to this hellhole?"

"Not a chance," came the soft reply.

Jazz could only guess at the thoughts — memories — going through his lover's mind. They'd met not far from the city. It had been Jazz's home for some time, an age ago. He'd fought hard to get away from its cloying hatred and mistrust. He'd sworn never to come back. Yet here he was, and willingly.

Memories of city life filled his thoughts — the hunger and thirst, the brutality of anyone unknown. The pack of people he'd been with had been close-knit and, in hindsight, vile. They'd as soon have slit a person's throat as reach out a hand — maybe even more so. They'd scavenged for enough to eat, stolen what they needed when they found it, beaten those who were weaker, been beaten when someone stronger came along and taken what they desired. There'd been little kindness or love, and no sense of belonging. He'd hung with that pack to stay alive. Even that hadn't saved him from the abuse he'd suffered when he was younger.

Yet he had fond memories, too. Not many, for sure, but important ones when he allowed them to surface. He'd found his first love in the city — a young man named Slash who'd been a little more experienced than Jazz and equally horny. They'd spent hours exploring and exciting each other until the climaxes they'd shared had been mind-blowing. The relationship hadn't lasted long. Too much tension and not enough food had sent the young Slash off on a search for something better. Jazz had taken to sitting alone and playing the flute he'd rescued from the wreck of a building. His love of music had grown by leaps and bounds from that moment. The 'alone' part was much harder to deal with.

He shook those thoughts aside, putting them back into the tiny cubbyhole he'd stored them in when he'd escaped. Finding Doc had been the luckiest day of his life. Being invited to join the tribe had been a close second.

"You lead the way, sweetie." Doc interrupted Jazz's thoughts. "This is your turf and I'd get us caught for sure."

"Stay close and don't make any noise." Jazz pushed up from his crouch, slowly, all the while keeping an eye out for any unexpected movement in the surrounding undergrowth. As unpopulated as the place looked, any number of animals could be stalking them, including men. He knew there was nowhere near the numbers there had been before the collapse, but even a hundred would be more than enough to take care of them.

Beside him, Doc rose to his feet and peered around. He reached for his bow but seemed to know the weapon wouldn't do much good in this arena and let his hand drop.

"Come," Jazz whispered, touching his finger to his lips as he ducked under some low branches and headed towards the centre of the city. He didn't know if he'd have to go all the way in — he hoped not, but it was the best place to begin their search.

The going was rough, as he'd known it would be. Creeping vines and roots tripped them up every five steps. If it wasn't some weird growth sending them stumbling, it was hidden holes or the remains of walls half-buried and broken, just waiting for a misstep. The old way of walking came back slowly — a shuffling gait that covered the ground fast enough but looked and felt odd after his years away. Doc stumbled behind him. Jazz worried that the other man would find it incredibly hard to adapt. And that he'd attract unwanted attention.

Come on, lover, where's the nimble-footed wonder I know and adore?

Roofs fallen in or pushed out by trees became scarcer and Jazz made the decision to enter one of the more stable-looking buildings. He guided Doc towards one and peered inside, knowing animals lurked in many of the ruins. Not just the animals of old who were supposedly native to the area, but escaped zoo animals and 'pets' that had survived the war.

It hadn't been much of a war, he reminded himself. A few nukes sent to the major cities of the world powers, half a dozen more to disrupt as much of the populace as possible, and the decline of civilisation had been assured. The pollution of the past few centuries had taken even more of a toll and guaranteed a weakened breed of humanity. Terror, starvation and disease had done the rest. Civilisation had collapsed.

Marauders, slavers and the underbelly of humanity, accustomed to fighting for their lives, had flourished. Inbreeding had become rampant and the surviving offspring were often infertile or, worse, prone to having enormous litters of young who lived for a few days before finally succumbing to some malady or other. Honesty, charity, respect and love had become almost non-existent, mere words, barely understood, especially in the city. Jazz hadn't seen any signs of real caring until he'd found Doc and his tribe.

"Hey, Doc to Jazz," Doc's voice again interrupted Jazz's thoughts. "You with me, lover?"

"Yeah, just remembering how it was, how this all came to be. The war, the disease, all the crap that made our world such a mess." He turned, facing Doc and, in a low voice, snarled, "I hated my time in this hellhole."

"I know." Doc kept his tone calm, obviously understanding the pain Jazz was going through. "I bet most of the poor souls trapped here feel the same. Cities have killed off some of the best people." He reached out and took hold of Jazz's shoulder, pulling him close. "But some of the very best find a way out." Leaning forward, he pressed a kiss to the bandage still covering the wound on Jazz's head. "Are you okay?"

Jazz's heart swelled with love. Doc had a knack of saying just the right thing at the right time. Jazz often wondered how he'd been so lucky. He inhaled the smell of his man and replied, "Sure. Just hate this place and want to get free of it as soon as we can."

"Me, too." Doc kissed Jazz's cheek, then his neck. "We'll find Robin and get her out as fast as possible."

"But not tonight." Jazz slid his hands up Doc's arms until he reached the man's broad shoulders. The rough woollen vest scratched his palms and he thrust it aside, baring the smoother material of his shirt. "Tonight we'll camp out in one of these buildings and hope it doesn't collapse on top of us." He massaged Doc's shoulders and chest, wanting naked skin instead of the patched shirt under his hands. There was nothing better, in his opinion, than making his lover feel good.

Doc looked around, then back at him. "Are you sure it's safe?"

"Hell, no, but it's what we've got to do. It'd be insane to stumble around here at night without knowing where we're going or who we might bump into." He bent forward and pressed his lips to Doc's, tasting the virility of the man and a hint of the rabbit they'd shared hours ago. "We'll start out early tomorrow."

Doc scanned the area. "Any ideas where we should bed down?"

Jazz did a slow spin, eyeing the remnants of the buildings he could see, and pointed at one not far away. "There. Brush surrounds it, so it'll be hard for anyone to sneak up on us. A little camouflage might hide our presence from the locals." He relaxed his grip on Doc's shoulders and grabbed an arm instead. "Come on, let's get inside before it gets dark. Shouldn't be anyone tracking us, but we'll see better in the light."

He led the way and Doc followed close on his heels. Jazz darted from the shadows of brush to the deeper crevices provided by the decaying structures. A flock of birds erupted from a large, overgrown expanse of flattened ground to their left. Jazz ducked into a deep cleft along with Doc.

"See anything?" Jazz whispered urgently, darting his gaze from one place to another. Nothing else moved.

"No, just the birds."

A soft kiss to the back of Jazz's neck made him shudder. "It could have been us that spooked them. Let's get under cover. I'm about ready to jump you."

A throaty chuckle came from behind him and Doc whispered, "Might be a tad difficult. I'm behind you."

Another kiss, along with a sensual grinding of Doc's crotch against his arse, encouraged Jazz to leave the safety of their hidey-hole and race for the shelter he'd spotted. He skirted a pile of rubble, attention everywhere at once, listening, looking and trying to predict where an enemy might emerge.

When they finally squatted beside the opening to the building, Doc on one side of the doorway, himself on the other, Jazz took a deep breath and held it. Exhaling, he looked at Doc, noticing how darkness had begun to fall already. He nodded and looked towards the gaping hole that opened beside them. "Let's go."

As if they'd practiced a million times, he rose to a crouched posture just as Doc did and they turned into the entryway. Jazz's senses were on high alert as, no doubt, were Doc's. Jazz spun to the right, peering into the dimly lit cavern that had once been multi-rooms in someone's home. Nothing stirred amid the piles of broken plaster and glass.

Doc moved from behind him into the dark recess of an alcove to the left. Jazz followed a moment later.

"Nothing," Jazz murmured and straightened up. He couldn't sense a thing and all he could hear were leaves brushing against the sides of the building. Water ran somewhere deeper inside. That was it.

"Do we risk a fire in here or do you want to rough it?" Doc asked from the deepest part of the alcove.

"Rough it. We'll finish off the rabbit. I can hear water running somewhere close. I'll find that and see if it's fit for drinking." Jazz turned his head, trying to zero in on where the sound came from. Finding it, he headed towards the far corner.

"I'll check the place out." Doc slunk into the darkness.

Jazz found the end of a surprisingly clean pipe at about waist height dripping into the remains of a dull white bowl. The overflow had rotted the flooring around it but he was quickly becoming accustomed to treading the special city way. Unlacing his water bottle, he filled it and replaced the stopper. He looked around, anxious to find anything that might be dangerous or harmful later on in the night, but again found nothing. The light was nearly gone, so he hurried back to the alcove. Doc was there, a blanket of sorts spread out over the pile of leaves and branches that had blown in.

"Been busy, I see." Jazz stepped closer and held out the flask of fresh water. "Here, it smells clean. Cleaner than a lot we've seen lately."

"Thanks." He took the bottle and drank deeply. When he'd half emptied it, he handed it back and said, "Yeah, I got a bed set up for us. The tarp's seen better days, but it'll keep the leaves from scratchin'."

Jazz fastened the much lighter bottle beside his pouch and took a deep breath, hoping to calm down. His heart thumped with excitement. Doc always got his motor running and the increased threat of danger seemed to add to the pleasure.

"I should check around," he stammered, feeling his cock thickening against his leathers.

"Already done." Doc took a step closer and slid a hand behind Jazz's neck, slowly drawing him in. "No one here and, from the look of the place, there hasn't been anyone in here for a long time."

Taking a moment to look around while he could still see a little of their surroundings, Jazz had to agree. Leaves were scattered from one end of the place to the other and dust, undisturbed but for their own footsteps, told the same tale. He looked back at Doc and grinned. "Why are you still dressed?"

Chuckling, Doc reached for the leather laces holding his jerkin closed and gave it a tug. "Just waiting for you, sexy." The woollen garment hit the floor and, a moment later, his shirt landed on top of it. Bare-chested, he reached for Jazz.

Stepping aside, Jazz managed to elude his lover's grasp, but only for the few moments it took to strip down to his skin. The cool evening air sent goose bumps up his arms and across his chest. His cock lifted off his sac, bouncing its pleasure at being free.

Doc stepped closer, a hand outstretched towards his crotch.

Jazz didn't try to evade him this time. Instead he shifted his feet, widening his stance and offering his entire package to his lover's touch. A heartbeat later, warm fingers cupped his balls, gently gripping and tugging on them while he bit back a groan.

"Anxious?" Doc asked in his sexy, deep voice. He gave Jazz's balls a gentle squeeze, then released them.

"Yeah." Jazz moaned, then gasped when his lover's hand left him. "Fuck, what...?" He took a step forward, hoping to regain the harsh stimulation.

"A second. Let me get out of the leathers. They're strangling me."

The dim silhouette and the soft hiss of leather sliding over skin reassured Jazz that Doc would quickly join him in his nakedness. Jazz slid a hand around the shaft of his cock and tightened his grip, making his pulse intensify. The head felt heavy and he could have sworn a drop of pre-cum oozed across the back of his hand the harder he squeezed.

Doc nudged his fingers and Jazz released his dick. "You took more than a second."

"So it would seem. You are horny, you sexy dog." Doc took firm hold of his cock and gave it a couple of hard strokes.

Jazz inhaled and rose onto his tiptoes. He bit his lip and hissed, straining for whatever control he could muster before Doc took him too far, too fast. A thrill of ecstasy raced up his spine. He clenched his arse cheeks. A low, guttural groan escaped from deep inside him as Doc worked his magic.

"Why don't we check out this bed? It ain't much, but it's better than I expected we'd find." Doc used Jazz's dick as a handle, guiding him onto the rough canvas he'd found and spread for them.

Jazz shuffled around, eager to please his lover yet gasping every time his cock got an extra jerk or squeeze. He slowly lowered himself, going to his knees and dragging Doc with him.

"Carefully, babe, or you'll break something," Doc teased, although he'd also dropped to the canvas.

Jazz reached for Doc's shaft, squeezing the hard length and stroking it firmly from root to tip until he forced a gruff moan from his lover. "Yeah, that's it. I want to hear you groan. I want to feel you jerk and tremble." Jazz grazed his thumb across the head of Doc's cock and gasped when the man mirrored the move.

Kneeling, face to face with their cock heads touched, sent a shiver of electricity up Jazz's spine. He shuddered and grinned. Placing his free hand on Doc's hip, Jazz caressed the firmly muscled flesh, first up over the man's ribcage, then down over his thigh as far as he could reach. Their stroking never stopped. The gasps of pleasure wafted warm gusts of breath over Jazz's face, and he supposed Doc received the same.

"I want to fuck you," Jazz whispered as his urgency mounted. "I want to make you crazy."

Doc chuckled. "You took the words right out of my mouth. I want that, too." He released Jazz's dick and, after thrusting his hips forward, giving himself one more stroke into Jazz's hand, he pulled back.

Jazz let him go and licked the droplets of pre-cum from his fist, savouring the taste of his man's juice.

Doc spun around and went to his hands and knees, his arse pointing towards Jazz. He looked over his shoulder and wiggled his bum. "Come and get me." As if impatient, Doc spread his knees and, reaching back, pried his buttocks apart. "I'm more than ready for that big dick of yours."

Jazz groaned and dropped behind Doc, gaze fixed on the man's smooth, muscular arse. Forcing down the need to simply plough ahead, he bent forward and ran a finger along the crease of Doc's buttocks. "You might think you're ready, but I'm about to make sure I don't hurt you."

I couldn't bear to hurt you, my love.

And, without another word, he nuzzled his face between the man's arse cheeks. He slid his tongue around the tight anus, pushing the tip in past the outer sphincter. The ring loosened, allowing Jazz to wiggle his tongue and force it in a little more. Jazz spat onto the puckered opening then used his fingers to loosen and lubricate his lover. Sure the crinkled hole was ready, he eased back and resumed his kneeling position behind Doc's bottom. Cock in hand, Jazz aimed for his target and pressed in.

"Yes, more. Push harder." A long, drawn-out exhalation followed.

Doc's hiss of obvious pleasure urged Jazz to greater depths. He thrust forward, slowly burying his cock to the hilt and remaining still. His erection throbbed, the smooth expanse of Doc's arse gripping him like a silken glove.

"Hold still," Jazz whispered as he slowly eased back. The pull of Doc's arse tore a groan from deep inside Jazz. When the head of his cock was all that remained held inside, he stopped and clenched his teeth against the pleasure he knew would come the instant he thrust ahead. The moment of respite ended just as he had predicted, yet he couldn't have kept still an instant longer. Ecstasy clutched at him and the groan turned into a growl as he sank his shaft in, balls deep.

Jazz worked his hips, swivelling them around while he tightened his grip on Doc's haunches. Sweat trickled from under his arms, tickled its way down his ribs and chilled him. He shuddered.

"Damn it, fuck me," Doc urged and pushed back against him.

Jazz bit his lip and pulled nearly completely out, but didn't stop this time. Slamming forward, he relished the grunt Doc uttered when their bodies collided. Jazz shifted his knees wider and worked his hips, gradually gathering speed as he sent his shaft in then drew it out repeatedly. Every ten or so thrusts, he churned his midsection, stirring his lover's insides.

"Come with me." Jazz thrust ahead, then swivelled his hips and gritted his teeth desperately, forcing himself to hold off. He wanted Doc to climax, too. "I'm close. Fuck, I'm so close," he whispered. He laid forward, his belly against Doc's arse, and reached beneath his lover for the man's cock. Once he'd wrapped his fingers around it, he stroked it in tandem with his fucking. The cock pulsed in his hand and Jazz knew Doc was as close as he was.

Doc growled some animalistic roar of completion just as Jazz's body went into its own spasms. Jerk followed shuddering jerk as Jazz filled Doc with cum.

The hand holding his lover's dick became slick with Doc's essence.

Gasping, Jazz leant forward a little more and kissed Doc's neck. "Love you," he murmured into Doc's hair.

Doc shuddered a last time then turned his head, coming eye to eye with Jazz. "Love you, too, my sexy dog." He chuckled at their private joke and clenched his arse, wringing a last gasp from Jazz.

The pair collapsed onto their makeshift bed and rolled to the side. Jazz wrapped his arms even more tightly around Doc's middle. The two lay quietly, still joined.

"I could stay like this forever," he whispered into Doc's ear. He knew he'd have to withdraw soon. The city was no place for extended love play, but he hated to pull out—hated to let go. The memory of how close he'd come to losing his lover—and how close he'd come to having his head smashed in—were all too clear. He raised a hand and carefully touched the bandage still covering the wound on his forehead.

"Me, too." Doc reached back and stroked Jazz's hip. "But I have a feeling we're both going to get mighty cold if we don't get some covering." He raised the hand he'd been caressing Jazz with and gave him a solid slap.

"Youch!" Jazz jerked away from the slight pain, withdrawing from his lover's arse more quickly than either of them liked. But it was done and, rather than grumble, he bent forward and pressed his lips to Doc's shoulder. "Bugger," he whispered, then chuckled.

"Yeah, I know. But you love me anyway." Doc turned over and faced him. "Go clean up and I'll drag this canvas up so we can at least have a rough cover."

Jazz gave Doc a quick kiss on the lips, then bolted for the pipe where he'd found water. He made quick work of cleaning up and dashed, still dripping, back to their alcove.

"Come on, get under here." Doc held the edge of the folded-over canvas up for him.

"You got our clothes under there?" Jazz clambered under the rough, heavy cloth and instantly felt warmer.

"Yeah," Doc replied, pushing a bundle against Jazz's belly. "Might want to get into them soon."

"Or later," Jazz added, slipping the clothes behind him and reaching for Doc. He pulled the man closer, sighing as their bodies pressed together. "I don't think I'll ever get tired of feeling you against me like this."

"Better not," Doc whispered. He reached up and touched the bandage. "I'll take a look at this in the morning. No more headaches, I hope."

"No, my head feels just fine. It itches, though."

Doc moved his hand up over Jazz's head, winding his fingers into the hair at the back of his skull. "That's a sign of it healing. Good."

Held in place, Jazz couldn't help but smile. "Better not pull too hard there, either. I think I lost a couple of handfuls already." He drew forward, straining for another kiss.

Doc relented, loosening his hold, but only enough to let Jazz press their lips together. Their hunger satiated for the moment, the kiss was soft and loving rather than lustful.

When Jazz pulled away, he sighed and laid his head on Doc's shoulder. The two men wound their limbs around each other.

"I'm surprised Zoe didn't argue more when you told her you wanted her to stay behind," Jazz said in a low voice. He was tired and knew Doc would be, too, but he wanted to unwind a little before he slept. Nothing unusual in that, he thought.

"I think she understands how much the villagers need her right now."

"She's a pretty amazing woman."

Doc didn't say anything for some time, perhaps thinking about how she'd been invaluable in their rescuing most of their people as well as the dozens of others who'd been enslaved by the rabble ruled by the Duke. "Yes, an amazing woman, and one I hope we'll share for a very long time to come."

Jazz chuckled, his reply from the heart. "Yes, I do, too. She's stolen my heart—or the bit you left unclaimed."

"Want to bet she's got more women trained as warriors by the time we get back?"

"Hell, no. I wouldn't touch that bet with a ten foot pole."

"As long as she's all right and the new people find a place for themselves, things should go smoothly."

"Yeah, I know. And Zoe's the one who can keep the women from killing some of the lazier men... I hope."

Doc chuckled and whispered, "She's winding up as the diplomat in our relationship. A role she might not appreciate."

"No kidding. She sees herself as a warrior—which we both know she is—but we all do what we have to."

"I love her, too."

They were silent for a few minutes and Jazz thought Doc might have fallen asleep. When the man spoke again, softly, Jazz started.

"Do you really think we'll find Robin unharmed?"

"She's a strong woman, but..." Jazz didn't want to sound as if he doubted they'd get her back, or that she'd be all right once they did, but from what they'd both seen, Robin's chances weren't good.

"It's that 'but' that worries me," Doc said in a strained voice. "Roll over. Spoon."

Jazz did as he was asked and turned over so his arse pressed against Doc's groin. The man's arm went around him and pulled him tightly against him. If he could have purred, he would have.

"She's tough, but she's also a woman. And we both know what happens to young, attractive women in the city. Unprotected, alone, she's fair game for any man big and mean enough to take her." Doc pressed his lips to Jazz's back, holding him as if that could somehow solve the problem.

"Things don't change much here, Doc. It's been a long time since I was in Victory, but I'm sure I'll be able to find a contact that'll help us locate Robin."

"I know you will. You're more than my man. You're invaluable in so many ways. I don't know what I'd do without you right now."

"Same. I love you, sexy brute. But we both need rest. Tracking the scum who took your sister isn't going to be easy from here on out. I'm pretty sure I know where to go, but seeing the head honcho might be tricky."

"We'll see him, one way or another." Doc shifted but didn't pull away. He seemed to be getting into a more comfortable position. "As long as we get to her before she's hurt, or worse—"

Cutting off any further talk of Robin dying, Jazz said, "She's valuable alive, not dead. She's young and smart. The guy who took her knows that, or he wouldn't have bothered. She's also beautiful, and that's what might, in the end, keep her breathing."

Doc's low growl warned Jazz to take their discussion in another direction. No doubt the he'd already thought of all the horrible things Robin might be dealing with.

"We'll head for the centre of the city in the morning. I can't imagine that stronghold will have moved." He shuddered, remembering the walls surrounding the Warlord's sanctuary and what went on inside. "Whoever's leading the worst of them will be holed up in there. Chances are she won't even be there, but it's the best place to start looking."

Doc lay quietly for a few moments, gently rubbing Jazz's shoulder and arm. "So you think Zoe is pretty special?" he asked in a lighter tone, apparently wanting to change the subject.

Jazz grinned and snuggled back, pressing himself more firmly against his lover. "Yeah, I do. She's stubborn and she's got a mind of her own. I have a feeling she's doing what you want only as long as it's what she wants to do."

Doc chuckled and replied, "I have a feeling you're right."

The conversation died. Only the occasional shuffling of some rodent among the leaf clutter and the trickling of water broke the silence of the night.

Doc kissed Jazz's back and whispered, "Sleep well, my love."

Jazz's eyes closed and sleep took him.

Chapter Two

"Here, it's the last of the rabbit." Jazz thrust the well-cooked meat into Doc's hand.

Doc yawned and sat up, the canvas falling to his waist. "Thanks. We'll have to see about finding some more food. Not sure how we'll go about cooking it. I'd hoped to sneak in and out of here unnoticed. A fire's a dead giveaway." He bit into the haunch and chewed thoughtfully.

A momentary rush of excitement swept over Jazz as he eyed his lover from the tip of his mussed hair to the mound of canvas tucked around his waist. The sight of Doc's body had never failed to arouse him, and he hoped it never would. A warm glow followed, the flush of love. He took a breath before speaking. "I'm pretty sure we can go unnoticed. You'd be surprised at just how many people are hiding in the city." He rose to his feet and held out his hand towards Doc. "Give me your water bottle and I'll top it up."

Doc fumbled for his bottle and passed it over. Their fingers brushed and Jazz felt a shock race up his arm.

It didn't appear to have affected Doc, who resumed eating.

The trickle of water hadn't diminished and Jazz wondered where it came from, but only while he filled both flasks. He bent forward and slurped up his fill, knowing it might be a while before they found any more as fresh or clean. Behind him, he heard Doc throw the canvas aside.

"You should have woke me," Doc muttered.

"You needed your rest. Besides, I've only been up and dressed for a few minutes." Jazz walked back to their alcove just in time to see Doc pull his leather pants up and button them. He waited and watched as his lover pulled on the worn boots and woollen jerkin that made up his usual attire. The pouch, filled with meds, soon hung from his waist and he reached for the water flask Jazz handed him.

"How's your head?" Doc grabbed him by the arm and peeled back the bandage covering the wound he'd suffered during the rescue.

"Feels good. The itching isn't as bad this morning." Jazz relaxed under the sure hands of his mate.

"Looks good, too. Leave it open. The air will do more good now." Doc squatted down and buried the white bandage under a loose slab of concrete. No need to advertise their presence if they could avoid it. "Let's get moving." He rose to his feet, gathered his pack and tossed the other one to Jazz.

They checked the area, making sure they hadn't left anything behind. Satisfied, they left the building with Jazz taking the lead.

Heading towards the city centre wasn't as easy as he'd hoped. The streets hadn't changed much, but it seemed like the populace had taken it upon themselves to make moving from one place to another as difficult as they could. Piles of rubble rose in mounds taller than they were. Shafts of rusted metal jutted out at all angles from ragged blocks of cement, and every time either he or Doc stepped less carefully than they might have a teeth-grating screech rose around them.

It was slow going. By midday, Jazz noticed shadows moving around in the nearby empty shells and knew they had someone on their tails.

Jazz ducked into a wide opening that might once have been a large doorway, and hauled Doc in after him. He pressed a finger to his lover's lips, signalling him to silence.

Doc nodded, obviously understanding. With his back to the door, he pressed his arm against Jazz's and nodded towards the skeletal remains of a large building across the rubble-strewn clearing.

Jazz peered in that direction and bit back a curse when he saw a rag-shrouded figure slinking through the shadows. Another followed a few steps behind. The two shabby figures seemed to be heading in the same direction they were.

A howl made Jazz jerk deeper into the crevice. His blood ran cold as he recalled the half-starved dogs he'd seen running through the city streets and alleyways in his youth. He leaned closer to Doc and whispered, "Dogs. There can't be many left. They run in packs and will take down anything they think is weaker than they are...babies, small kids, even some not so small if they're hungry enough, and any dog not in their own pack. Vicious bastards."

"Got it," Doc replied tensely.

They waited. Jazz wanted to see which way the duo went before venturing on again. When it became clear the other two were travelling more slowly and veering to the south, he shrugged — *they won't be a problem.* He got up from his crouch and resumed their trek. The piles of refuse grew more numerous yet smaller and easier to clamber over as the day wore on.

"There are more people skulking around," Doc said in a hushed voice.

The sounds of movement came from behind them and Doc grabbed Jazz by the shoulder, pulling him into the shadow of a fallen wall. "How far to the city centre?"

"We'll get there today, providing we don't run into any big trouble." Jazz glanced around, aware and uncomfortable about those who might be listening. "Newcomers to the city attract them. Fresh meat. There usually aren't that many so close together."

"Okay, let's move, then." Doc slunk into the open and looked over his shoulder.

Jazz hurried ahead, listening for his lover's light tread behind him. A cry of anger from their right drew his attention, but only for a moment. Mounds of rusted metal rose in large piles along their way and they circled each one carefully.

A dark figure moved, shadowing them. The outline of a person limped along beside the pair and stayed there. Jazz tried to put some distance between them, but failed. Too many obstacles barred their way and the shadowy figure seemed more adept at avoiding them.

A dog howled nearby. Another, much closer, snarled.

The figure tailing them cursed.

It was a male voice, Jazz was sure of it, but higher pitched than he'd expected. He looked towards the person.

A large dog came into view, not many paces away from the shadowy figure. Its gait quickened as it lowered its great, wolf-like head. The beast crouched so low to the ground that its pink, lolling tongue nearly touched the broken pavement. Another joined it, appearing to come out of nowhere, but soon trotting by the side of the first. Three more emerged, each one as brutal looking as the first but not as big. Trailing them were three much smaller dogs, the young of the pack.

In a swirl of dingy robes, the limping figure dodged towards the nearest opening. A curse hissed across the distance separating him from Jazz and his lover. The gap led to a rubble-strewn door that refused the man's frantic efforts to open it. He turned and peered around, then lumbered into the next gap.

The lead canine lunged after the man. The beast growled and leapt. It landed with a thud and crouched, snarling, halfway to the fleeing figure. The rest of the pack paused but only for a split second. As if some invisible thread joined them, the four adults raced ahead silently.

"He'll be killed any second," Jazz whispered, a stab of concern for the lone figure transfixing him. The figure had vanished, but even as Jazz thought that it — he emerged again a few dozen paces from where he had disappeared.

"Maybe not. He's—" Doc gasped; his hand gripped Jazz's arm.

The lame figure stumbled and went down. The canine was on him in a flash.

Without thinking, Jazz took off at a flat-out run. He leapt over a pile of broken cement blocks and raced towards the fallen man.

"Hey, what the—" Doc's surprised voice came from behind him. An instant later, footfalls clambered after him and Doc growled, "Jazz, you crazy son of a—"

"Save your breath," Jazz barked, veering around the last object between himself and the fallen man. It was a vehicle of some kind, he thought. The sound of snarling dogs grew louder, intermingling with desperate, fear-encrusted curses.

"Roar!" Jazz jumped and landed a pace or two away from the cowering man. Raising his arms, Jazz waved them around wildly and kept yelling.

The dog pack whirled away from the downed figure, their bellies nearly touching the dirt as they faced Jazz.

Doc roared and landed beside him but didn't stop moving ahead. He swung his arms and continued past him. Their crazy antics must have scared the hell out of the pack. With Doc getting closer, they turned tail and raced for the cover of the wreckage.

Jazz knelt beside the ragged fellow. "Hey, are you all right?" He placed a hand on the man's shoulder. For a moment, nothing happened. Jazz wondered if the man was hurt more than he'd anticipated. He was just about to manhandle him on to his back when there came a soft shudder.

"Yes, I'll survive—this time." The man—or, more precisely, youth—rolled over and gazed up at Jazz. "Thanks. I'd be feeding their pups if you hadn't shown up. Damn dogs."

Jazz settled onto his haunches and took a good look at the young man. He judged him to be in his late teens or early twenties. Shaggy, dark hair surrounded a long, thin face that looked like it hadn't been scrubbed in months, possibly years. Steady brown eyes peered back at him, showing not one whit of fear.

Garbed in an assortment of rags, he looked like he'd fallen into someone's wash pile and scrambled out wrapped in half of the clothes. Even his legs and feet were wrapped in dull grey or brown cloth. One arm lay across his belly, seemingly held there by yet one more scrap of cloth wrapped around him.

"Did the dogs get your arm?" Jazz reached for the arm, but the man quickly pulled away.

"No, fuck off, mister," the stranger growled. His leg, however, also seem injured. A bright splash of blood seeped through the material covering his ankle. "Shit!" he yelped and pulled his feet in closer to his body. With his good hand he stroked the obviously injured limb.

"I'm not here to hurt you." Jazz sat back on his heels and looked around for Doc. The dogs were long gone, even their yelping howls fading into the distance. He turned and quickly spotted his lover approaching from the far side of the clearing, a smile on his face. Relieved, he returned his attention to the young man and smiled. "I'm Jazz. And you are?"

"Sam," the young man answered in that slightly higher than usual male voice.

"Well, Sam, that leg is going to attract more dogs — or worse, if it's left untended. My partner, Doc, is…well, a doctor of sorts. He's the closest thing there is to a healer."

"Yeah, that's me," Doc said from a few feet to the side.

Sam spun around and scooted backwards awkwardly. His face blanched when he inadvertently bumped his ankle on a sharp-edged piece of masonry. He gasped and bit back the curse he no doubt had on the tip of his tongue.

"Easy, we're friendly. Or at least we're not out to hurt you." Doc held his hands up, empty, as if that might reassure the injured man.

"You're not city peeps," Sam said in a hard voice. He'd backed himself up about as far as he could go without climbing over more of the rubble. Looking around, he seemed to take comfort that no one else was going to come at him. He pulled himself into a sitting position and, with his good hand, checked out his lower leg.

"No, we're just passing through," Doc said before Jazz could think of something rational to say without giving their true reason for being in the city. No reason to give information away that could come back to bite them in the arse.

Sam looked from Doc to Jazz, then back again, as if he hoped one of them would add to the comment. When neither did, he asked, "Going somewhere, or just travelling? Seems people either stay put or they're searching for something they'll never find."

Ignoring the question, Jazz said, "Yeah, I've seen that."

"Peeps don't leave the city. It's like they been told for so long there's nothing but death in the outside world, they quit asking about it, even looking out there. Even when they're starving, moving into the forests or plains just doesn't enter their minds. It's like when horses are in a burning barn. You have to pretty much beat them to get them to leave. Same with these peeps, only no one around to do the beating."

Jazz nodded. He'd heard the same story before. He'd left, but very few others ever did. He shrugged and leant forward, trying to get a look at his lower leg. He turned and looked up at Doc. "Sam needs someone to look at his ankle."

Doc dropped into a crouch. Without trying to touch the man, he peered at the injured limb. "That looks ugly. Mind if I check it out?" He pulled his med pouch to the front and opened it. "I've been trained. My mother was a healer. She showed me a lot."

Sam released his leg and extended it. "Can't hurt any more than it does already."

Jazz backed off a little, giving both the newcomer and Doc room to breathe. The material around Sam's ankle had both dry and fresh blood staining the outside of his foot. When Doc held up the injured limb, Sam inhaled sharply and gritted his teeth.

"How'd it happen?" Doc asked as he worked the rough cloth around, unwinding it slowly, carefully. He pulled the worn shoe from the man's foot and continued.

"Caught it in some rubble. Bunch of metal scraps I was rummaging through shifted and I fell," Sam replied through clenched teeth.

Doc doused the blood-sodden cloth with a bit of water to moisten the dark clot. Gentle pressure soon revealed the wound. Jazz sucked in his breath at the ragged edges of the gouge in the man's ankle. Blood seeped rather than pumped steadily, so he was sure Doc would be able to work his magic as long as infection hadn't set in. That was always a danger and rusted metal made the threat even more perilous.

"How much has this thing bled?" Doc turned the leg from side to side, apparently judging how best to deal with it.

"When I first did it, last night, it bled a lot. Got me worried for a bit. Finally slowed when I decided to get off it and bed down."

"Pain, how bad is it?" Doc held the wrapping to his nose and took a good whiff.

"Bad right now. Been walking on it a lot and those fucking dogs chasin' me didn't help."

Doc nodded and looked at Jazz. "Doesn't smell like there's any infection. Jagged but clean. No rotten colour or swelling." He looked at Sam and added, "I think you lucked out. It could use a stitch or two to help close it up, but it'll heal without."

Sam's shoulders sagged and he took a deep breath, exhaling slowly. "Thanks. I was worried. Any sign of weakness can get a guy killed fast here."

"I've got clean bandages and an ointment that should help it mend faster." He drew a small tub from his bag and held it up. "That okay with you?"

"Yep, I'd be crazy to say no." Sam gave Doc a tired smile. "You two in a hurry to get somewhere?"

Doc looked at Jazz and slowly nodded, then went to work bandaging the wound.

"No, why?" Jazz sensed something important was on the man's mind.

"My mother and two younger sibs were taken. I've been trailing them for a week."

"Taken?" Jazz said, his thoughts racing. "When? By who? Are you sure they came here?"

Sam lowered his head and Jazz noticed the young man's shoulders shuddering. "Yes, taken. And yes, I'm sure they came this way." He dug into one of the many folds in his threadbare clothing and pulled out a piece of bright red cloth. Holding it up, he said, "See this? My younger sister had this in her hair." He clutched the material to his face and closed his eyes, as if fighting back tears. "I have to rescue them."

"How old are you, boy?" Doc finished wrapping the younger man's leg and began returning his meds to the satchel at his waist.

"Old enough." Sam thrust out his chest and forced a stern look onto his too-thin face. "Twenty summers, most of it hard living on the road and here in this hellhole of a city."

"Easy son, we've all had it rough. I just wanted to find out a little about you." Doc patted the man's leg and added, "You can put your boot back on and see how this feels now." Getting to his feet, he looked down at Jazz. "What do you think?"

Jazz straightened up and watched Sam carefully manoeuvre his foot into his worn boot. He was young, but for some reason Jazz wanted to trust the young man. He nodded and said, "Might prove useful. Sounds like he's got the same troubles we have."

"My thoughts exactly." Doc pushed the med pouch around to the middle of his back again and adjusted his bow. "Not bad looking, either." He smiled when Sam spun his face towards him.

"Thin, but with a bit of meat on his bones...who knows?" Jazz returned Doc's smile and wondered what his lover had in mind. Trust him to be thinking about sex even when things were a little hairy.

I wonder what Zoe would think of him? She's as horny as Doc.

The thought of her and Doc with the young man gave Jazz an added kick to his flash into fantasy land. One he quickly squelched, knowing he had to remain focused.

Sam's face suddenly turned a deep shade of red and he spluttered, "What the fuck...? I'm not... You're fucking crazy." He finished wrapping his leg and ankle in rags, then scrambled to his feet. "If you think I'm going to—"

Jazz closed in and rested his hands on Sam's shoulders. "Easy, now. We're not going to do anything."

Sam stepped back, nearly falling when he slipped on the uneven footing. "You're damn right you're not."

Doc said, "Sam, I'm sorry. Neither one of us will touch you unless it's something you want."

Sam glared at the man, then looked at Jazz with a little less hostility. "You said you have the same kind of trouble. What did you mean?" He readjusted his oversized coat of rags and thrust his hands into the folds, apparently checking to be sure he hadn't lost any of his goods.

"Doc's sister, Robin, was captured then traded or given to someone from the city," Jazz said in a serious tone. "We're looking for her. We've been tracking her for some time."

"So, you're not just 'passing through' at all. You're looking for a slaver?"

"Yes, if that's what you call them. This...man, he acquired Robin from a band of marauders. This happened a few weeks ago."

"The trail's pretty cold, then. She could be anywhere by now." He looked up at Doc. "She could be dead." He fell silent.

Jazz followed his gaze and frowned, his heart nearly breaking for Doc and the truth of what Sam had said. He'd also thought about how long they'd taken to come after Robin. He knew Doc had, too. They just hadn't used those words. She could be anywhere — alive or dead — by now.

"I know what the delay might have cost," Doc said glumly. "I couldn't have done anything differently. I'm not going to give up hope, though, until I see her — one way or the other."

Sam nodded and said, "Yeah, I understand. Perhaps we're looking for the same man, this trader."

"Perhaps." Jazz's take on the young man went up a notch. "But, there could be dozens of minor despots with a few men to ransack the countryside and drag women away."

"There are. The city peeps are inbred. Too many women are infertile, deformed or give birth to…something less than human. There are always raids into the nearby lands, looking for women who can breed true, or children.

"There's one real slaver to worry about in the city now. Warlord Black." Sam shuddered, then went on. "He's got a garrison in the centre of the city. It's about the only place where there's enough upright buildings that can be guarded and enough land to farm and feed his hoard."

"Guarded…which means this Warlord has some manpower." Doc turned and looked in the direction they'd been travelling. "Any idea how many men he's got with him, followers?"

Sam looked thoughtful for a moment. "It's not just the followers, his guards. He's got families inside this sectioned-off area who can't leave. They do what he says or any number of bad things can happen to them. He's not above killing children or women who don't do like they're told. He controls the production of food. The slaves do all the work, but he makes sure only the ones who obey him get fed."

Jazz's blood ran cold. This guy sounded like someone they should steer clear of. Yet he knew they couldn't. Not if Robin was there. "About how many do we have to worry about?"

"A couple of hundred, maybe a few more or less." Sam stomped his foot, then walked around, testing his injury. "It's not so much the numbers. He's got arms, guns and ammunition."

"Live ammo? Reliable stuff?" Doc stepped close to the young man. "How is that possible?"

"Look. I only know he's got it. I don't know where it came from or how much he's got. I've been picking up information where I can. That's all."

Jazz reached for Doc's arm, gently pulling his lover back. Sam stood his ground, but he was obviously uncomfortable looking up into Doc's angry face.

"You say you've been trailing your family for about a week," Jazz said, more of a statement than a question.

"Yeah, and the only reason I'm telling you anything is so maybe—just maybe—we can help each other out."

Jazz nodded and glared at Doc. Looking back at Sam, he said, "I understand. Have you been close to this garrison?"

Doc pushed Jazz's hand away and added, "Three men against a couple of hundred, with arms, is crazy."

Sam's face grew stern. "No shit, it's crazy." He looked from Jazz to Doc, then back again. "And, yes, I've been close. I can take you."

Doc nodded and looked around. "Let's get moving, then. We've got about half a day before we have to find shelter for the night."

"Shelter's no problem. It's the locals you have to worry about." Sam glanced around. "They're city peeps, and are adept at surviving here."

"You've managed okay. I'm sure—"

"I've managed to hang on to whatever I have in my pockets. I started out with a pack full of food. That's gone." Sam scowled and thrust his hands deep into his pockets. "Anything I couldn't hang on to is gone."

"And that's why the three of us have a better chance." Doc laid a hand on the young man's shoulder. "Will you take us with you? I want to see what we're up against."

Squaring his shoulders, Sam seemed ready to take on anything. "Yes, but it's not going to be easy. Three make more noise. Are easier to spot. There are lookouts we'll have to get past without being seen."

"Figured as much," Jazz replied.

"Might as well get moving." Sam turned and headed off. "Keep your eyes and ears open."

Doc looked at Jazz. "Looks like we've found a guide."

"Yeah, but let's not get too friendly until we know him a little better." The attraction Jazz felt for the guy could be dangerous. As long as he knew it, he hoped he'd be able to guard against anything stupid happening. He hoped.

"Let's go," Doc muttered and took up a spot behind the man.

Jazz took a last look around the debris-strewn area, partially to see if the dogs had returned but also to let his lover get a few paces ahead. Travelling bunched together had never been a good idea. Finding out their possible adversary had functioning weaponry made a little separation mandatory.

They spent the remainder of the day picking their way over mounds of rubble or around it if the going was easier. Twice they skirted blocks of tumbled-down high-rises when one of them spotted smoke billowing from a window or two. Smells of rotten meat or unwashed humans made Jazz gag a couple of times as they made their way deeper into the city.

He daydreamed about their village and the happiness they had there. His love for Doc was boundless, endless, and he wanted nothing more than to get back to the simple joy of loving him. A sudden twitch of Doc's buttocks sent a thrill up Jazz's spine. He wanted the man, always. A flash of their last fuck-fest made him smile and his cock pulse. The firm thrust of his lover's shaft deep in Jazz's arse would be just what the doctor ordered. He smiled at his idiotic witticism.

"Down!"

Jazz dropped to the ground, the daydream forgotten. The voice had been Doc's. Jazz looked around, trying to spot whatever it was his lover had seen. Ahead of him, Sam also crouched behind an irregular block of cement and peered into the nearby rubble. Nothing seemed out of the ordinary, but he remained on his belly, waiting for Doc to explain.

"Damn." Doc's tight, quiet voice came from the right. "I keep getting the feeling we're being watched."

Jazz swept his gaze around the broken slabs around them and tried to peer into the darker crevices. He couldn't see anything or anyone, but once or twice he thought he'd caught movement out of the corner of his eye, as if a person was keeping to the shadows while trailing them. He trusted Doc's instincts. They'd saved both of them more than once.

"What do you want to do, babe?" Jazz slithered across the rough ground towards his mate.

"It could be nothing." Sam moved closer as well and the three of them slowly sat up, their backs forming a triangle. "It could be one of the locals, too."

"Keep going. We don't have much choice." Doc slowly rose to his feet, still obviously uneasy. "Sitting here isn't going to do any good. Just keep your eyes open."

Jazz stood and whispered to Doc, "I've been getting the same feeling. An itch at the back of my neck."

Sam cocked his head. "Both of you? I could take you a different way. Maybe some of the locals don't like us travelling through their territory or something."

It made sense and Jazz nodded. The young man moved off. Doc grabbed Jazz's arm and pulled him close, whispering, "It could be someone Sam knows. I just have an uneasy feeling about him."

"Okay, we'll just have to be alert. We need him for now." Jazz gave Doc a quick peck on the cheek, then turned and followed Sam. Doc brought up the rear.

Jazz had just begun to think they were going to make it through the day without any trouble when a stink of rotten meat cooking wafted by him. Sour bile rose in his throat. He retched. The other two men didn't fare any better. Doc vomited. Sam managed to keep his last meal down but, from the sound of his gagging, not by much.

Jazz looked in the direction of the smell and his stomach rebelled again. He swallowed and gritted his teeth. The room he saw reminded him of a cave. But what caught his attention and held it was the gathering of half a dozen raggedly dressed, malformed people huddled around a fire. The 'meat' spitted and turning slowly over that fire was one of the dogs that slunk around the city. The carcass was half eaten, and more than a little rancid from the look and smell of it.

"Fuck!" Doc's voice echoed the thought stuck in Jazz's mind.

"Come on, run." Sam's young voice cut through the haze of disgust and revulsion Jazz felt.

He tore his gaze away from the partially consumed canine and blinked at Doc, then at Sam.

How could they eat something that rotten and survive?

Sam took off at a hobbling run. Doc raced after him and Jazz, after taking one final look into the dwelling, chased after them.

Behind him, a guttural roar erupted and the sound of several sets of feet scrambling across rubble followed.

Jazz looked over his shoulder once and quickened his pace. Two men, thin beyond anything he'd seen alive before, shambled after them. Both had the deep-set eyes and splotchy skin of malnourishment.

A few moments later, the sound of their pursuit died.

Doc was the first to stop. Sam and Jazz joined him but no one said a word. The haunted look Doc shot Jazz said it all. Survival was precious, but to live like that, it was like they'd taken a step back in evolution.

"We've got to get further away from that bunch," Sam advised. He looked over his shoulder, then moved on.

Doc grabbed Jazz by the arms and pulled him close for a brief hug. "Are you okay?"

"Yeah, I think so." Jazz gave Doc's arm a squeeze. "I want to get as far away from them as we can."

"I'm with you, babe." He nodded towards their guide and said in a quiet voice, "I'm not sure how far I trust him, but we don't have a lot of choice for now. Keep your eyes open." Doc gave Jazz a push and quickly followed.

Jazz hurried on and wondered why Doc had such a mistrust of Sam. So far, the young man had done nothing but show them the way—or *a* way—towards their goal. Hopefully, they'd get there before they ran into any more city dwellers like those they'd just outdistanced.

Chapter Three

"Yes, more," Jazz whispered urgently. "Take it all."

Doc shuddered, his teeth grazing the shaft of Jazz's cock. Sucking harder, Doc eased the last inch into his mouth, the tip pushing against the back of his lover's throat. He swallowed and the pressure nearly drove Jazz over the edge. He dug his fingers into Doc's bulging shoulder muscles and groaned. Desperately trying to keep from coming, Jazz forced himself to remain still, to not thrust his hips or clench his arse cheeks.

His struggle seemed to go on for an age. Doc continued to tease him, nibbling and sucking his cock. When his lover's hand gripped Jazz's balls, the battle was lost and he thrust forward, driving his length deeper. The tension in his thighs grew. He tried to take a deep breath but found it impossible to do more than gasp. He strained for release, but wanted the pleasure to go on forever.

Doc slid his mouth to the tip of Jazz's cock and held it firmly between pursed lips. Using just the tip of his tongue, Doc teased the crown by flicking it back and forth over the sensitive tissue.

"Fuck, you're driving me crazy, babe." Jazz closed his eyes and immersed himself in the sensation. A gentle tugging of his balls forced him to groan.

Doc pulled his mouth off and whispered, "Want me to finish you?"

Before Jazz could reply, Doc slid his lips over the tip of his cock and gently sucked.

"Yess." Jazz's thoughts whirled. He couldn't think of anything but his lover and the mouth driving him crazy.

Something snapped in the brush outside the opening in the crumbled wall.

Jazz glanced in that direction, but the disturbance couldn't stop the explosion of cum shooting from his cock. The muscles in his belly tightened and another stream gushed into Doc's mouth. His fingers still gripped his lover's head, clenched in the man's long hair.

Jazz searched for whatever had made the noise.

In the moonlight, he saw Sam, naked from the waist down, gripping his impressive erection while he stood gazing in.

The sight of the man sent Jazz into another fit of shuddering bliss. The vision of the young man's hand tightly clasped around his cock took his breath. The slender hips, the too-thin legs and that look of lust on his face were forever scorched into his brain. Jazz grunted and sent another stream of cum into Doc's mouth—the last. Only shivers of ecstasy followed, one, two, three of them, leaving him gasping.

When the sensation of Doc's mouth became too much to bear, Jazz gently pushed his lover away. Doc looked up at him and smiled, then wrinkled his brow, obviously seeing something on Jazz's face.

"What?" Doc mouthed and wiped his lips with the back of his hand.

"Look." Jazz nodded towards the hole in the wall where Sam still stood, seemingly oblivious to the new situation.

Doc turned his head and Jazz knew exactly when he'd spotted their new companion by the way he did a double-take. "Oh," he whispered, and when he looked up at Jazz again the smile was much bigger. "Think we should get this guy into bed with us?"

"Yes. I wasn't sure until now, but his excitement is pretty obvious." Jazz knew Doc was still concerned about Sam's motives. "He'll be more willing to talk once we've bedded him."

Doc nodded and slowly got to his feet, the pronounced bulge in his leather pants clear evidence of his arousal. "You'd enjoy yourself a whole lot more if you joined us, Sam."

Jazz remained as he was, shirtless, his pants unfastened and around his knees, his cock still partially erect and pointing towards their peeping travelling companion. He slipped a hand around his damp cock and gently stroked it, shuddering at the sensation. "We told you we wouldn't force anything on you. That still stands true." Jazz shifted his gaze towards the man and smiled.

Sam froze; his face went white. As Jazz watched, the man's cock wilted. "Fuck, I'm…"

Jazz rose from his seat and took a stumbling step towards Sam, his hand still gripping his cock. "You're alone. We're inviting you to join us. No strings, if you don't want them."

Doc strode forward a few paces, then stopped. It wasn't until his pants slid down over his hips then down his legs that Jazz knew what his lover was doing. "Just sex, for now. Okay?"

For a moment, it looked like Sam would bolt. He glanced from Doc to Jazz then back again, while still holding his penis. He finally took a deep, shuddering breath. "You're not pissed?"

Doc chuckled. "Does this look like I'm pissed?" He looked down and shook his hips.

"Or this?" Jazz slowly masturbated, encouraging his own flagging dick to resume some stiffness.

Sam's eyes went to Jazz's mid-section and a smile pulled at his mouth. He licked his lips and looked up. "I ain't getting between you two, right? No blaming me for fucking you guys up?"

"There's no way you can get between Doc and me." Jazz couldn't imagine anything or anyone with the power to do that. He adored his mate and would do anything for him. He knew Doc felt the same.

Doc jumped in and said, "Might be us fucking you up, but we'll talk about the ins and outs of who does what to who later." He chuckled and held out his free hand. "Come on, you know you want to."

That last comment seemed to be the icebreaker. Sam pulled his ragged pants up and clambered through the opening. He stopped a few paces back. "I'm not real experienced. Just know I like guys, too."

"That's enough for us," Jazz said, and stepped closer to Doc. *For now*, he finished silently. Side by side, he and Doc opened their arms to the slender man.

After a moment's hesitation, Sam took a few steps forward.

Feeling as if he was opening a gift, Jazz slid a hand over the man's rough clothing, tugging at the sleeve then searching for buttons or clasps to get inside. With Doc's assistance, they soon had enough skin showing to encourage Sam even further.

Doc moved to Sam's rear, his hands continuing their relentless exploration of all available flesh as he went, while Jazz leaned in for that first heart-stopping kiss. With his hands on Sam's newly revealed slim hips, Jazz pressed his lips to Sam's mouth. Soft, trembling lips touched his and opened. Their breath mingled as Jazz pushed his tongue deep into the warm depths. He slid his hands forward until the crinkled hair at Sam's groin tickled his palm. He didn't stop there. While inhaling the salty sweetness of the man's mouth, Jazz took hold of the freshly engorged shaft and slowly worked the tight skin up and down it.

Sam's lusty moans persuaded him to step it up a little, and it must have done the same to Doc. Suddenly, the clothing that had hampered his exploration fell away, and Doc's hands joined his on Sam's cock.

A sudden inhalation from their new lover sent a thrill of excitement straight to Jazz's cock. Over the young man's shoulder, Doc growled softly.

"Get some clothes off," Doc muttered and pulled his hands away.

Taking a couple of steps back, Jazz quickly shed the rest of his clothing, leaving only his boots on. When he stood up straight again, his cock rose, pointing its round head skyward. Doc grinned at him, then at Sam, who was soon as naked as they were. He wasn't quite as comfortable, though, and slid his hands over his crotch.

"None of that," Jazz whispered and pushed the man's hands aside. "You're too late to be bashful." He replaced the rough hands with his own and again began that gentle masturbation he'd seen earlier. Leaning down, Jazz blew a gust of warm air over the head and smiled when it leapt upward.

Sam shuddered, then sighed.

Jazz looked up just in time to see Doc standing close behind the young man and wrapping his strong arms around him, Doc's body pressed against him.

"Oh, fuck," Sam whispered as he slid his hands into Jazz's hair. He tightened his grip and pulled Jazz's mouth towards his body.

Jazz moaned and allowed Sam to guide him. The taste and smell of the man sent his thoughts racing. He knelt, taking the role Doc had several minutes ago and relishing every moment of it. A new lover always added an extra element of excitement, of pleasure for both of them, and Sam was somehow special. Jazz sensed it, but didn't understand it yet.

The soft cock head touched the back of his throat and he fought to keep from gagging. He swallowed, knowing full well the sensation it would give Sam. His grunt and the clench of his fingers in Jazz's hair indicated the desired reaction.

Jazz swallowed again and again, milking the upper shaft like Doc often did for him.

Doc's gruff voice came from far away, or so it seemed. "Sam, you ever had a cock inside your arse?"

"Yeah, once. It hurt."

The young man's body tensed beneath Jazz's hands.

"Well, we're not here to hurt anyone. Just askin'."

Doc must have shifted his approach because almost immediately Sam relaxed and began gently thrusting his cock in and out of Jazz's mouth. He sucked and tongued the underside, then carefully nipped at the head a few times. His own cock pulsed in its futile attempt to get attention.

"Oh my fuckin' lord!" Sam's words came out in a soft, husky whisper.

"That's it, just let it happen," Doc said in his lust-thick voice. "No pressure. No pain. Just pleasure and more pleasure."

Sam's body shifted, his legs spread, and he leant forward, moving his hand from Jazz's head to his shoulders. Jazz continued his oral assault on the stiff and throbbing shaft, enjoying every moment of his ministrations.

Above, he heard Doc's voice droning on, the gentling words blurring as Sam's thighs tensed and relaxed. Every time Doc added a different kind of stimulation, Jazz knew it. The subtle shifts and trembling, a whisper of sound or the sharp inhalations of excited breath, all made Jazz feel as if he was about to explode. His cock ached. His mouth filled with saliva, which soon enough dripped down Sam's cock into the sparse spattering of hair around its base.

"Yeah, that's it. You'll be begging for my cock in no time. Trust me, Sam, you're going to love it."

For an instant, Jazz felt a pang of jealousy. Doc's mouth and tongue always drove him insane with need. He wanted to feel them, knew how much pleasure his lover could deliver. But, the sweet taste of the cock quickly pushed that thought aside. Sharing this new lover was a treat they both craved.

He took the chance and pulled free of Sam's erection. Before he could protest, Jazz stood up straight and spun around. With his back to Sam, he ignored the sudden gasps and the fingers gripping his arms. He quickly positioned himself, leaning over the piece of wall Doc and he had spotted earlier but had never quite got to use. Only a couple of steps away, he wasn't surprised when he felt hands on his hips.

Warm, trembling hands whose fingers dug in with a desperation he hadn't felt in some time.

Looking back, Jazz smiled. "Easy, Sam. I'm not going anywhere."

Wide-eyed, Sam stared at him. With a nod, he loosened his hold, but not by much. Over Sam's shoulder, Doc's face appeared. He grinned and placed a hand on the young man's shoulder. "Spit—that works as well as any grease."

Spinning around, Jazz resumed his place, bent at the waist and waited. A cool dribble hit the top of his arse crack. His heart pounded in response. He knew he was about to get fucked and couldn't control a slight trembling in his limbs.

A finger probed along the cleft of his arse, forcing a deep shudder to shoot along his spine. He clenched his cheeks but quickly relaxed them in order to allow further exploration, insertion, mind-blowing pleasure. "Yes," he hissed when that finger found his opening.

He was ready—more than ready—and eager for the digit to press inward. He didn't have long to wait. The tip circled, then slowly wiggled its way past the outer ring of muscle. Clenching, he held Sam's finger captive for a second, then released it. The digit slid free, circled his anus again, then pushed back in, deeper, harder, until the flat of the man's palm lay against Jazz's buttock. With tiny sideways movements, Sam stretched Jazz's anus until a second finger slipped easily in alongside the first.

"More spit," Jazz whispered when a tiny stab of discomfort made him cringe.

"Sorry."

A guttural moan followed, as did another trickle of saliva down the crack of Jazz's arse.

"Stay bent over," Doc said in a gruff tone.

Again, Jazz looked back. He was just in time to see Doc, a tight grip on his erection, aim and slowly enter Sam's rear.

"Sweet Jeez..." Sam's voice gave out and his mouth sagged open.

"My turn," Jazz suggested, and squatted just enough to slip beneath Sam's bent-over figure. A soft jab of the man's cock against his leg urged him on. He reached back between his legs and took hold of the dangling shaft.

Sam shuffled his feet, but didn't pull away. He slipped his fingers from Jazz's well-stretched hole and held his cheeks spread wide.

"That's it," Jazz whispered, an unexpected gruffness in his voice. He'd already come, so he shouldn't have been so desperate to feel a cock inside him. Yet he was. And when Sam placed the tip against Jazz's hole he wasted no time in backing onto it.

In a matter of moments, Sam's cock filled him. His own cock pulsed, its head tapping the flesh of his stomach and leaving a sticky dab of pre-cum. Glancing down, he saw the glimmering thread joining his belly to the head of his cock.

"Fuck yeah," Sam groaned and thrust his hips.

Jazz gave his cock a few firm strokes then let it go. Shuffling his feet wider apart, he grabbed a knee in each hand and steadied himself. Behind him, Sam did much the same, or so it seemed.

When the men behind him moved, Jazz felt it. It didn't matter who shifted or pushed forward, he felt it intensely, intimately. When Doc began thrusting, a steady, slow motion, Sam wasn't the only one who groaned. Jazz's body gripped the younger man's erection. Wanting to add to his new lover's pleasure,

Jazz reached back and gently cupped the round, dangling sac.

"Oh my fuckin' God!" Sam's body went into a fit of trembling.

His shudders sent a ripple of pleasure straight into Jazz's rectum, and he, too, groaned. Carefully, Jazz caressed the man's balls, and grinned when he felt something warm and furry brush his knuckles. Doc's sac, he thought and pushed against it.

The three men worked at finding a rhythm. Jazz, being on the receiving end, had little control over it, but did his best to provide Sam with as much stimulation as he could. Doc seemed to be in control, although Jazz knew he was close to shooting from the grunts and shudders his man exhibited.

They finally found their pace and worked at it for several minutes, before Sam's body betrayed him. A long, shuddering cry was the only warning he gave. A strong thrust forward sent his cum deep into Jazz. Doc grunted and jammed his cock in deep, sending Sam more firmly against Jazz's arse. Another hard stab made Jazz lose control and his hand went to the shaft of his cock, giving it a few lusty tugs. A moment of blissful tension gripped him. His heart hammered in his chest. A hearty gasp and a rush of relief filled him as he shot his load all over the floor. He inhaled and dizziness struck as another gush of cum shot forth.

Long moments of urgent thrusting passed too quickly. Too soon, Jazz exhaled a huge lungful of air and realised he was cold. The body lying across his back held some warmth, but not enough. He eased out from under Sam and looked back. "Get dressed, you two—the weather's turning cold."

Doc wrapped his arms around Sam and gave him a final caress before he, too, eased back and out of the man. If Doc hadn't held him, Jazz was sure the younger man would have collapsed. He staggered, then grabbed for the tumbled wall.

"You all right?" Jazz took Sam's arm and held him while Doc moved away, gathering his clothing.

"Yeah, knees shakin', that's all." Sam took a deep breath and squared his shoulders. "Leg's still sore. But I'm good." He smiled at Jazz, then lowered his eyes. "Didn't think I'd be joining you two. Jeez, that was…"

Off to the side, Doc chuckled. Once he'd wiped himself down with a damp rag and was dressed again, he returned to stand with Jazz. "Yeah, we're amazing. Now, why don't you get dressed so we can get some shut-eye? Unless you're used to freezing your arse off." He held the cloth out to Sam.

"No, no. Thanks, Doc." Sam used the cloth to clean himself as best as he could before pulling his ragged clothing back over his thin frame.

Jazz smiled and took the rag from Sam, tucking it into one of the many crevices in the wall, then reached for his own garments. The chill had settled in by the time he was dressed and he flung his arms around himself to get warm.

Doc grabbed both Sam and Jazz by the arm and hauled them into a more sheltered area. "We'll share the blankets. Two will work well enough."

The men settled down for the night, Doc with his back to a partially erect wall, Sam in the middle and Jazz on the outer side. When Sam's breathing grew softer and slower, Jazz whispered, "Feel more like trusting him now, Doc?"

"Shut up," his lover growled softly.

Jazz snuggled down and pulled the rough blanket they shared more tightly around his shoulder. His nose was cold, but his body was warm. Sleep reached for him.

Just before his thoughts fled, he heard Doc say, "Yeah, I trust him. Not sure why though. Love you, Jazz."

"Love you, too, Doc." After he'd said that, the world seemed to fade. Just before his inner lights died completely, he thought of Zoe. Was she all right? He missed her dearly and hoped they'd re-join her soon. Very soon.

* * * *

"I realise we need to get into the city centre as soon as we can. My family's there, too, you know." It was Sam's voice and he sounded angry.

"So why are we sneaking around, ducking into every dark corner or alley when we think someone might be around?" Doc's tone was just as irate. "We should head in a straight line. We'd be there in hours, instead of the days it's taken us."

"Because there's three of us against hundreds skulking around the wreckage. Any one of them would attack if they thought they had a chance in hell of getting the food, weapons, meds…whatever else we've got." Sam's voice was more determined when he continued. "And if we march straight ahead we'd be dead in an hour. There are territories you know nothing about. Trust me — I'm alive because I've learnt to go around the worst of them."

Jazz rolled over and gazed at his two companions. A small cooking fire separated them. Each sat on a chunk of cement, elbows on knees, leaning towards the other. Both of them looked like they were ready to pounce.

"Ahem." Jazz sat cross-legged, and tucked the blankets around his waist. "Did I miss anything important?"

Doc turned and scowled for an instant before his face brightened into a sheepish grin. "No, we were just talking." He crawled towards Jazz and, when he got close enough, kissed him soundly on the lips. "Mornin', babe."

"Morning, sexy." Such a feeling of love gripped Jazz that, for a moment, all he wanted to do was sink into his lover's eyes. He caught movement to Doc's rear and smiled.

Sam had moved closer, but didn't join their morning greeting. That was until Jazz reached out and hooked his neck, drawing him forward. "Good morning, Sam." Jazz pressed his lips to Sam's mouth, his tongue quickly finding entrance. Doc shuffled back to the fire and was waiting when Jazz pried himself away from Sam's embrace.

"What've we got left to eat this morning?" Jazz asked Doc, and winked at Sam.

"Just heating up some water. We've got a little of that dried venison we brought with us."

While Jazz clambered out of the makeshift bed, Doc tossed the meat into the small pot of boiling water along with some herbs he always carried. "Won't be much, but it'll keep our bellies from making too close an acquaintance with our backbones."

Sam picked up the blankets and rolled them, handing them to Jazz and Doc. By the time they'd stowed them, the meal was ready. It wasn't much, and in no time the three of them were ready to move on.

Jazz kicked the last embers of the fire around to be sure they'd go out rather than spread.

"If we're careful, we should be able to reach the Warlord's camp by tonight. Maybe sooner." Sam tucked the last of his belongings into his pockets and patted the bulges.

"Let's work on sooner," Doc said in a calm voice. "We thought it'd only take a day to get there."

Jazz glanced at his lover, then at Sam. The younger man simply nodded and scrambled out of their temporary shelter.

Sunlight warmed his face as soon as Jazz made his way into the open. A slight breeze ruffled his hair. Ahead, Sam trudged towards the centre of the city, Doc on his heels.

It wasn't long before they caught the smell of decaying meat. Sam quickly turned away, detouring around whatever — or whoever — had made that smell. Doc grumbled, but not too loudly, and Jazz patted him on the shoulder. Jazz knew Doc's thoughts continually went to his sister and what might be happening to her. Each minute's delay could be her last.

Several hours later, the heat of the sun reminded him more of an oven than anything else. Ahead, Sam suddenly ducked into a deep cleft in the side of what had been a large building. The noise that had sent him into hiding reached Jazz and he, too, slipped into a narrow crevice. Doc chose a shadowy hole close to Sam's retreat.

The voices of men arguing came from ahead and to their right. Many men, or so it seemed to Jazz. Metal clashed and an angry retort blasted from someone. Jazz couldn't make out the words, just the tone and the stomping of feet marching away.

When the noise died down to a faint rumbling in the distance, Doc slid out of his hiding place, followed by both Jazz and Sam.

"We're close," Sam whispered, and shrugged. "Those might have been some of the Warlord's men. Guards, maybe, walking the perimeter of what he likes to call his kingdom."

"We'll have to be extra careful now." Doc peered around, then nodded at Sam. "Lead on. Let's get closer before it's too dark, if we can."

"I can get us closer. Just be quiet. These guards aren't dumbass yokels. They're good and fucking dangerous." Sam slunk ahead, his head swinging from side to side as if it was on a swivel.

For an instant, Doc looked like he was going to say something. He must have thought better of it, because instead he nodded for Jazz to move on.

Jazz followed their young companion, taking great care not to stumble or scuff his feet. A couple of times, he heard voices close by. Sam must have heard them, too, as he slowed his pace to a crawl but kept them going in the same direction.

The buildings took on a newer, less run-down appearance. Some structures stood nearly intact, only the windows gaping like empty squares of blackness. When Jazz peeked inside one such opening, he was surprised to see walls and a proper floor. A broken chair sat in one corner and another lay on its side across the room.

A daydream struck—Doc, naked and bent over that chair, his arse presented for Jazz's pleasure. His lover peered over his shoulder, that come-fuck-me look he'd snagged Jazz with countless times. His heart raced.

Doc's whispered voice brought him back to the present. "Hey, move your butt before I swat it."

Jazz cursed under his breath and hurried after Sam's retreating figure as he slipped around the corner ahead. Silently, they raced from one shadowy hiding place to the next. Figures of armed men appeared more frequently and the danger of discovery rose.

Heart pounding, Jazz rested his head against the brick wall of the building they'd just come to. Sweat trickled down his face and back. He fought to keep his breathing from getting too loud. That was all they needed, for him to attract unwanted attention by gasping for breath.

Beside him, Sam looked up nervously. Eyes wide, mouth agape, his face shone with sweat as he blinked up at Jazz.

"We're losing light," Doc whispered from Jazz's other side.

Jazz looked into the sky and saw how close to sunset it was. "Yeah, we need to find somewhere to hole up for a while." He looked back at Sam and shrugged. "Any ideas?"

"Follow me." Sam headed down the next alley.

On his heels, Jazz had to slow his pace to keep from making too much noise. Litter and rubble lay strewn from one side to the other and as far ahead as he could see. A great deal of noise came from the far end of the passage.

Sam sank to his belly, crawling the last few paces. He stopped when he got to the opening and waited for Doc and Jazz to join him.

Jazz fought down the desire to flee when he saw what lay ahead. The alley opened onto a large circle of empty space. Three, perhaps four dozen men, armed with everything from rifles to crossbows, marched in unison down one street and came back on the next.

Others, singly or in pairs, walked or sat around talking.

He also saw captives—men and women in chains, toiling over cooking pots, washing clothing or doing other menial tasks.

"Let's back out of here, for now." Doc tapped Jazz's arm and nodded towards a building in the previous block.

Nodding, Jazz tapped Sam and indicated the building. Without waiting for him to reply, Jazz turned and crawled back down the alley. The scrape of booted toes and soft grunts followed him. The trio had almost made it to the end of the alley when a small group of men marched by.

Jazz lowered his head and froze. He recognised Doc's soft grunt as he did the same. Sam wasn't so quiet. His curse seemed loud enough to wake the dead, let alone attract the soldiers.

Taking a chance, Jazz lifted his eyes just enough to peer ahead. He was just in time to see two men dragging a flat-bed, wooden cart across the mouth of the lane. On it and aiming skyward was some kind of rocket launcher. His blood ran cold. If they had shells to fit that thing, there'd be no stopping them. He saw no artillery, but for all he knew they could have that stored somewhere else.

He lowered his head and waited until the noise of the cart's wheels faded to silence. He could still make out men yelling in the distance, but for the moment they'd lucked out and could carry on.

From behind him, Doc hissed urgently, "Let's move, before more of those guys show up."

Jazz got to his feet and raced ahead, crouched as low as he could and still move quickly. Doc came behind him, and he assumed Sam brought up the rear. At the end of the alley, he stopped, back pressed against the rough wall, Doc beside him, and finally Sam.

Peering out, Jazz saw nothing and no one moving. After taking a deep breath, he darted across the wide road and into the dark opening he'd targeted. His foot skidded and he nearly went down. Doc, who'd come right behind him, grabbed his arm and kept him upright. Sam skittered in and bumped into both Doc and Jazz.

"Made it," Doc whispered, and looked around the empty room. "Check the windows. I want to see if there's one that'll show us what's going on in that yard." He moved stealthily across the rubbish-strewn floor and through a doorway. "Keep it quiet."

Jazz nodded and looked at Sam, who simply shrugged his shoulders. Jazz headed for another room. There, he found a large opening facing away from the spot they wanted to spy on. He turned and made his way down a long hallway. A staircase led up and he climbed it carefully. Surprisingly, the floors seemed solid, and he crossed into a room he thought might give him the view they wanted. He spotted pairs of guards at the corners of most blocks around the central plaza and was shocked at how close they'd come to being seen — or worse, captured. All of them were armed, and from the way they stood at attention these weren't anything like the lazy scruffs who'd made off with many of the villagers. These were more like a proper, well-disciplined army.

He also saw enclosed areas that held chickens and pigs. He was sure that in the distance he could see either cows or horses — it was difficult to say for sure. He noticed fields outside the city proper, some closer, some in the distance, where corn and other crops grew and people worked. Men on horseback dotted the fields.

He returned to the main floor and found Doc peering through a window but obviously having little success at spotting anything. He scowled at Jazz, then at Sam, who'd followed Jazz into the room.

"Upstairs there's a window that shows the square and some of the guards in the area. We're in for one hell of a time getting Robin out. We'll be lucky if we can find her. This place is huge."

Doc's scowl deepened. "Show me." He pushed past Sam, heading for the front of the building.

"This way," Jazz said, just loud enough for both men to hear. He turned and walked towards the stairs.

He never made it.

A cry of rage came from the doorway, several more from the windows they'd only moments ago peered through. Men—too many scrawny, ugly, and in some cases deformed men—raced into the building, swinging clubs or firearms carelessly around.

"Grab 'em. Hold 'em for the Warlord," yelled one enormous fellow wearing an outfit of tight, black leather. His bald head and bushy, black moustache on a lumpy, malformed face gave him a sinister appearance.

Jazz turned to flee, but something hard slammed into the back of his head. The world turned dark, and he sank into oblivion.

Chapter Four

Jazz came to with a gasp and a sputter as cold water rained down on him. He twisted and a sharp pain in the back of his head tore a grunt from him. Ignoring the sharp agony nearly blinding him, he struggled, trying to escape, but something or someone held him.

Fingers dug into the muscles in his shoulders; more gripped his wrists and forearms, pulling him to his knees. Waves of nausea hit and he clenched his jaw to keep from vomiting. His knees burnt; his ribs felt as if someone had danced on them.

"Get his face up," a deep, booming voice growled.

Fingers slid across his skull and clenched in the long hair just above his forehead. An instant later, he found himself looking up at a raised platform where the most repulsive man Jazz had ever seen lounged on an enormous, ornate chair—or throne. He looked like he'd once been firm and muscular—neither heritage nor time had been kind. Or perhaps it was simply his debaucheries catching up with him. The ringletted hair looked greasy against the too-pale flesh of his cheeks and forehead. One eye appeared higher than the other on a skull too small for the man's bulk. Black silken robes clung to his bulging stomach and thighs, leaving his plump arms bare from just above the elbow down. Strapped to his naked feet were sandals that looked too small. This guy was obviously someone important, Jazz realised when he saw how everyone kept their distance and bowed to the man's every move.

He caught sight of a lot more than just the chair and its occupant. The room was breath-taking, overwhelming in its grandeur. Plush carpets and overstuffed couches formed small, intimate areas where people could chat, if the lord of the manor permitted. The walls were plastered with paintings and artwork, haphazardly, as if merely having them was enough to raise the owner's status to the next level. Bowls and basins of bright coloured jewels lay scattered on tables bowed with their burdens.

"Bring 'em here. I want to see the face of this useless waste of flesh," the fat man snarled.

Jazz hung limp between his captors. Two bore his weight forward, while a third held his head up, as he'd been ordered. Dragging his toes across the floor, the two men quickly brought Jazz to the foot of the two steps leading up to the platform. They didn't release him, but the strain in his shoulders lessened when they sat him back on his heels.

Jazz's thoughts reeled.

What the fuck happened and where am I? Where's Doc?

He twisted his head around, trying to find his lover and Sam. He saw men and women all around him, some clothed, some not, most of them deformed in one way or another. All cowered before the seated man. The dark wooden walls and tall windows with their rich coverings of amber and gold made his head spin. But he couldn't find Doc or Sam.

"Listen, dumbass, Warlord Black wants to see you," the man behind him growled into Jazz's ear, then pulled on his hair, forcing Jazz's head upright and still. "So quit your fuckin' around and do what he says."

Jazz felt like his hair was being torn from his scalp, but he refused to let the bastard get another groan from him. He struggled, trying to get free, then stopped dead.

Robin, naked and in chains, knelt beside the robed man's throne. Her dark hair hung in a tangle of knots and what looked like dried blood, along with other assorted bruises, cuts and scrapes covering her body. He couldn't see her face clearly, but it was her. He'd seen her often enough with Doc and their mother to know every curve of her body, every curl in her long, dark hair.

"Bastard," Jazz roared and lunged forward, nearly tearing his arms from their sockets in his attempt to free himself.

A hand appeared to his left, upraised into a fist. The hand in his hair held him for the blow. His cheek exploded with pain. His vision blurred, but he remained conscious.

"Silence, or you'll be gagged, scum," the fat man yelled and shifted forward in the oversized throne. He glared down at Jazz, obviously unaware of why he was outraged.

Clenching his jaw, Jazz looked up at where Robin knelt. He focused on her, willing the young beauty to lift her chin and look his way. It took forever, but finally she raised her face. He knew the instant she recognised him. Her eyes got big and her mouth opened, as if she was about to speak.

She cringed and closed her mouth. Jazz was sure she'd learnt silence the hard way. He'd bet some of her bruises were from teaching her that lesson. Like her brother, she was stubborn. Unfortunately, she didn't have the strength Doc had, but her stubbornness might have stood in its stead.

Robin nodded towards him, then quickly glanced around. No one was paying attention to her.

"A bit thin for the fields," the fat man said in a nasal voice.

"My lord, we've got plenty of field hands. He might be of better use in the stable, or swilling the pigs." A grey-haired man with eyes that bugged out so much they threatened to pop out of his head stepped forwards, his hands clasped in front of the multi-coloured jacket he wore. A long, snug-fitting skirt covered the man's lower body but left the bottom half of his skeletally thin calves bare and showed off large, new-looking boots.

"He'll pleasure a few people when he's been softened up. A few weeks of working in the fields should do the trick," huffed the rotund lord. "He's thin, but he's pretty."

Jazz snarled and fought the men holding him. "Come here, you fat bastard and I'll show you pleasure!"

"Hold him! Don't let the animal go, for God's sake," the rotund man snarled, and scooted back onto his throne. He held out a long, slender silver rod, pointing it at Jazz. "Guards, teach him who's boss. I will not have a slave of mine show such animosity towards me. After all, I am the Warlord, and he is…nothing. A vagabond who has nothing and knows nothing."

Anything else the so-called *Warlord* said was lost to Jazz. The guards holding him lifted him to his feet and several others came forward. Each had their fists raised, until they began his beating.

The last thing he saw was the chunky, robed Warlord rising to his feet. His face was a mask of demented lust. Even as the world faded, Jazz watched the man reach down and wind his fingers into Robin's long, dark hair.

* * * *

"Argh!" Jazz rolled onto his back and groaned. Every muscle in his body protested. Even his hair hurt. The coppery taste of blood filled his mouth and he moved his tongue around, exploring for missing or loose teeth. All were present and firmly implanted, but he noted a new gash along the inside of his cheek and the taste lingered.

He opened his eyes, to darkness.

"Jeez, not again," he muttered, and turned on his side. Waking up a prisoner wasn't a great habit to get into, he thought. Surprisingly, his arms were free and he pushed himself up until he could sit. He swung his arms wide, trying to find a wall. When his hand touched something solid, he scooted that way. He ran his fingers over his head, but couldn't detect any blood. "Guess being hard-headed isn't always a bad thing," he mumbled.

Jazz stretched out his legs and laid his head back against the wall, carefully. He squared his shoulders and revised that last thought — the *rough, cold* wall. When he closed his eyes again, he realised the wall wasn't the only discomfort in the cell. The smell was horrendous. Mix the stench of an outhouse with several weeks' worth of human sweat, and that would be close to what assailed his nostrils. His stomach churned.

He shuddered, but forced himself to take stock instead of puke. He ached from head to toe, but nothing seemed broken, just bruised. Everything moved as it should, even if a bit stiffly. He touched his nose and grunted. That might be the exception, he mused, as he carefully ran a finger from its tip to the swollen bump in the middle. He inhaled and thanked his lucky stars there weren't any issues with taking a deep breath. A few bumps on his head sent warning signals when he ran his fingers over them, but all in all he couldn't complain.

"Wouldn't do much good if I did," he muttered softly.

"What 'er you bitchin' 'bout?" a hoarse, male voice rumbled from some distance to his right.

Jazz jumped, then turned that way, shocked there'd been no sounds from the man. Listening more carefully, he became aware of other noises he'd obviously missed — the scraping of movement, the soft, repetitive hum of people breathing.

He peered into the darkness but was unable to see anything but the utter blackness of the chamber he'd been left in.

"Who's there?" He shot the question towards the voice.

"Name's Zeb. Been here some time."

A scuffling sound came from where the man named Zeb was, and Jazz realised he was moving closer.

"You'll get used to the dark, if you're here long enough," came Zeb's voice, only this time much closer. "Who're you?"

"I'm Jazz. And I'm hoping not to be here that long, friend." Jazz pushed himself to the side, trying to keep a little distance between himself and anyone else trapped in the cell. He bumped into something soft and pulled back when that something grunted.

"We all said that when we was put here." Zeb's voice had stopped moving and seemed to be about a dozen paces away. "Most of us are still here, or been carted off to work the fields. That's where us slaves is needed most."

Jazz didn't like the sounds of what his future might hold, and hoped Doc was close and working on getting him out.

"How many are in here?" Even trying to judge the size of the place was difficult, with just the echoing of their voices as a guide. It wasn't very big, that he was sure of.

"'Bout a dozen, give or take," Zeb replied. "There's usually 'bout that many. There's more cells, though, so who knows."

"Shut the fuck up, you two," grumbled a fellow captive from farther away.

Zeb whispered, "We don't get enough rest, so we best shut up or talk quiet."

Jazz wasn't willing to have the man too close, so whispered back, "We'll talk later, when it's safer."

Zeb chuckled and said, "Ain't never safe, but you got it." He shuffled away, leaving only a wall of silence behind.

Jazz let his head fall back against the wall again and tried not to breathe too deeply. The smell was something he was sure he'd never get used to. He prayed he wouldn't be there long enough to test that theory. He wasn't sleepy, but he knew he'd better rest.

Eyes open, he listened to the breathing of his fellow cellmates.

Light—not a lot of it—coming from the floor across the room got his attention when he turned his head. It came from under a door—the cell door. Then he saw bars in the small window opening at the top.

From the other side of the door he heard gruff cursing followed by the shuffling of feet coming towards him. "Come on, bitch, quit dragging your fuckin' feet or you'll pay dearly." The harsh voice of a guard filtered in. Muffled groans and sobbing intermingled with the shuffling of feet accompanied his demands. "I ain't had me a bit of pretty slut for way too long." The commotion got closer.

Jazz scrambled to his feet and glanced around. His eyes had grown more accustomed to the dark by then. Bodies shifted, crawled towards the door and clambered upright all around the room—men and women, all in decent shape from what he could see. One shape near him caught Jazz's attention. "Zeb," he whispered.

A slender man with long, scraggly, dark hair and beard nodded, then moved closer to the doorway.

The lock rattled. The door opened, letting in more light, blinding Jazz before he could make out who'd entered.

"Stupid cow, hold up."

More whimpering followed. Those already in the cell grumbled, adding to the noise level. A man snarled, "Get up, you fuckin' moron. Shift yerself before I whack ya."

Jazz blinked against the light and, when he could see, he focused on who the guard was holding. His temper soared. Robin, gagged and with her hands bound, was held by the hair and bent double beside the large figure of a guard. Luckily she had been given a smock to wear, so her generous curves were hidden.

"Lookit what the Warlord sent us, mates," one of the prisoners cried gleefully. "She be normal. No messed-up bits or scabs."

Jazz strode forward, stopping only when his body blocked that of the eager captive. "Not going to happen. She's mine." Two others wound up in front of him, between Robin and himself.

The guard laughed uproariously but released his hold of Robin's hair, letting her fall to the floor. She grunted upon landing and rolled to her side.

Jazz pushed past the two men who'd zeroed in on her. Holding his arms out from his sides, he barred them from getting any closer.

The guard chuckled, thrust his toe under Robin's body and pushed. "The Warlord said she needs some tenderising. Too spunky for his taste. He likes 'em obedient. And this one don't want to learn."

Robin rolled over, coming to a stop only when her body touched Jazz's feet. Her whimper angered him, but he held his tongue. The burly guard turned and walked out, taking the light with him.

One of the men who'd tried to get past Jazz said, "She's clean. No deformed parts."

"Yeah, I know, and she's mine, so let her be." Jazz wasn't sure what the fellow meant, but he was determined to keep Robin away from any further harm.

"No harm, mate," the man replied, and moved away. "Can't blame us for wanting her. She's a beauty. She'd breed true."

Jazz shuddered, suddenly understanding the city peeps' need for good breeders. He pushed that thought aside and bent down, reaching for Robin.

When he found her with his fingertips, she scrambled back, escaping his grasp.

"Robin, it's me. It's Jazz." He swung his hand from side to side, trying to find her again before someone dragged her away.

A muffled cry came from ahead and he reached that way. His fingers connected with warm flesh and he took hold. Pulling her close, he stood up and took her with him. With her in his arms, he shuffled them both back to where he'd been sitting against the wall. Once he got her there, he held her close while untying the gag from behind her head.

"Come here, luv," a woman's voice said softly. "I'm not pretty like her, but you and me always get along."

"Aw, Red, you know how to treat a man."

The sound of soft shuffling soon faded to that of heavy breathing and groaning. Jazz tuned it out, but smiled. Even in the worst conditions possible, couples found pleasure.

The mutterings of the others grew in volume for a few minutes, then died to a general rumble of people trying to get some more rest. No one came near them again, and that was all Jazz cared about.

"Jazz, I'm... They..." she stammered a few words, but nothing more intelligible.

He slipped his hand behind Robin's back and searched out the rope around her wrists. While she pressed her face against his chest, he fought the tight knots until he freed her. As soon as the rope fell away, she wrapped her arms around his neck.

Jazz held her until her sobbing turned to soft shudders and finally her breathing deepened. He stroked her hair, feeling the knots and dried *something* against his palm. Her breast pressed against his ribs and he marvelled at the softness. How had she survived the horrors of the last few months?

"I'm here now," he whispered, and kissed her hair. "You're going to be all right." His stomach lurched.

Can I get her out of here? Where the fuck is Doc? He slid down the wall, taking her with him, until they both sat on the rough stone floor.

"Where's Doc?" Robin whispered, barely loud enough for Jazz to hear.

He debated whether to tell her he was close, or pretend he hadn't heard. She took the choice from him when she pushed herself out of his arms enough to look up into his eyes.

"Is he all right?"

"Yes, he's all right," he said, reassuring her even though he knew it wasn't entirely true. He'd *been* fine—but. It was that 'but' that worried Jazz. When he'd been knocked out, he hadn't seen what happened to Doc or Sam. Ignoring his deception, he ruffled Robin's hair gently and pulled it back to his chest. "Let's see if we can get some rest now. We'll need it for the long trek home."

He wasn't sure if she'd let it go. When her body moulded to his again, he breathed a sigh of relief. Her breathing deepened and her body relaxed against him as sleep overcame her. The soft snores around him urged him to do the same. Sliding down the wall, he crossed his legs at the ankle, hoping to get a little more comfortable. His head still ached and he knew he must look horrible, but he smiled anyway. They'd come to rescue Robin, and he had her in his arms. Hopefully, the rest of it wouldn't be so painful.

* * * *

The next thing Jazz knew, he opened his eyes after an unsatisfying amount of sleep. He sat quietly, listening and not moving. His arms still held Robin, and the memory of the other prisoners wanting her flooded back. The old war still held the city in its grip. Deformities were the norm, clean women – men, too, for that matter – were rare. The breed was dying here, and they couldn't leave. For some reason, they didn't have the courage to break away and find new homes.

He lay there thinking. The woman named Red had shown how humanity still cared for its own. He hoped she'd find a way out of the city, but didn't hold out too much hope. Life was hard here, but it was a life they all knew. That ancient saying, 'Better the demon you know than the one you don't', held a tragic meaning here.

When he was sure no one else had roused, he eased away from Robin and climbed to his feet. He oriented himself and realised he could see light coming from where he was sure the doorway lay. The barred window at the top was much brighter than the cell he was in.

Being careful not to step on or kick anyone, he shuffled that way. The short walk reminded him of how many sore spots he had. Every movement stretched an abused muscle or bit of flesh. His head didn't pound too hard, so all in all he wasn't too upset.

Stopping in front of the wooden door, Jazz leant forward and peered into the uncommonly wide hallway. It wasn't well lit by any stretch of the imagination, but he could make out the stone walls and the floor. Across from him, he spotted a set of leather handcuffs and, above them, a rough torch thrust into a holder. It looked like someone had wrapped burlap around the end of a heavy stick.

Scuffling noises came from the left and Jazz pulled back from the opening. He could still see, but hoped whoever was approaching couldn't see him. Voices, one deep and booming, the other higher pitched and soft, reached him.

He waited, straining to hear the words, his fingers curled into fists.

"Jazz!"

The soft, feminine voice caught him by surprise. It was Robin, of course, and he looked towards where he'd left her. He fought the need to return to her right away. He wanted to see who was in the passageway. The noise from the hall won and he turned back to the opening, peering through the bars.

Sam, walking beside one of the guards, approached. There weren't any restraints, the young man wasn't struggling or angry; they simply walked side by side.

Jazz stumbled back a step and tried to put it together. The young man and the burly guard marched on, oblivious to his confusion. As the pair passed the window, Jazz noticed the guard's hand on Sam's arm, and for a split second wondered if he was guiding him or 'taking' him.

"Jazz, are you there?" Robin's tone was fearful and held the promise of panic.

He hurried back to her, again careful not to kick anyone on the way. "Yes, I'm here. Sorry. I heard something and wanted to see what was going on." He stopped there, unwilling to worry her any more than he already had.

Where is Doc?

The thought raced through his mind and he pushed down the fear threatening to overwhelm him.

Sam, caught?

He'd been talking pretty amicably with the guard, or so it had seemed.

What the fuck is going on?

Settling down beside Robin, he asked, "How are you?"

The light filtering in through the small opening in the door allowed him to see her face, although not easily. The bruise he'd seen on her cheek earlier wasn't the only one. He thought he saw another on her neck. One arm had a large, discoloured patch from just above the wrist up to her elbow—another bruise—but the lighting made it impossible to see more.

"I'm better now that you're here." She scooted as close to him as she could. "I thought you'd been dragged out while I slept." Peering around, she added, "I don't usually sleep so soundly."

"It's all right, hun," Jazz reassured her, and hugged her close. "I'm here. We'll get out of this, somehow."

"Dream on," one of the nearby prisoners mumbled.

Glowering, Jazz growled, "Shut the fuck up. We'll get out. Trust me on that."

A rumbling of sleepy, disgruntled voices swept across the cell, and Jazz took note of them but tried to ignore the possible threat. He knew people who'd reached their limit could turn on their cell mates if they thought it would make their own lives better or more secure.

From his right side, Zeb's familiar voice snarled, "Don't be a bunch o' jackasses. Ya'll would jump at the chance to get outta here."

The door to their cell rattled. The bar holding it closed scraped as someone lifted it.

Beside him, Robin gasped and tucked herself in close behind him. Her shivers only intensified Jazz's determination to protect her.

A guard shambled in. When the fat brute had completely entered the cell, Jazz peered past him. His heart lurched.

Doc, naked from the waist up and held between two very large, burly guards, knelt on the other side of the entrance. Head down, it looked like his lover had given up—or had been beaten into semi-consciousness.

Jazz couldn't see much more than that. The light, although better, still wasn't good enough to make out details at a distance. But he was sure it was Doc. There could be no mistaking that mop of shaggy, dark hair or the cut of his leather pants.

From behind him, Robin cried out and thrust herself forward. "Doc," she screamed, and struggled to get to her feet.

Jazz grabbed her and held her back. She fought him, but he refused to let go.

"Ah, I see our young recruiter has brought us more than a simple traveller." The fat man seemed very pleased about something. "So, the man's name is Doc. Sam said as much, but one never knows what to believe." He strode forward, stopping only when he'd reached Jazz. "You know this man?" He scowled down at Jazz.

Jazz was silent, refusing to give any information and hoping Sam hadn't completely destroyed their hopes of freeing Robin, and now themselves.

The fat guard reached down and ran a hand over Robin's hair. With a malicious snarl, he thrust his fingers into the mass and grabbed a handful. He dragged her forward, right out of Jazz's arms. He hauled Robin to her feet and deftly bent her backwards, forcing her to stand on her toes while arching her body painfully.

Her yelp of pain brought Jazz to a half crouch. He would have gone further, but a hand gripping his arm tightly stopped him. Looking back, he scowled at Zeb, but knew the man was right.

"Who is he, bitch?" The ponderous, malformed guard growled, holding Robin's face inches from his own.

"Fuck you, moron," Robin snarled, pulling futilely at the man's hands in her hair. She kicked at his legs, but with bare feet the damage she did was minimal at best.

The guard bent her back even further, and snarled into her face, "Might try a good fucking later, bitch." With his free hand, he leisurely explored Robin's curves, paying special attention to her up-thrust tits. "Now, before I get pissed, who the fuck is this guy to you?"

Yelping in misery, Robin wriggled and fought, but was no match for the brute. After several minutes of stubborn silence, she cried out and snarled, "He's my brother."

The brutal guard laughed and tossed her back onto the straw near Jazz. "Yeah, that's what the young guy said."

"Bastard," Jazz hissed under his breath, and gathered Robin into his arms.

She came willingly. When she looked up at Jazz, he saw tears glistening in her eyes.

In the hallway, pandemonium broke out. Jazz looked up in time to see Doc explode into action. The two guards holding him seemed to suddenly fly into each other. A blood-chilling crunch reached Jazz's ears, followed instantly by a loud shriek of pain. One of the men grabbed his arm and howled. He rolled across the floor and stopped only when he hit the far wall.

Jazz lunged forward, but the fat guard in front of him raised his fist. An instant later, it felt like the left side of Jazz's head had slammed into a stone wall. The wall won and Jazz sagged to the floor.

"Jazz!"

Robin's cry of anguish shocked him and he fought back the threatening unconsciousness. She bent over him, her newly shed tears dripping onto his face.

"Best save this fer when it might do some good." Zeb's deep, masculine voice held a tone of reason, whereas Jazz wanted nothing more than to release his rage. "Come on, friend." Large hands grabbed Jazz's arm, and he allowed Zeb to draw him away from the action, towards the wall. Other hands joined his. The prisoners, who a while ago had been only too eager to take Robin for their own use, now seemed keen to help them.

"Ain't no use getting yer head bashed in for nothing, mate."

Softer hands stroked his cheek. A woman's voice whispered, "Hold on."

Jazz's senses returned quickly and he realised the ruckus had died down. The malformed guard who'd struck him was again at the entrance, but now he peered into the hallway. With his wide back towards Jazz, for a moment Jazz thought about jumping him. The opportunity passed when the big man turned and smiled into the room.

"So, big brother comes to rescue his little sister. How touching." He frowned, but the tender-hearted expression didn't reach his eyes. The cruelty fairly leapt from them and Jazz promised he'd make an extra effort to find this man, later, to teach him a much needed lesson.

The malicious guard turned his attention to Jazz and the frown deepened, yet the eyes remained like burning embers of hatred beneath the thick, dark brows. "And you — another brother, perhaps." He cocked his head and looked thoughtful. A vicious smile appeared as he snarled, "No, you're not a sib. More than that. You're fucking lovers. Fucking pervs." He took a step back, as if being in close proximity might, in some way, contaminate him.

Jazz took note of the man's reaction and stored it away for possible future reference. The prejudice wasn't new to him, but it wasn't a common concern. There were too many other things to worry about. Who a person loved or had sex with wasn't all that important when you were worried about starving or trying to find shelter.

"You dickhead," Zeb said with a note of derision in his voice. "You'll fuck anything that's warm. I've seen you." The slave retreated into the nearest dark corner before the guard turned his attention away from Jazz.

Jazz, unwilling to let the man suffer for aiding him, said, "I do the fucking, dumbass."

The guard growled and took a step into the cell. Behind him, another of the guards snarled, "Scar, you fat slob, quit messin' with the slaves and give us a hand. Dirk is one-armed now, thanks to this one."

It wasn't until then that Jazz noticed a long scar running all the way from the man's left eye to below his jawline. When Scar turned back to the doorway, Jazz sighed with relief.

"Let's get this new one softened up — he's way too snarky to just release," Scar said and nodded to the leather cuffs hanging from the wall. He looked back at Jazz and Robin. "Maybe you two wanna watch?"

Before Jazz could get to his feet, Scar stepped out and slammed the door closed. The resounding thump of a bar across the front told Jazz they were again confined.

Jazz raced for the door, unwilling to believe Doc was still captive. His lover had been fighting. He'd injured one.

Glaring through the small window in the door, Jazz grabbed the bars and pulled. It was locked, as he knew it was, but he had to try. Again, he hauled on the door, but it held.

He spotted Doc, barely able to stand, held by Scar and the unwounded guard. The wounded man was gone.

Together, the guards manhandled Doc to stand beneath the torch. The unnamed guard lifted one of Doc's arms and held it while Scar buckled the leather cuff around his wrist. A moment later, the men had Doc's other wrist cuffed over his head.

Scar backed away and stood with his arms crossed over his chest, looking at Doc. His fellow guard sauntered over to the opposite wall where Jazz couldn't see him. While he was out of sight, Jazz heard the unmistakable sound of metal on metal, and something else. When the guard returned to Scar, he held a long bar that had leather straps on either end, plus a short whip.

Before Doc resumed full consciousness, the two guards buckled his feet to the ends of that bar, holding him spread-eagled. His feet touched the floor, just.

"Hey, you two dimshits. Cowards! Can't even take on one man when there's two of you," Jazz raged, knowing what was about to happen. Perhaps Doc hadn't been so easily captured and they wanted to make a point. Perhaps the Warlord had simply chosen him for the guards to practice on. It didn't matter.

Scar snarled and stomped over to the window in the cell door. "Might drag your arse out here and do some damage to your hide, too, if you don't shut your fucking yap." He raised the whip and brought it down across the bars. A good forearm's length of the slender leather reached through the bars, forcing Jazz back a step.

The scarred man laughed but didn't repeat the act. Instead, he returned to Doc's side. "Wake the bastard up," he said to his fellow guard, who stood leaning against the wall.

The man grinned at Scar and stepped in front of Doc. While Jazz and Robin watched, he grabbed a handful of the front of Doc's hair and lifted his head. With the back of his free hand, he slapped Doc across the face.

Doc finally responded, jerking his body erect and his head back. He howled.

The guard dropped Doc's face and stepped to the side, obviously awaiting Scar's instruction. It seemed Scar had some small authority and loved to use it.

"Step aside. Give me a little room." Scar repositioned himself and raised the whip. It came down hard and a line of red appeared across Doc's chest. Scar raised the slender whip again and the beating proceeded.

Jazz heard movement from several places behind him, but couldn't take his eyes off the brutal spectacle in the hall. He held Robin against his chest, determined to keep her from witnessing the worst of the ruthless cruelty, but the sounds were something else. Something he couldn't shield her from. Doc didn't cry out for the longest time. A grunt or curse reached them, but not until Jazz saw Scar send his knee into his lover's groin did a cry of anguish erupt.

Jazz groaned, anger and frustration tearing at him. He pushed Robin behind him and grabbed the bars again, tearing at them.

"Jazz, stop." Robin pulled at his arm and shoulder. "It's no use. The bastards do that with most of the new prisoners."

"Fucking, motherless, useless, fucking perverts," Jazz snarled, rattling the bars savagely, then releasing them. He turned and strode across the cell, careless of whom he stepped on or where he was going. Nothing mattered but getting Scar to stop. But how?

Red came up beside Jazz and he saw her clearly for the first time. The red hair gave her away, but the colour of her skin would have done the same. She looked like she'd been burnt. Her flesh looked like it was pulled tight over her skull. Holding up a hand, she stroked his face and said, "Your Doc will survive. They can't use a corpse."

Robin stood beside Red. "She's right, Jazz. They'll put him in here, or one of the other cells, when they're done with him. But we'll be able to talk to him soon." She went on trying to reason with him, in a completely unreasonable situation.

He knew they were right. They'd been here longer and knew the ropes. Even Robin knew what went on a lot better than he possibly could.

His thoughts raced. Sam! What was his role in all this? He was obviously involved. He stomped to the back of the cell, not as careful as he might have been to avoid tromping on a fellow prisoner. When he turned, Zeb was there, standing in front of him.

"Better stop kicking your cellies or you're liable to wake up with a few extra bruises."

The man's warning caught Jazz by surprise. He'd been completely unaware of the people he'd walked over. He glanced around and cringed. They were prisoners, just as he was. None of this was their doing. Even Red stood looking at him, a frown on her face.

"Zeb, you're right. I'm sorry." Jazz walked over to the nearest wall and stood with his back to it. He curled his fingers into fists and simply stood listening to the whip hitting flesh. Doc's flesh. Robin came and pressed her cheek to his chest. Tears wetted his skin, trickled down his chest. He wrapped his arm around her and bent to kiss her head.

Zeb came and stood beside him. "Not long now. He'll be in rough shape for a day or so, but they don't kill the new slaves."

Over Zeb's shoulder, Red shuffled her way back to the corner she shared with her man. Jazz watched her until the darkness became too great. He looked away and waited.

The beating went on for a few more minutes, then stopped as quickly as it had begun. Jazz hurried back to the cell door and peered into the hallway. Robin joined him and gasped.

Doc hung from the cuffs, his upper body criss-crossed with crimson. Even his arms bore the evidence of Scar's brutal beating.

As Jazz watched, his anger held in check only because he had no choice, Doc got to his feet and raised his head. He didn't say a word. He just stood there and waited for whatever came next.

"Get him into the cell," Scar snarled and threw the whip to the floor. "We'll see just how perky he is in the morning." Without another word, or even a glance towards where Jazz and Robin peered through the cell door, the man marched down the hallway.

The remaining guard picked up the discarded whip and returned it to its place. Then he removed the leg spreader from Doc and leaned it against the wall before releasing the man's hands.

Doc staggered but didn't fall.

"Come on, you heard what Scar said," the man grumbled, and gave Doc a push towards the cell Jazz was in. "Time to join your sib and your pervy boyfriend."

Jazz pulled Robin away from the door. He wasn't sure what the guard would do if either of them got too close. He didn't want to take any chances of Doc being forced into another cell.

The bar scraped along the wooden door, and a moment later, Doc entered. He took two steps, just enough time for the guard to slam the door, then fell into Jazz's arms.

"I've got you, babe," Jazz whispered, grateful for the weight. For an instant, he thought of Zoe, and was glad she'd decided to stay in the village. He didn't think he could take having her in the kind of danger they found themselves in.

Chapter Five

Jazz groaned and opened his eyes. The dull, grey ceiling and the stink of people were a quick reminder of where he was. He tried to turn over and groaned again when he realised someone was on his arm. He looked down and spotted a head full of shaggy, brown hair.

Doc!

His heart raced. He forced himself to remain still but looked around, trying to find Robin among the other captives. He spotted her almost immediately, a dozen paces away, sitting with Zeb and quietly talking.

Robin must have sensed him, or seen him, and turned his way. "How's Doc?" she asked, just loud enough for him to hear.

"Don't know yet. He hasn't moved," Jazz replied.

Loud footfalls sounded in the hallway, and the rest of the captives stirred. Robin scuttled back to where Jazz and Doc were, but not before the bar holding the cell door closed rattled.

The door banged open and three guards rushed in, two of them holding rusted-out rifles at the ready. Big, shambling brutes with oddly small craniums and sloped foreheads, stood in the entrance, all searching for something. Or someone. That someone turned out to be Robin. One of the guards lumbered forward and grabbed a handful of her hair, stopping her before she got to Doc or Jazz.

"Bastard," she yelled, then yelped when the man pulled her close. He forced Robin to bend forward, keeping her head at his hip.

Zeb rose to his haunches and snarled, but got no further before one of the other guards stepped forward and backhanded him. He crashed into the wall and slumped to the floor. He was still conscious, but groggy.

Doc sat up and Jazz felt his muscles tighten, as if he, too, were about to leap at the guards. Jazz grabbed his arm, and hissed, "Stop! You'll just get her killed. Doc, we'll get her back."

"Fuck!" Doc growled, but to Jazz's great relief, halted.

The guards hauled Robin towards the door. One turned and snorted, then in a deep, guttural voice said, "Food come shortly." He lifted Robin's face, presenting her grimace to Jazz and anyone else looking. "The Warlord wants her now." He turned on his heel, pushing Robin's face back to his hip, and strode out.

The other guards followed, rifles held across their chests. The door slammed shut behind them and the bar fell into place.

Doc roared and raced for the cell door. Grabbing the bars, he looked one way then the other, obviously trying to spot which direction the four of them had gone.

Jazz joined him and placed a hand on Doc's shoulder. "Hang on, Doc. We'll find her. We made it this far." He peered through the opening, but couldn't see anything but the wide hall.

"If she's with the Warlord, she'll be back," Zeb said from across the room. "He uses his slaves, but he doesn't do any of the killings. When he's had his fill, he'll send her back here. She's been here a while; she knows the drill. She'll be alive when he finishes with her."

"And that's supposed to make it all right?" Doc snarled at the man.

"No, but it means she'll be alive when you get her back." The man got to his feet and looked levelly from Doc to Jazz. "Seen it before. Sucks, but there ain't nothing to do for it."

The other prisoners moved. Most of them leaned against the walls; one or two went to a corner and relieved themselves. The stink made Jazz gag and he hoped they'd be released soon.

From the hall came the rattling of metal on metal and wood creaking. A deep, masculine voice came from around the far corner. "Hurry up, young'un, or we'll be sharing cells with the louts we feed."

"Yes, sir," a young voice replied.

"Best get away from the door," Zeb suggested. "The guy won't come in till we on the far side of the cell."

Jazz gripped Doc's arm and pulled. His lover followed him, although he sensed reluctance. When they'd reached the wall, Jazz heard the bar rattle then drop to the floor outside the cell. The door opened.

A wooden cart was wheeled in, pushed by a short, frail-looking man with a mop of filthy, white hair and bright blue eyes. He wore the remnants of what might at one time have been an apron, but now was more like a rag around his waist. His rough pants and shirt were sizes too large, and did nothing to hide the fact that his legs were miles too long for his frame. He stank of rotten food.

Marching beside the cart, a boy of about ten peered around. The youngster's black hair poked out all over; his grimy face and limbs appeared too thin for his size. The large lump on his back didn't seem to bother him, yet it must have weighed him down considerably. Over his shoulder, a rope was threaded through the handles of a couple of dozen cups of varying sizes and colours.

The boy unslung the cups and unfastened the knot holding them all together. He handed one to the old man, who shuffled around to the side of his cart. Reaching in, he pulled the lid off the large pot inside.

The smell made Jazz's mouth water.

"One at a time," the old man said, as if he'd said the same line a million times before. Maybe he had.

The progression of peeps took time. When Jazz got to the side of the cart, most of the others had already been fed. Jazz held his cup of thick stew and waited while Doc got his allotment before they both returned to their place by the wall. Zeb sat close by and nodded as Jazz slurped his food.

The meal was surprisingly good. When they were done, the mugs went into the empty pot and the old man and his helper quickly left the cell.

As if their departure was a signal, half a dozen guards entered the cell. One, a well-muscled and well-armed fellow, yelled, "On your feet, scum. The fields need watering and you're it."

Doc and Jazz got up. Zeb joined them and whispered, "They'll march us out. Just tag on to the end of the line. Two abreast. No talking." He backed away and shuffled over to a place in the double line forming.

Jazz watched for a minute, then went to the end of the line. Doc joined him and, after a short wait, the guards led them out.

* * * *

"What do you mean, Sam got you captured?" Jazz was dumbfounded at Doc's announcement. Kneeling in the dirt, pouring a water pail over a corn plant, he tried to grasp how the young man had fooled him. "But he... I... Fuck!"

"Yeah, pretty much my reaction when it happened." Doc quickly looked around to be sure there were no guards within hearing. "Sorry, Jazz, but it's true. When I saw you being dragged off, I grabbed Sam and we took off. No biggie there. I figured we'd come back later that night and see about getting you out. And finding Robin."

"Makes sense," Jazz interjected as he poured the last of his water over the corn plant.

"Yeah, and it might have worked, except when we were coming back in Sam led me straight to where a couple of guards were posted.

"Seems he's one of theirs. He brings them new slaves so the Warlord won't hassle him or his family. He's got a younger sister, and you know what happens there." Doc ran the back of his hand across his sweat-drenched forehead.

"Yeah," Jazz said thoughtfully. "Do you know if she's normal or deformed?"

"Normal—or from what he said she's as normal as they can be here."

"So he lied about his mother and two sibs being taken?"

"Not sure. Might be he's trying to free them from wherever they're being held, or housed. He could be trying to trade them for new bodies or something, too." Doc straightened up and limped to the nearby water wagon, where he filled his pail. Instead of returning to Jazz's side immediately, he poured some of the water over himself, sighing as the cool liquid drenched his face, hair and sun-bronzed flesh. Refilling the bucket, he strode back and bent to the task of watering.

Jazz, on the row beside Doc, upended his pail and went for a refill. Returning, he said, "Might have lied about the entire family thing. Might be just one more city peep out for himself. Survival isn't easy here."

"It's not easy anywhere." Doc cringed, his right side badly bruised from the beating he'd got earlier. "I think he's got a sister. Not sure about the rest."

"He seemed pretty chummy with the guard I saw him with," Jazz added and moved along his row.

They worked silently for a while. Jazz was deep in thought.

Where is Robin? Will we see Sam again? Was the kid just using us?

Questions, questions! He'd thought Sam was going to be more than a few hours of fun. How in hell were Doc and he going to get Robin out of there in one piece?

Hours dragged by. Young men delivered wagon loads of water and drove the empties away while Jazz, Doc and the slaves carried pails to the plants. Row upon row of corn. More of potatoes and other hearty vegetables. In adjacent fields, Jazz saw trees — fruit trees, he thought, but he wasn't a gardener. Or he hadn't been.

His back ached. Hunger tore at him, and at the others, he was sure.

In the row beside him, Doc toiled on. The man didn't complain. Even though angry, red marks criss-crossed his upper body, he just carried on. Jazz knew he'd be watching, though. Keeping his eyes peeled for any opening in their enemy's defences. Looking for a weakness — an unsecured gate, a guard asleep when he shouldn't be, some means to escape or cause damage and give them a way out.

In the back of his mind, Jazz thought of another time they'd spent in a garden. The harvest had been good. The weeks of backbreaking work had ended and the evenings had cooled. Doc had dragged him out for an evening's walk, or so he'd said. The rock he'd taken Jazz to had been just the right height to lean against while his lover had dined on his cock. It had proved even better to sprawl across while Doc rode his arse an hour later.

He shuddered and again thought of how much he loved his mate. Doc was kind and loving. He never seemed to tire of caring for others, even when it meant going without himself. His sister's rescue was delayed, just for that reason. Others came first.

His thoughts wandered while they worked, hour after hour. When the sun reached its height, the guards marched them over to where a group of trees separated one field from the next and ordered them to sit down and wait. Doc sank to the soft grass and lay gasping. Jazz sat beside his lover, too exhausted to do more than run his hand across Doc's arm. The slaves helped each other settle down, comforting their weaker members as best they could.

A group of older women, some obviously deformed, others hiding under layers of rags, trudged towards them from the nearest of the run-down buildings, large baskets balanced on their heads. When two of them reached Jazz's group, they stopped and placed the baskets on the ground a few paces away. The rest carried on towards the next group of slaves. The two who'd stopped retreated a dozen or so paces and knelt quietly, heads bowed and their arms behind them.

A guard tore into the baskets, pulling out large, flat loaves of bread. He broke each loaf in half and passed each man the meagre offering. A pail of water was passed around and helped wash down what turned out to be stale bread.

Choking down his allotted meal, Jazz looked back at the Warlord's garrison. The buildings were surprisingly intact. Some had obviously been rebuilt to some extent, or patched haphazardly with whatever rubble was available.

His exhaustion finally wore him down and he followed Doc's lead, lying back on the grass. For a few minutes, he closed his eyes and simply allowed himself to think of nothing but soft grass and Doc's presence. He turned onto his side and pressed his lips to the underside of Doc's arm.

"Hey, you're tickling me." Doc rolled over, tucking his arm under his head. "You all right?"

"Yeah, so far."

"We've got to get out of here. That Warlord is insane."

"No kidding," Jazz replied.

"I can't figure out why he's got so many followers." Doc shifted, the ground obviously digging into the bruises on his side.

"He controls the food and the guards. Not sure what he has on the guards, but most of them seem to be…uh…less than bright."

"That could be all he needs. That and the rod he carries. It looks like some kind of cattle prod."

Jazz remembered the rod, but hadn't thought much about it. He looked Doc in the eye and asked, "Does it work? He didn't use it on you, did he?"

"Yeah, it works. And no, he didn't use it on me. He did use it on one of his slaves, though. The poor bastard bit his tongue nearly off." He shuddered and rolled onto his back again. "When Black let up, the slave collapsed. I don't know if he was alive or—"

"All right, you lazy bunch of useless fuckers," yelled the guard who'd fed them. He strode towards them, his whip at the ready. "Get up and let's get a move on. Work is waitin'."

Groaning, Jazz sat up. Doc wasn't as fast and Jazz worried. His lover had been hurt—not badly, but enough to slow him down. As long as he was left alone and given time to heal, Jazz was sure everything would be fine. But the guards didn't seem inclined to leave anyone alone. Doc kept up, but it would take its toll. At least he wasn't being brutalised any further.

Jazz held out his hand and Doc took it and grinned crookedly at him. "Thanks, babe," the bruised and battered man said.

The guard organising them yelled, "Form a line, two by two." He strode to the front of the line and crossed his arms, the whip dangling from his hand.

The slaves slouched into a rough line, Doc and Jazz at the end. Ahead of them, Zeb took his place beside a slender, middle-aged man covered in scabs, who looked like he could barely put one foot in front of the other. None of the slaves looked like they'd last long. Jazz had watched them all during their morning's work and the guards had whipped several of them repeatedly to keep them moving.

Another guard took up position at the end of the line and shouted, "March!"

The first guard turned and headed for the main buildings. The slaves followed, helping each other, some nearly carrying their companions. Jazz and Doc brought up the rear. Behind them, the guard whistled a tuneless ditty, occasionally punctuating a line with the slap of the whip against his leg.

When they got to the buildings, Jazz peered to each side, looking for an escape route or refuge. He spotted a few peeps, some bent and in rags, the odd one not. That stopped him, and he gaped at the lone man standing just inside one of the nearby hovels. It was next to the first really tall building they had come to, at least five floors high and with a statue of a woman at the front. The man looked familiar.

"Move your slimy arse," the guard behind him snarled.

An instant later, Jazz yelped. His back burnt where the whip had landed. He hurried on but still couldn't shake the feeling that he'd seen that figure before. Looking back, the man he'd spied was gone.

Doc grabbed him by the arm and whispered, "What the hell are you doing?"

"Nothing. I saw someone in there." He nodded towards the run-down building and added, "I swear, the guy didn't look like he was a city dweller — too clean, too well dressed. And he looked familiar."

"You're crazy," Doc muttered, and continued walking.

Jazz noticed, however, Doc's head turning now and then, as he, too, checked the ruins around them. Doc's pace faltered once, but he resumed walking without the guards whip *encouraging* him.

The group went past several inhabited buildings before they reached their next job.

"Carrots and beans," yelled the first guard. "Half go left, the rest of you on the right. Baskets in there." He pointed at a small shack they'd walked past. "Don't pick enough, you don't eat."

Zeb and his partner went for baskets; Jazz followed. Doc stood waiting and looking back at the buildings they'd passed.

"Come on, babe," Jazz said to Doc, and urged his lover to the tall bean plants on the right. Bending down and pulling carrots would be backbreaking. Pulling beans would be a lot easier.

Zeb nodded and headed for the beans as well, his partner in tow. Jazz watched them for a few moments and got the gist of the best way to pick. He went down one side of the row, Doc the other, each pulling beans and tossing them into the basket Jazz had set down. With guards walking up and down the rows, they had no chance to talk.

They filled one basket, then, while Doc rested, Jazz carried it to the end of the row and got another. There was no water this time, and thirst became an issue. A breeze helped a little, but raised dust devils where the soil was dry, which added to the torment.

Several hours and a dozen baskets filled with beans later, the guard called them into the shade beside the small shed. Jazz wrapped his arm around Doc and together they trudged down the row towards the promised rest.

Sitting on the ground with his back against the cool wood, Jazz gazed towards the buildings. He noticed that one seemed to have more guards patrolling around it. A cement structure, or brick, it was hard to tell from where he sat.

The water cart approached from the direction he'd come to recognise as where it filled up with its precious liquid. He nudged Doc and nodded towards the old man pushing the wooden handcart and his young helper, who carried a pail.

"Finally," Doc whispered in a hoarse voice. "Wasn't sure I'd make it."

Jazz looked at his lover and sighed. The bruises on his face and upper body gave him a sinister appearance. Sweat trickled and left rivulets of grime from his hairline to his waist. His lips were cracked. One eye had swollen nearly shut. The man really did look abysmal.

Doc, love, I need to get you out of here.

"Can't see them going to all the trouble of acquiring slaves to simply let them die of thirst out here." His own voice didn't sound much better than Doc's had. "Besides, I'd never allow you to die." Jazz smiled at Doc, a big, cheesy grin he knew must look insane in light of their situation.

Doc gaped at him and his mouth sagged. He blinked, then tried to speak, unsuccessfully. He tried again and managed to say, "You are insane. Either that or you've had too much sun."

"Bit of both, I guess," Jazz leaned in and pressed his lips to Doc's cheek, close to his lover's ear. Keeping his lips there, he whispered, "Spotted where they keep their arms."

Doc nodded and replied, "Yeah, a small brick building. Lots of guards around it."

"Yeah, that's the one."

"Gawd, I just feel like shit." Doc kissed Jazz on the side of his face, then pulled away.

"'Fraid you look a bit like it, too, babe."

The water carrier arrived and the boy lugged the pail full of cool liquid to the group of men resting in the shade. Starting at one end, each man took a turn, drinking his fill then upending the remaining water over his head.

Jazz scooted around to the other side of Doc, which allowed his lover to drink first. Once he'd had his turn, Jazz guzzled as much water as he could, then slowly poured the rest over himself. The cold felt good, but didn't last long enough.

As soon as they'd all been watered, their guard urged them up and marched them to the next field over.

At first, Jazz couldn't figure out what the job was going to be. It was late afternoon and everyone was close to falling down from exhaustion. There were no crops — it was just an empty meadow of rough weeds and grass. When he spotted the half a dozen wooden contraptions sitting beside the field, his confusion grew.

"Time to plough this baby," the guard said, and Jazz's heart missed a beat.

What the fuck? The sun was at its hottest. The men were stumbling from the work they'd already done. And now these morons expected them to plough?

"Teams o' two. Each team do four rows. We head back to compound then." The guard strode down the row of slaves, whip at his side, slapping his leg for punctuation.

Doc grabbed Jazz's arm and whispered, "Stick with me. Together we might be able to do this. If I get stuck with one of those used-up blokes I'm sure I'll wind up fertiliser."

"You and me both, babe." Jazz might have been in better shape than Doc at the moment—he didn't have the bruises or scrapes his lover had—but he knew Doc. The man was stubborn, and that made up for a lot.

A little farther down the row, the man Zeb had been teamed up with fell to the ground, sobbing. "I can't. I'm so tired. I—"

The words were cut off when the guard nearest the kneeling man brought his whip down. And again, and again.

Crying out, the fellow rolled to his side and curled into a tight ball. He continued sobbing as the guard cursed and beat him into unconsciousness. Apparently satisfied, the brute kicked the downed man, then turned away, going again to the end of the row.

Zeb gaped, but didn't try to interfere.

Jazz assumed the event wasn't as uncommon as he'd like to think. But knowing what would happen if they faltered was a lesson no one needed to have repeated.

The guard giving instructions said, "One pulls, other works the plough. Move it."

He turned and said to Zeb, "You, help them harness up. You the spare."

Jazz quickly got into the harness, thinking he'd save Doc's battered flesh from rubbing on the leather. Straps crossed his chest and went over his shoulders. The plough was attached to the heavy leather band buckled around his body. When he tried an experimental tug, he groaned. The thing was going to be hell to pull.

Zeb came to Jazz's side and said in a hushed voice, "You get the plough going, it gets easier. Don't stop till you get to the end o' the row. Stopping and starting are what kill you."

Jazz looked at the man and nodded. "Thanks."

Zeb hurried to Doc's side and, while handing him the reins, said, "Don't put too much weight on this thing. It digs in and will tire him out fast."

"Got it," Doc said.

The rig shifted behind Jazz.

"Get movin'. We ain't got all damn day, you lazy, useless…"

The rest was lost to Jazz, who had leaned into the leather harness. The plough seemed stuck in the dirt. When it let loose, he made sure to carry on. He veered into a straight line and trudged across the field, another harnessed man beside him.

The late afternoon wore on slowly. Painfully.

Jazz's shoulders ached. His back burnt from the sun's heat. His thighs trembled from overuse. Sweat and grime clung to him. He fell to the ground once, and thought he'd never make it back to his feet. Limbs trembling, he struggled and failed. He remembered the poor man who'd been beaten into oblivion and swore it wouldn't happen to him. He gritted his teeth and fought the fatigue, the heat, and rose. Lumbering on, he kept his eyes on the goal.

Doc did his best to help, Jazz was sure of it. Still, it took aeons to get the rows done. Longer than he'd thought he could pull the plough, but not as long as it took some of the others.

When he finally stood at the end of his fourth row, he could barely see because of the sweat in his eyes.

Gasping for breath, he swiped the back of his hand over his face and peered around. Vision blurred, he made out two other teams along the end of the row — both kneeling in the dirt, as he soon was.

Doc hurried to unfasten the buckles, fumbling with the stubborn leather. Finally freed, Jazz fell onto his side and lay gasping, trembling.

"Fuck me," Jazz moaned.

Doc collapsed next to him, an arm across Jazz's back. "Maybe later, babe. Much too tired."

Jazz chuckled.

The guard approached and, with the toe of his worn boot, jabbed Jazz in the side. "Not bad for a new boy." He walked away and stood with the other guards, waiting while the other teams finished.

The march back to their cell seemed much longer than the march out. Doc's legs gave out just as they reached the outer edge of run-down buildings on the outskirts of the Warlord's 'kingdom'. Jazz caught him, barely, before he collapsed completely. With his arm under Doc's, Jazz supported, almost carried his lover towards the cell block.

"Look over there," Doc said, and pointed towards the window of the building nearest them.

When Jazz looked to where Doc had pointed, he saw a man watching them. He whispered, "Yeah, that's the guy I saw earlier."

"I've seen two more who look sort of like him." Doc peered around, obviously looking for more. He looked back at Jazz and shrugged.

Once the guards had escorted them back to their cell and locked them in, Doc stumbled into the corner with Jazz right on his heels. The others found their niches or the spots they had claimed as their own and fell to the straw, exhausted. The soft murmur of voices was the only sound.

Doc sat with his back to the wall. Jazz joined him, getting as close as he could.

"Any thoughts on where Robin is?" Doc asked, his concern evident in the tone of his voice.

"No. All I can think of is she'll be with that Warlord character. When I got here, that's where I came to. She was right next to his big ol' throne chair." He laid a hand on Doc's arm, hoping to reassure him.

The bar across the cell door scraped over the wood, stopping any further conversation. The door opened and a dishevelled Robin stumbled in.

She stood in the centre of the cell for a moment before Doc pushed himself up and staggered over to her, pulling her to their corner. He sat down, drawing her along with him by the arm.

When she was safely cuddled against him and next to Jazz, he whispered, "Are you all right, hun?" Doc stroked her hair.

"Yes, I'm fine." Her voice was strained yet strong, despite her obvious maltreatment. "I'll be better when we get out of here." She looked up at Doc, then shifted her gaze towards Jazz. "We are getting out, right?"

"Course we are," Jazz replied, although he wasn't sure how. Not yet. "Are you really all right? You look like you've been beaten again. Nothing broken?"

Robin shifted but didn't seem to favour any one place more than another. "I'm really all right. Just bruises and a few cuts. The bastard will have a few new scars to show after today, too." She smiled grimly at him.

"Good." Jazz said.

"I'd have slit his throat if I could."

Jazz opened his mouth to reply but quickly shut it when something slammed into the cell door. He looked up in time to see the cart with its large pot of food come into the room. The skeletally thin attendant shuffled in and halted the cart. The young, hunchbacked boy followed with his string of mugs slung over his shoulder.

It was feeding time.

While he sat and slurped down the stew, Jazz pondered the cell door. The bar was what held them up — or in — so how could they get past it? The bar would stick out beyond the metal cup it sat in.

A hook or loop. Something to draw it up with. Something strong enough to hold the weight. Something easily manipulated.

He might as well wish for a third arm, bent in all the right places. Oh, and an eye so he could see what it was doing.

"Fuck," he muttered, and drank the last of his stew.

"What?" Doc looked at Jazz, confused.

"Nothing. I was trying to figure out how we could open that door. We need to find a hook, or a loop of some kind."

"Right, and we've got all kinds of places we can look for this stuff." Doc upended his mug, finishing off his own stew. "A loop," he said thoughtfully. After a few minutes of silence, he turned to Jazz. "You're right, babe. But, I don't have a clue. Sleep on it. Maybe one of us will come up with something." He glanced down at Robin, who was nearly asleep, and smiled. "She's exhausted." Carefully, he shifted her until she was over him, so he was next to Jazz, Robin closest to the wall.

Jazz nodded and slid down until he was flat on the floor. He turned and shuffled forward, entering Doc's arms. "Love you, babe," he said, just as Doc whispered the same thing.

They didn't dare do anything, not with so many people close by, but their gentle caresses and kisses were enough for Jazz. It took him some time to fall into a deep sleep.

He came awake instantly some time later. It was pitch black and the only sounds were the snores or grumblings of the people around him. Doc's head rested against his shoulder and the soft touch his breath against Jazz's flesh made him shiver.

"A loop," he murmured, and knew he'd figured out how to get out of the cell—or at least he hoped so.

He shook Doc's arm. "Babe, I've got it. I need some cloth strips." His heart raced. They could get out if he could just get his plan moving quickly. He didn't have a clue what time it was. It could be the middle of the night. He could have minutes before sunrise.

"What? What the hell are you—"

"Just listen for a sec. I just need some long strips of cloth," Jazz mumbled, trying to control his excitement. "It can't be that simple."

Doc squirmed out of his arms and sat up. "You're not making a lot of sense, babe."

"Yeah, I know." Jazz ripped off his shirt and tore it into strips. "Any idea what time it is? How much time I have before the guards show up?" He reached for Doc and pulled at his woollen jerkin, then muttered, "Not sure I can use this. Fuck, fuck! Fuck!" He let the material go, frustration mounting.

From close by, Zeb's sleepy voice asked, "What are you doing? What do you need?"

Jazz lurched, but thought he might as well dive in. "Cloth. I need long strips of cloth."

A moment later, Jazz sensed Zeb moving closer. In the darkness, all he could make out for sure was the man's outline. But it had to be him.

"This do?"

Cloth brushed Jazz's hands and he grabbed it. Holding it out, he spread out what appeared to be a shirt, then nodded. "Yeah, it's good. Hopefully I'll have enough." He tore the material into strips, then braided it all into one long strip of stronger cord.

"Anyone got an idea what time it is?" Jazz murmured urgently. "Daylight coming soon, middle of the night—what?" He fumbled the makeshift rope, forming a loop in the end and fastening it as best he could in the dark.

"It's a couple of hours to light." Zeb shifted around until he was closer to Jazz. "What the fuck are you doing?"

Jazz chose to ignore the question. He wasn't sure if his hare-brained idea would work, so best not to raise hopes, or wake any more prisoners. Finished, he tugged at the loop and judged it would hold.

He hurried over to the door and peered into the hall. He listened for movement or sound, but heard nothing. Slipping the loop through the opening, he swung it and prayed. Drawing the rope back in, he sighed and tried again.

Time after time, he let the loop out and swung it back and forth, hoping it'd catch. Finally, when his patience was nearly gone, the loop held—something.

Please, let it hold. Let it be the right place!

He slowly pulled the end of his makeshift rope and felt the weight of something at the other end.

"Jazz, you're a fuckin' genius," whispered Doc from behind him. "Steady, don't pull too fast. I'll reach down and grab it when I can."

Jazz shuffled forward carefully and waited for Doc to get into position right behind him, bodies touching. When his lover had his arm thrust through the cell window, Jazz continued drawing the braided cloth in.

Several heart-stopping moments later, Doc hissed, "Yes, got it."

Jazz let out a breath and felt lightheaded.

I'll be damned, it was that easy.

Over his shoulder, Doc said, "Let's get the others up. They've got to be quiet or we're all done for."

Zeb, who'd stood by and surprisingly kept quiet, said, "I'll do that. Might be easier comin' from me. They all know me. And if I tell em to shut up, they'll do it."

"Go—just be quick and be quiet."

Jazz helped pull the door open and listened for a guard doing his rounds or simply walking around to kill time. All was quiet.

Inside the cell, rustling became soft words, hastily spoken. The sounds of others moving followed, some approaching the door.

"Doc, Jazz, where are you?" The terrified voice came from where they'd left Robin. She'd been exhausted and had slept through everything until then.

Jazz darted to where she sat and squatted. "Hey, girl, it's okay. We're going to get out of here."

"You're crazy. We're all—"

"Never mind," he interrupted and took hold of her arm. "We've got the door open. It's just a matter of getting everyone out."

"Open. But how?" She sounded dumbstruck but quickly gathered her wits. "I can get us out. I know the way."

"Good," Doc said from close by. "We'll need someone we trust to get us out of here."

It wasn't long before Zeb returned to Jazz's side and said, "Everyone's awake. None in great shape. Won't fight much. But they're all eager to run."

"That's all we need," Doc said. "We'll have Robin lead us out."

Jazz pulled Robin's arm, keeping her close. Standing beside Doc, they were ready for whatever happened.

Doc pushed the door the rest of the way open and released his hold on the braided cloth. The bar dropped down and made a soft thudding sound.

Jazz grabbed the braided cloth as he entered the hall, his lover and Robin on either side of him. Behind them, the slaves followed, Zeb in front. Robin pointed to the left and they hurried that way.

Robin tiptoed around a corner and stopped dead in her tracks. A soft gasp reached Jazz's ears. Doc reacted instantly, rushing ahead.

Sam, the traitorous young man, stood dumbstruck in their path.

Doc grabbed him. Before he could cry out or run, Doc had the young man's arm cranked up behind him and an arm around his neck, effectively silencing him.

Chapter Six

Jazz leapt after Doc and slammed his fist into Sam's stomach. The young man grunted, but couldn't fold because of the hold Doc had on him. It did keep him from calling out.

Zeb came to Jazz's side and whispered urgently, "Is he alone?"

Jazz glared at him but raced down the hall to the next corner and peered around it. Even in the darkness, he was sure nothing and no one was ahead.

He turned and went back to where Doc held their former friend. "Clear."

"Give me that braided rope." Doc held out a hand.

Jazz handed it over and held Sam while Doc quickly bound his hands. Robin supplied another strip of cloth, enough to form a gag. By the time they had him secured, Sam was able to stand up straight and glare around. He shook his head, as if disbelieving they could escape.

"Robin, lead on," Jazz said levelly.

The former slaves huddled around, comforting each other and anxious to get moving. A taste of freedom wasn't enough.

Robin moved ahead and hurried down the corridor, slowing at each new bend or doorway she came to. When they got to the main entrance, she stopped and turned. "What now?"

"Time to split up." Doc nodded at Sam, who'd given up struggling almost as soon as he had been captured. "Do you think you can control him?" Doc asked, and held the young man forward.

"You bet." Robin reached for Sam and, using the rope around his wrists as a handle, pulled him close. Leaning in, she whispered to Sam, "Behave or I'll slit your throat."

Sam cringed but didn't put up any further fight. He, of course, had no idea if Robin was armed or not.

"Zeb, I want you and the others to release as many of the slaves as you can. No use just us getting away."

Zeb stepped up. "You got it. And if we run into any guards along the way...well, they won't need to worry about what's for breakfast."

"Understood," Doc said. He looked thoughtful for a moment, then asked, "Where can we all meet?"

"Why not the armoury?" Zeb suggested.

"Because it's not going to be standing for long," Doc replied tightly.

Jazz was about to argue, but when he saw Doc's face he changed his mind. There were some things he could talk his lover out of, but he recognised there were also things Doc would do, period. This was one of the latter.

"This so-called *Warlord* needs to lose whatever hold he has over the peeps in the city. The armoury should take care of some of that. Taking out his guards, or most of them, should be enough to do the rest."

"How about the first tall building we saw when we came back from the fields today?"

"Yeah, beside where I spotted that familiar-looking dude," Jazz offered.

"Huh?" Zeb cocked his head and looked from Jazz to Doc.

"Never mind," Doc said, then added, "I know the building you mean. There's a statue out front, right? Yes, we'll meet up there." He clasped Jazz by the shoulder and hugged him for a moment.

Jazz's heart raced. "Yeah, the statue of a woman." They'd be free soon. And Robin was with them.

"Zeb, make sure you team up with Robin. I'm relying on you."

"You got it," the slender man replied, then turned and headed back into the dark hallway. The others followed. After the initial hum of their departure, silence fell over the place.

"Robin, do you know which building we were talking about?" Jazz asked her.

"I think so. There's only one that I can think of in the area. And I remember seeing that statue. I'm sure of it."

"Okay, you just get yourself there, with Sam if he behaves, and wait for Doc and me." Jazz took a deep breath. Things were moving fast—hopefully not too fast.

"I'll see you there." Robin dragged the docile Sam after her. She opened the door to the world outside and peered around it. A moment later she exited, along with her bound and gagged charge.

"The armoury isn't going to be standing?" Jazz said to Doc. "I suppose you've got a plan?"

"Not exactly." His lover grinned at him and grabbed him by the shoulders. Drawing Jazz close, Doc whispered, "I've wanted to do this for hours. Fuck, I was scared, Jazz. Twice is two times too many."

Jazz leaned in and pressed his lips to Doc's, tasting his breath. When he pulled back, he said, "I wasn't captured that first time. I was just trailing them. This time...well, it won't happen again. I hope." He smiled at his lover's look of mock annoyance and added, "You're the one who should take better care of himself. Hell, you got beaten up, I didn't."

"Never mind." Doc pushed Jazz away playfully, then said, "Let's go. We've got work to do."

Jazz listened for a moment, sure he'd heard something from the direction Zeb and his crew had gone. Nothing more came, so he followed Doc to the entrance. They slipped outside after looking around for guards posted nearby. Doc sank into the shadows with Jazz on his heels.

On their way to the armoury, they detoured around two sets of guards patrolling the area. More of the sloped-forehead type who didn't seem to have many smarts. The four man teams seemed oblivious to anything but their path ahead and the loud bantering about the women they'd had earlier that night.

Finally, the armoury stood across the way. Doc settled into the shadowy depths of a crevice in a nearby fallen wall. Jazz slid into the dark opening next to Doc's hidey hole.

Across from them, the small brick building looked well-guarded. Two men stood at the door, another two shambled around the structure. None of them seemed overly alert.

"Doesn't appear to be an easy way in," came Doc's whispered report.

"No windows this side. Have you seen the other?" Jazz watched as the guards went around the corner and left only two on this side of the building. He wondered if they'd have to get by those two.

"No, but I think we're going to have to check it out."

Before Jazz could respond, Doc darted out and along the wall. Jazz followed. Crossing the open space proved easier than Jazz thought it was going to be. They backtracked to where they'd passed a pile of rubble and simply used it for cover. Coming out only a dozen metres from the armoury, Jazz waited until he judged both guards were looking away, then scampered across.

He hit the wall and stood with his back to it. He listened for anyone approaching.

Unexpectedly quickly, Doc arrived next to him against the wall. "Fuck," Doc whispered, barely loud enough for Jazz to hear.

"What?" Jazz asked, equally quiet as he looked anxiously around. Had one of the guards spotted his lover?

"It's okay. Thought I heard the guards coming around. But I think it was a cat or something."

Doc headed around the side of the building, following the way the guard detail had gone. When they reached the back of the cement structure, Jazz spotted something near the base of the wall — a metal plate, about the width of a man's shoulders.

Jazz tapped Doc's shoulder and waited for him to turn around. "Here, look." He pointed down and Doc dropped to his knees.

Jazz joined him and Doc whispered, "It's some sort of hatch. It's got four latches." He reached down and fiddled with them.

The hatch dropped open.

Jazz leapt to his feet, Doc beside him, and spun his head around, instantly on the lookout for anyone who'd heard the small clatter of metal hitting concrete. Both he and Doc waited, listening for anyone approaching.

When he was fairly sure no one had heard, Jazz dropped to his knees. Doc stayed erect, apparently wanting to give Jazz time to see what was inside. His stomach in knots, Jazz leant down even further and peered into the rectangular opening. Rough edges of cement bit at his fingers as he held on to one side.

The lighting was crap, but Jazz could make out shelves piled high with boxes along the far wall. On the right side, a rack held dozens of rifles. A pallet of boxed ammunition sat in the centre of the room and he could just make out a bin, filled with who knew what, sitting on the left. Not a soul was in sight. It seemed the Warlord, or the head of his dim-witted guards, assumed patrolling outside was enough.

"What's inside?" Doc asked urgently.

"Arms, weapons, just like we both thought. Guns, ammunition, boxes and crates of something…explosives maybe."

"Perfect." Doc squatted down and tried to peer into the hole. "Think I can get through that?"

Jazz shrugged, but thought he could, if he exhaled and pushed hard. "Yeah, but if Zoe were here, she'd have a better chance of slipping in without losing skin. For you, it'll be tight." He flipped around and pushed his feet through the opening.

Doc grabbed Jazz's shoulders, stopping him from going in. "Zoe's not here, but you're right. She'd fit easy. Doesn't matter—I'm going in and you're not. You know tracking and music. I know meds and how to make things go bang."

Jazz wanted to protest. This was going to be dangerous and he desperately wanted to protect Doc. He'd come too close to losing him and wasn't sure he could deal with the heartache again.

"It's okay, babe." Doc stroked Jazz's shoulder then leant forward and kissed his cheek. When he pulled away, he whispered, "The sooner I get in there, the faster we can get out of here and back home."

"I hate it when you sound so fucking logical." Jazz slid his legs out and made way for Doc.

"I'll be fast," his lover said as he slipped into the opening, feet, legs, then the rest of him. He dropped to the floor, which wasn't really a drop at all. His head remained level with the hatch. He turned and looked back at Jazz. "Keep your eyes open for guards. Whistle if you see or hear anyone."

"Just hurry up and do whatever it is you were planning." Jazz got to his feet, but remained crouched to minimise the chance of someone seeing him. He leaned away from the wall, checking both ways and listening for any sounds. In the distance a dog barked, but that was all.

Doc seemed to take far too long inside, and Jazz grew anxious. He forced a growing fear of discovery aside. Every tiny sound had him jumping around to see what it was. By the time Doc poked his head out of the opening, Jazz was about ready to chew nails.

"Done." Doc grinned up at Jazz.

"About fucking time, babe." Jazz leant down and offered his hands.

Doc took hold and allowed Jazz to pull him out. "We don't have much time. There wasn't a lot of choice. I had to trust some of the newer-looking fuse, but who knows how old it is or how fast it'll burn." Doc wriggled his legs out, then quickly got to his feet.

Jazz listened carefully and realised Doc had rigged the place to blow up. His stomach clenched and he whispered, "You're fucking crazy. I thought you were going to grab some ammunition or weapons. We'd blow it later… Something. Fucking crazy!" He felt giddy with fear.

"Nope, the guns are old. I have no idea how much good the ammo is, or anything else in there."

"Let's get out of here," Jazz urged and, with his back against the wall, made his way to the corner.

Doc scrambled to his feet and quickly scooted along the wall after him.

Jazz stopped at the turn and took a deep breath. The guard could be close, or he could be anywhere. They should have watched the men's routine for longer. Still holding his breath, Jazz peeked around the corner and he exhaled.

"Come on, it's clear," he whispered over his shoulder. Without looking back to see if Doc was following, he raced for the next corner. A quick glance around that one, and he deemed the time was now or never. He raced for the pile of rubble they'd started from.

Footsteps hurried after him, Doc breathing more heavily now as they scrambled around the mound. Jazz dropped to his hands and knees. His heart was beating so fast he couldn't hear anything else for a moment. He lowered his head and just breathed for a few minutes, hoping the place didn't blow up—not quite yet.

"We better keep moving, babe," Doc said breathlessly. "We're too close."

"Lead the way." Jazz got to his feet and wasn't surprised to see Doc heading towards the building where they'd told Robin to meet them. They got to the nearest alley and skirted an enormous pile of rubble from a collapsed building before they caught up with Doc. His lover seemed determined to put as much distance as possible between them and the armoury.

Partial walls loomed in the darkness, offering shelter or the danger of city peeps waiting to steal what they had. Any openings in the run-down buildings threatened ambush or promised sanctuary – they couldn't be sure.

Jazz followed Doc, skirting hazards he could see, stumbling over those the darkness hid. Ahead, two, maybe three blocks away, the building they were heading for appeared.

"Nearly there." Jazz hoped he wouldn't be overheard. They'd been lucky so far. The city peeps were asleep or elsewhere. Even the mangy dogs they'd run into on their trip in were absent, hopefully far away.

"Yeah," Doc gasped. "I hope Robin's there. I honestly don't want to go looking for her in the dark."

"No shit. I've stubbed my toes more times than I can count," Jazz replied in a quiet voice.

They ran across another street and kept on going. Jazz zigged when Doc zagged, leaving them separated by a pile of rubble for a few seconds. Enough time for Jazz to become nervous and quicken his pace. Breathing hard, he came around the other side in time to see Doc sidestep a large slab of cement as he headed for the next street.

They were just about to cross the last street when Jazz spotted Robin in one of the many openings. Her white skin seemed to shine in the darkness.

Doc must have spotted her at the same time. "There – Robin and Sam." He pointed to where the two stood.

Jazz stepped off the boulder he'd climbed onto in order to see better just as the city shook. A roar like thunder blasted them. Flashes of brilliant light lit the sky behind them and made it seem as if daylight had arrived hours early. A few seconds of silence followed, but Jazz knew it wouldn't last. Explosions, one after another or piled one on top of the other, jarred the city's quiet. Dogs howled, adding to the din. Ammunition—rifle shells for the most part—rat-a-tatted haphazardly into the air in a wild volley of deadly fire.

Peeps in the surrounding buildings screamed and ran into the streets. They'd have been better off staying behind the solid walls of their run-down dwellings.

Jazz watched a woman in rags race for shelter and nearly make it. A chance bullet sent her sailing through the air. She landed several paces away, dead before she hit the ground.

A child peeked out from behind a crumbled wall, only to dart back and perhaps save his own life. A woman grabbed him and cuddled him into her arms. The man behind her pulled both child and woman close while they all gazed out into a city gone crazy.

Doc grabbed Jazz's arm and pulled him into the crevice formed when a building had fallen in. Brick and mortar shielded them while mayhem raged in the outside world.

"You okay?" Doc asked, and ran his hands over Jazz's naked chest and sides.

"Yeah, fine. You, babe?" Jazz shuddered at the tender touch of his lover and allowed him to continue his examination.

"Good, but man, did that place blow!"

"No shit." Jazz snuggled in closer to Jazz and waited for the din to die down. "Did you see if Robin took cover?"

"Yeah, just before I ducked in here, I saw her run for cover. She's a smart girl."

The din died down a few minutes later and Doc got to his feet. "Come on, we'd better get moving."

"I'm sure the Warlord will be sending patrols out as soon as he cleans his drawers." Jazz chuckled at the thought of the big man filling his pants, if he had any on.

Chances are, he shit the bed.

Doc headed for the street, aiming towards where they'd last seen Robin. Jazz raced after him and they reached the opening at the same time. Jazz went in first, listening for any noise he could follow.

"Hey, Jazz," came the excited voice he'd hoped to hear.

Robin came out of nowhere. The next thing Jazz knew, she'd wrapped her arms around his neck and was kissing his face.

Sputtering, his arms automatically going around her, he grinned and waited for her to calm down. It took a few minutes. Long enough for Doc to enter and chuckle at his sister's antics.

"Doc!" Robin's excitement hadn't lessened at all. In fact, when she launched herself at Doc she very nearly knocked him over.

"Where's Sam?" Jazz asked quietly and looked around. He needn't have worried. When he went a few paces deeper into the interior, he saw the young man sitting behind one of the sturdy cement foundation walls. Sam cringed and pulled away when Jazz reached down and took a firm hold of his arm. Pulling the man up, he got him on his feet, then dragged him towards where Robin was still hugging her brother.

"We'll wait for the others, but not for too long," Doc said, while trying to disengage himself from Robin's bear hug. "Warlord Black will have searchers out looking for us as soon as he can get them under control. If he can."

Robin seemed to think otherwise. "Those arms. The cattle prod thing he used — that was the only hold he had over any of the scum he had guarding him. That and the farms, where the slaves provided food. He organised it all. That was it for him. Now it's gone, he's most likely on the run."

"Interesting," Doc said thoughtfully. "That is, if he's survived at all. For all we know, one of those blasts or a stray bullet could have taken care of him."

"Now, what to do with this character?" Jazz thrust Sam forward. "We trusted you."

Sam stumbled and would have fallen if Doc hadn't grabbed him by the scruff of the neck. "He was just trying to save his family," he quipped, and tore the gag from the man's mouth. "Am I right?"

The young man squirmed but quickly realised he wasn't getting anywhere. Bowing his head, he shook it and said in a dull voice, "No family, not now. Everyone's dead but me. Just trying to keep life and limb together."

"As we all are," Robin stated matter-of-factly.

"So why trick people for Black to enslave?" Jazz snarled, not quite as eager to forgive or forget as the others might be.

Lifting his gaze, Sam looked Jazz in the eye and replied, "Because if I didn't, I'd be one of those slaves. You've seen me. How long do you think I'd last out in the fields?" He looked from Jazz to Doc. "I learnt a long time ago to take care of number one—me—because no one else will."

"And now that Black is dethroned?" Doc released the hold he had on Sam and crossed his arms over his chest.

"I guess I'm going to have to find a place somewhere that won't kill a stranger on sight." Sam shuddered, but from the way his shoulders shook he was terrified.

Jazz knew the prospect of the young man finding some kind of sanctuary before he was killed weren't good. The city peeps kept to their own. It was how they stayed alive.

Just then, a clattering of rubble against rubble sent Jazz and the others into hiding. Sam joined Jazz behind the same wall he'd been hiding behind with Robin. Doc and Robin seemed to vanish into thin air.

"Doc, Jazz," came the tentative call from just beyond the entrance.

Jazz peeked out from behind the wall and called, "Zeb, is that you?"

"Yeah, me and as many slaves...er, ex-slaves as I could bring. About thirty."

Doc materialised just this side of the entryway and hopped over a small pile of rubble. Standing a few paces from Zeb, he held his hands out and said, "That's great. Bring 'em in here so we can plan."

Zeb waved an arm behind himself, indicating that the others should follow him. He was right—about thirty men and women slunk out from behind mounds of debris and into the building. They huddled in a semicircle around Doc and waited for him to say his piece.

"It's like this. Jazz, Robin and I are leaving the city. You're welcome to join us, if you can keep to the rules of our home. Simple rules—civilised rules. You can come with us, or you can remain in the city."

One of the women, a good looking femme with surprisingly pale skin who looked furtively around while she spoke, said, "Will I have to obey some man?"

Robin stepped forward and replied, "Only if you want to. Or you can live by yourself. No one will make you do anything you don't want to. We expect people to pull their own weight. We don't allow bullies to force the weaker ones to do more."

The woman nodded and stepped forward. "I'm with you."

A dozen people stepped forward—a mixture of both men and women, some deformed, others appearing normal.

Sam approached. "What about me?" he asked, and Jazz sensed his nervousness.

Doc said, "Up to you. Although you have to realise we'll be keeping an eye on you for a while."

Lowering his gaze, Sam replied, "Understood. I'm with you."

After several questions, some arguing from an older man who simply couldn't understand why anyone would—or could—leave their beloved city, an hour had passed. Of the thirty or so people there, twenty wanted to join Doc and Jazz and find a new home. The rest would remain in their familiar city.

The first rays of dawn were just brightening the city when Jazz slipped his arm around Doc and whispered, "Think we'll be able to find a nice secluded spot for some down and dirty sex?"

Doc chuckled softly. "Might do. Might take a day or so, though. Hard to tell."

"Yeah, hard as hell here, too." Jazz grinned at Doc, then leaned in for a kiss. When he broke away, he murmured, "Let's go, babe."

Doc went and stood at the entryway, looking out over the city. Jazz came up behind him and shivered. He couldn't wait to be free of the place, one more time.

"Everyone ready?" Doc looked back at the small group of city peeps.

Jazz turned towards where Robin stood beside Sam. The fellow seemed satisfied with how things were going. Robin smiled, a lot.

Doc headed out and Jazz quickly joined him. The city seemed quieter than when they'd entered it such a short time ago. They saw the occasional half-starved dog, but no peeps crossed their path. Hours of stumbling over rubble strewn from one end of the streets to the other proved hard on the ex-slaves. The pale-pale woman who'd asked about her freedom soon found herself supporting a man who'd twisted his ankle. Another fellow nursed a bad gash in his leg where a sharp-edged piece of metal had torn it. Zeb helped those who seemed to need it the most, and Jazz knew the man was going to be a huge asset to their village. Red was there, her and her man. They kept to themselves mostly, but helped when it was needed.

By nightfall, Jazz could see the end of the city streets and the beginning of the forest. A great green wall of trees and brush he couldn't wait to get into. He hugged himself and shivered. He hadn't been able to replace the shirt he'd torn up for braiding and the air chilled him. He refused to complain, though, and simply continued walking.

"Are you sure we won't get eaten by wolves or bears?" asked one of the women behind Jazz.

He smiled, but realised these were indeed city peeps and knew next to nothing about the life outside Victory. He'd been much like her when he'd left.

He turned and offered his hand to the distraught woman. "No, the dangers in the city are as bad, if not worse, than anything you'll find out here."

"But the stories—"

"Are just that, stories." He pulled her along, joining Doc in a few steps. "You trusted us when you decided to come with us. Nothing's changed."

The forest closed around them, its branches and foliage brushing against Jazz's naked chest and arms. He sighed, relieved. They'd have to find the trail they'd followed in, but there was no hurry. They were out of the Warlord's reach.

Stumbling over an exposed root, Jazz cursed.

"Fumble-footed moron," came a husky, feminine voice from deeper in the woods. *A female voice.*

Jazz spun around, facing a rich growth of berry bushes. "Zoe, is that you?" he called, knowing it was.

Zoe—curvaceous, dark-haired Zoe—strode out from behind the bush. Her eyes shone with mischief. "Who else would follow you two this far out of the way?" She entered Jazz's arms, pressing her warmth against him.

"Damn woman," Doc said from behind Jazz. "I thought you were going to stay and help in the village."

"Yeah, you thought." She pulled free of Jazz's hold and held her arms out to Doc. When he'd lifted her high and twirled her around, she laughed softly and added, "I had to see if you needed rescuing again."

Robin approached, dragging Sam with her. She looked at Zoe, a quizzical expression on her face for a moment. When Jazz slipped his arm around her shoulder and hugged her close, he noticed the puzzled look quickly faded. She suddenly smiled, obviously recognising Zoe.

"I might need rescuing from you, woman," Doc said, didn't let go of her.

"No way." She looked from him to Jazz, then back again. "Neither of you have a hope in hell of rescue this time. I've missed you both so much. I was scared you'd get into some kind of trouble and I wouldn't be there to get you out."

"Oh, nice. Don't think we can find our way." Jazz slapped his forehead and grimaced. "Woe is us. We need a woman to guide us home."

Zoe chuckled and said, "And that's what I'm doing here. Came to make sure you didn't get lost." She pulled Doc's head down, bringing his lips to within kissing distance. Standing on tiptoes, she pressed her lips to his.

Jazz waited, feeling a pang of desire and love.

"Looks like I missed some important changes while I was...away," Robin said, with a note of whimsy in her voice.

Zoe stepped away from Doc and extended her arms. "Robin, I'm so glad they found you."

Robin entered Zoe's embrace warmly. They held each other for a few moments and Jazz heard them exchanging words but couldn't make out what they said. The hug went on for some time and, when they separated, both were smiling. "And who is this?" Zoe pulled back, and stepped around Robin, her attention on Sam.

"This is Sam." Jazz moved closer and took hold of Zoe's arm before she got too close. "He's one of the city peeps. Not sure if he's a good guy or not, yet. He did help us find Robin, sort of."

Zoe eyed the young man, and licked her lips. "Sort of?" She walked around him, sliding her hand across his rag-covered shoulders. "Why is he bound? No one else seems to be."

"He got us captured, too."

"He did? Did he say why?" From her demeanour, it seemed Zoe might be more willing to forgive than either Doc or Jazz. She couldn't seem to keep her hands off the man.

"Survival. He needed food, shelter. We were his ticket to both." Doc crossed his arms over his chest and smiled down at his lovely partner.

Jazz stepped beside Doc and let Zoe check Sam out.

"But he didn't hurt either of you, right?" She raised her eyes and looked at Jazz, then at Doc, expectantly.

"No, not directly. We actually spent a little time together. He's a great..." Jazz stopped before he got himself into trouble.

"He's a great...what?" Zoe caught his omission and apparently wanted to know the rest.

Doc interjected, "Why don't we get the rest of these poor people to the village before we go into this. Robin's been through a lot. So have the rest of these peeps."

"Sounds like the best idea I've heard all day," Robin said, in a strained voice. She'd been through a lot and had managed to put on a brave face. With Zoe's arrival, that face was showing some strain.

"Perhaps we could find some shelter a little closer." Doc went to Robin's side and slipped his arm around her, holding her up.

Zoe looked thoughtful for a moment. "Shelter ahead. A mile or so. I think it might have been a barn. Its roof is still standing, some of the walls. It's shelter for the night."

"Sounds perfect, babe," Jazz said, and winked at Doc.

He nodded and asked, "Zoe, which way to this barn?"

"Follow me, sexy." She turned on her heel and strode into the underbrush. They followed, Robin held in Doc's arms and Sam directly behind her. Jazz made sure Zeb and the others didn't fall behind. When it became apparent that more help was needed than he could provide, Sam moved in beside him. "Jazz, let me help."

Jazz looked at the younger man and was about to tell him to fuck off, but changed his mind. They weren't about to guard Sam for any length of time. They didn't have the manpower or the desire for it. He looked at the man's eyes and nodded. "Turn around."

Sam spun around and held up his arms. In a flash, Jazz untied him and pushed him towards Red. "She's exhausted. Help her and anyone else you can. Screw up and it'll be one hell of a long time before I offer you my trust again."

"You won't regret it. I promise," Sam said and hurried off to help the failing Red.

The barn was a dilapidated ruin, but at least it had walls and most of a ceiling. The refugees shambled in and soon enough found comfort in each other's arms. Zoe had brought some food, but not nearly enough to fill their bellies. It was more than some had been used to.

"We'll let them rest until this afternoon. We should be able to get them all home by dark, if they can manage the trek," Doc said softly.

Jazz looked across the empty space separating them and smiled at Zoe, who'd wrapped herself around

Doc as if afraid he'd vanish. "I turned Sam loose," he said, and waited for Doc to say something.

"Yeah, noticed that." Doc looked around the room.

Jazz followed his gaze and stopped when he saw Sam sitting with Red. He was looking at Doc and had a soft smile on his face.

"We'll see how it goes. He's young. Hell, we don't know what all he's had to deal with."

"Too true," Zoe said, and sneaked her hand into Doc's shirt. "And you never know what you'd do in the same circumstances."

Jazz watched her hand move upwards until it stopped at chest level. "I think we can sneak out of here for a little rest of our own, don't you?"

Doc grinned at him, then flinched when Zoe did something to his chest. "I think this one needs a good..." He reached down, slipped his fingers under Zoe's chin and lifted it. Leaning close, he whispered, just loud enough for her and Jazz to hear, "Fucking."

"What about the guy, Sam?" Zoe asked, her attention going to where Sam watched them.

"Later. We'll talk about Sam, and us, later." Doc grabbed her hand and pulled it from under his woollen jerkin. Not releasing her, he took hold of Jazz with his other hand and headed out of the door.

In the open, he sniffed the air and sighed. "Much better than the city air."

"Sure is. Now, where can we take this to?"

Zoe took the lead, bringing them to a rough circle of long grass that promised to be soft and fragrant. She lay down and held her arms up to both men. "I've been so worried about you two."

"No need. I told you we'd be careful," Jazz said, and remembered saying exactly those words – had it only been a few days ago? He dropped to his knees on one side of her and Doc followed suit on the other.

"Yes, you did. I somehow think you'll have stories to share, though." She arched her back and pulled off her leggings, baring the smooth, white expanse of her shapely legs. Her shirt came next, tossed to the grass above her head.

Doc stripped quickly, throwing his clothes into a pile next to him. Jazz wasn't as fast, but he wasn't far behind. Still without a shirt, it only took a moment. He'd simply been caught up watching his two lovers and marvelling at his good fortune.

"You're covered in bruises and welts!" Zoe whispered when she got a good look at Doc's handsome hide.

"Yeah, I'll tell you about it, later," he replied, and spun his body around so when he leant forward he lowered himself onto her. "For now, I just need to feel your body, your arms around me."

Jazz's cock stiffened and he wrapped his fingers around the shaft, stroking it from crown to base. He wanted to be part of the couple's pleasure, but equally, he wouldn't have dreamt of interrupting. He splayed his knees and continued masturbating, watching his mate and the woman they both adored stroke and tease each other with eager fingers. Doc winced when Zoe's exploring touch slid over a wound. Zoe kissed her way down his chest, suckling at the tight nipples and tugging at them ever so gently.

"Come here, Jazz," Doc murmured, then gasped at something Zoe had done.

Jazz joined them, touching and kissing where he found sweaty skin in need of pleasuring. His cock slipped into Zoe's mouth. He kissed his way along

Doc's spine while teasing his anus with a stiffened finger.

His hips jerked, his cock pulsed and he groaned as his climax approached. Zoe slid her tongue across the crown, poking the tip into the slit. He shivered and tremors gripped him. He wanted to come. His body, abused and sore from the mistreatment of the last few days, craved an easy release.

Her mouth slipped off him and he heard her soft, whispered voice. "Come for me. I want to taste you."

A heartbeat later, she was back on him, driving him crazy with her oral pleasuring.

Doc grunted and hissed as he thrust deep into Zoe's pussy. He withdrew and clenched his arse around Jazz's finger, then thrust again.

They formed a triangle of thrashing body parts, each trying to outdo the others. Each strained for release, while their hearts beat wildly. Nothing mattered but the touch and taste of the others. Sweat trickled down Jazz's sides and he couldn't have said if it was his or the others'. It didn't matter. Nothing did but their pleasure.

He lurched forward. His arse muscles clenched. His balls shifted, moving in tight to his body. He lunged ahead. The shaft of his cock swelled.

Beside him, Doc roared his release.

Zoe cried out and sank her teeth into Jazz's arm. The pain sent him into that slippery slide to oblivion. He thrust forward and came.

Trembling, he pushed his hips forward again and sent another stream of hot cum deep into Zoe's mouth — and another.

"Yes, fuck, oh, fuck," Doc muttered as his body thrashed in orgasmic bliss.

When Jazz's thoughts returned to something akin to normal, he realised both Doc and Zoe were watching him. He smiled and sank to his side, his body pressing against Zoe's. Doc had collapsed and still lay atop her, his face in her hair.

"Almost home, babe," Doc said in a husky voice.

"This is home. You and Zoe." The words had come easily, but once he'd said them, Jazz realised how true they were. It didn't matter where they were, as long as they were together. Doc – the man of his dreams. The man whom he loved beyond anything or anyone else. And Zoe – the woman who'd stolen a piece of his heart.

"We'd better get back to the group. No one there is bush-wise. A raccoon could scare them all to death," Zoe said, then chuckled. She eased herself out from under Doc and reached for her clothing.

While she dressed, Jazz and Doc climbed into their own clothing. Jazz shivered. "Don't suppose you brought an extra shirt?"

"Here." She tossed him a vest she kept in her small pouch. "This'll have to do you till we get home."

He slipped into it and sighed at the welcome warmth. "Home. With both of my lovers. I can't think of a better thing to do."

Doc leaned in and pressed his lips to Jazz's. When he pulled away, he looked deep into Jazz's eyes for the longest moment.

"I love you too, Doc." Heart close to bursting with pleasure, Jazz turned and looked at Zoe, her face bright with love, and said, "I love you, Zoe."

"I love you, Jazz." The two voices came as one.

About the Author

Jude's imagination frequently leads her astray and she eagerly follows while trying to keep out of trouble, or at least, not get caught. For those of you who know her, you'll know that's not always easy. A picture, a smell, an unexpected glimpse of flesh, or a load of soil in the back of a pick-up, are all fodder for her writing. Her male characters run the gamut from the dominant male ruling his women with an iron fist, to a simpering purple-clad boy-toy whose only desire is to please. As diverse and as richly depicted, her women find themselves in a myriad of exotic and erotic situations.

Jude Mason loves to hear from readers. You can find her contact information, website details and author profile page at http://www.total-e-bound.com.

Total-E-Bound Publishing

www.total-e-bound.com

Take a look at our exciting range of literagasmic™
erotic romance titles and discover pure quality
at Total-E-Bound.